NOT A DROP TO DRINK

NOT A DROP TO DRINK

Mindy McGinnis

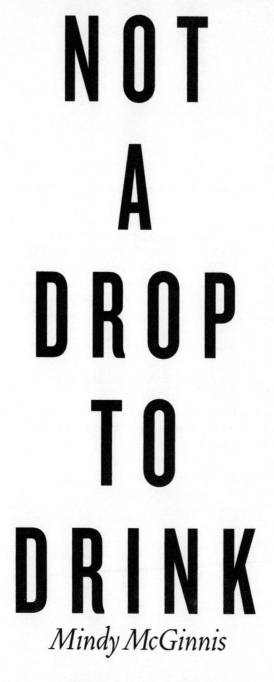

KATHERINE TEGEN BOOKS
An Imprint of HarperCollins Publishers

Katherine Tegen Books is an imprint of HarperCollins Publishers.

Library of Congress Cataloging-in-Publication Data
McGinnis, Mindy.
Not a drop to drink / Mindy McGinnis. — First edition.
pages cm
Summary: "Sixteen-year-old Lynn will do anything to protect her valuable
water source, but the arrival of new neighbors forces her to reconsider her
attitudes"— Provided by publisher.
ISBN 978-0-06-219850-1 (hardcover bdg.)
[1. Water supply—Fiction. 2. Survival—Fiction. 3. Self-reliance—Fiction.
4. Mothers and daughters—Fiction.] I. Title.
PZ7.M4784747Not 2013   2012051737
[Fic]—dc23   CIP
                                                                        AC

Typography by Erin Fitzsimmons
13 14 15 16 17 LP/RRDH 10 9 8 7 6 5 4 3 2 1
❖
First Edition

For my parents. They read to me.

One

Lynn was nine the first time she killed to defend the pond, the sweet smell of water luring the man to be picked off like the barn swallows that dared to swoop in for a drink. Mother had killed the people who came too close to their pond before, but over the next seven years they fell by Lynn's gun as well, their existence easily wiped out first by a bullet, then by the coyotes before the sun could rise. Death and gunpowder were scents from her childhood, but today the fall breeze brought something less familiar to her rooftop perch, and her nose wrinkled.

"What is that?" Lynn asked, nerves pricking. "Smells like smoke, but there's something wrong with it."

Mother jerked her head toward the binoculars lying beside her. "East."

Lynn picked up the binoculars to see a thin line of white smoke rising above the trees there, barely visible in the gray evening sky.

"They're burning green wood. That's why it smells funny. Doesn't make much heat, just a smoky mess." Mother kicked at an errant pinecone on the roof, sending it plummeting to the ground below. "I don't think they know a lot about being outside." She shaded her eyes against the last red rays of the sun. "They're also burning at all times of the day, not just when they'd need it for cooking, which to me says they're keeping somebody warm who can't take it—somebody sick maybe, or could possibly be children in the group."

"Looks like they're down by the stream," Lynn said. "Shouldn't be a bother to us. They have their own water."

"Until the stream dries up, like it always does in the summer. Then they might take an interest."

"Dries up," Lynn agreed, "or washes them away in spring like it did that last poor cow that was wandering around."

The firm line of Mother's mouth went even thinner. "Can't count on that stream. There's a reason why nobody's set up there permanently. Doesn't look like these people know the ground from the sky. I doubt there's a hunter among them. . . ." She trailed off, watching as the white smoke dissipated. "I'd give them three snows. Then we'll see no more smoke from the east."

Lynn let the binoculars hang from her neck. "That the same fire you've been seeing?"

2

Mother shook her head and pointed due south, where no smoke rose above the treetops, no birds raised an alarm.

"I see nothing."

"Exactly," Mother said. "There's been smoke to the south consistently in the evenings and the mornings. Yesterday it was gone. Today, nothing."

"So they broke camp, left."

"There's no reason. They're set up at a tiny town called South Bloomfield. It's at the bend in the stream, plenty of water, plenty of trees for cutting. It's a good location," Mother admitted. "It's where I'd be, if I weren't here."

She fell quiet and stretched into the prone position, raising her rifle to watch the world through the scope. Lynn sat silently beside her, waiting for whatever explanation would come.

"Past three times you went for water in the evenings, you notice anything?"

Lynn shook her head.

"You know the momma raccoon? The big one that cuts through the field behind the house every night?"

Lynn nodded. The raccoon was hard to miss, her hunched back rising high enough to be seen above the grass that grew in the abandoned fields surrounding the house. "Yeah, what about her?"

"She hasn't been going out. Doesn't want to cross the field."

Lynn felt the hairs on the back of her neck rise, a primordial response to danger that she had learned to never ignore. "You think they're watching us? You think they got someone in the fencerow?"

"I think maybe. And whoever they are, they stopped building fires because they want us to think they're gone. Without fire, they're not eating much of a supper. People won't go long without a hot supper if they don't have to. They'll be coming soon."

"Coming for us?"

"For everything."

Lynn pulled her own rifle into her lap, the cold metal bringing more comfort to her than Mother's touch ever could. Her finger curled around the trigger, hugging it tight in the life-taking embrace that she'd learned so long ago. She slipped onto her belly beside Mother, watching the sunlight bounce off the twin barrels of their rifles. Waiting was always the worst part, the crack of the rifle a relief.

Years before, Mother had shown her pictures of the thirsty dead. Their skin hung from their bones like the wallpaper that sloughed from the walls in the unused upstairs hallway. Swollen tongues were forced past lips cracked and bleeding. Eyes sunk so deeply into sockets that the outline of the skulls was evident.

"Do you want to die like this?" Mother had asked that night and every night since then.

Lynn's answer never changed. "No."

And Mother's response, their evening prayer. "Then you will have to kill."

Regret was for people with nothing to defend, people who had no water.

When Lynn was ten years old, Mother had fired up the shortwave radio in one of her sporadic fits of optimism. Whether she had hoped to hear that normalcy had been returned somewhere in the world or that the cities had begun to loosen their grip on water supplies, Lynn did not know. But the news that came caused Mother to smash the radio, not caring what the outside world had to offer anymore.

Cholera. Mother explained that it had once been the most feared disease in the world, striking people in the morning and killing them by nightfall. It was waterborne, contagious, and deadly. Clean water sources and antibiotics had banished it for decades, but desperate people were now drinking brackish water, and the demand for medicine far outstripped the supply. Now thousands died from a disease that had been laughable a decade before.

With dead bodies dropping all around the countryside, and the water table rising with the spring rains, Mother had decided that the pond water could kill them as easily as save them. Mother's purification system was a simple strategy she learned from an issue of *National Geographic*. Sheets of tin roofing from the old red barn were laid out in the yard, the ends weighted with rocks to prevent them from blowing away. Bottle by plastic bottle, all the water collected from the pond rotated out to the tin sheets. They could only purify on clear days, when a full eight hours of UV rays would kill any bacteria in the water.

Even though it had lately been cooler in the evenings, the morning sun pounded on the back of Lynn's neck as she made the early water run to the pond. It would be a purifying day, for sure, which meant hours of labor. She pushed the lip of her first bucket under the surface of the water, trying not to disturb the muddy bottom. No matter how careful she was, there were always flecks of dirt and algae that settled in the holding tanks. She moved along the bank to a new spot to dip the second bucket.

When it was full, she set both buckets on the muddy bank and raised her arms to show Mother she was ready for the trek to the barn. Sunlight flashed off the barrel as Mother followed her progress, scanning the horizon for the slightest hint of someone watching. Lynn's upper arms were quivering by the time she covered the hundred feet to the barn doors. She set both buckets down to rest before sliding the massive door open.

The water tanks sat there in the darkness, motes of dust settling onto their long white bodies. They had once carried chemicals to the fields that were now fallow. Mother said she had rinsed and re-rinsed them, terrified she and Lynn might be poisoned by the very water she was depending on to save them.

As Lynn climbed the ladder to the top of a tank, she remembered Mother's story, how she had run a hose from the tap and left it running into the tanks right up until the water had been turned off. Lynn knew that her first few sips had been from those tanks of tap water, clear as crystal. But she could not remember. The only water she'd ever known was laced with dirt and tasted slightly of fish. And she was grateful for every drop.

She twisted the plastic cap off the top of the tank and dumped both buckets into it, listening to the tone of the falling water change as the level rose. This tank was the unpurified pond water. The other stood half full of water that had already been rotated out to the tin sheets, and would be drawn off through the winter to fill the smaller thousand-gallon tank that was in the basement, where they lived.

Lynn snapped the cap back on the tank and sat astride it for a moment, weary at the sight of all the work waiting for them. She hadn't slept well last night, staring at the cinder-block walls of the basement but seeing only the twin spires of smoke in the sky. Mother had not slept at all. Lynn could hear Mother's fingers tapping against the barrel of her gun as Lynn had finally drifted down to sleep. Yet Mother was on the roof before Lynn was even out of her cot, eyeing the horizon and waiting for a target.

Lynn cut through the long grass of the yard to the rusty antenna on the side of the house, ignoring the thistles that snagged her jeans as she went. She was covered in a thin film of sweat by the time she climbed to the roof. She swiped a few drops out of her eyes and slipped to the shingles beside Mother.

"Warm day."

"Good for purifying," Mother said idly, her eye still tight to the scope. Lynn slid her rifle strap off her shoulder, bringing the gun around to see what Mother was seeing.

"No smoke this morning," she said. "Do you think—"

A persistent buzzing sliced through the air. All her muscles tensed, but years of handling guns prevented Lynn from jolting the trigger. "What is that?"

Mother's thin line of a mouth turned upside down. "It's Stebbs," she said. "He's got a log splitter."

Lynn turned her scope to the southwest where she could see their only neighbor, his dark silhouette barely discernible from the edge of the forest.

Mother's voice was hard, matching the shape of her mouth. "Your leg bothering you more as you get older? How far did you have to go to find that?" she asked, and Lynn knew the questions weren't meant for her.

"A log splitter," Lynn repeated, finally drawing Mother's attention away from Stebbs. "What's it do?"

"Splits logs."

Lynn switched out her rifle for the binoculars to get a better view of Stebbs and his log splitter, watching as he heaved an enormous tree stump onto it. The splitter reduced it to half, then fourths, in seconds. "Looks handy," she said.

"I'm sure it is. Also runs on gasoline. Not easy to find."

"We've got the tank." Lynn gestured toward the metal tank nestled beside the barn, completely obscured by juniper bushes.

"That's for emergencies."

"Emergencies." Lynn reiterated. "What would make you use the gas?"

"The truck." Mother didn't look at her as she answered. "To go south."

"I won't go," Lynn said, fists instinctively clenching against an unknown fear of things not seen. "I won't leave."

It was an old argument that arrived every year with the autumn: stick by their sure source of water through the frigid months to come, or head south to warmer climates and trust that drinkable water could be found there, unguarded, unclaimed. For Lynn it was never a question. She knew where the wild blackberries grew in the spring, which bank of the pond the fish preferred for their spawning beds. She listened to the frog songs in the evening and felt a fierce pride that she could hear a sound so rare in their world, and that her bullets helped keep the pond safe. Her feet were confident on the slope of the roof in a way they never would be on the flat surface of an unending road.

"Gathering wood is a lot of work, cutting even more," Mother said. "We go even a few hundred miles to the south and we won't freeze to death in the winters."

"A few hundred miles with no water will kill us deader than the snows."

Mother sighed. "I should've gone before you could speak, and I could still carry you out of here. We'll talk about it again another time. I'm not getting any younger, you know."

"And I'm not getting any less stubborn," Lynn shot back.

Mother rose from the shingles, and Lynn followed, aware that the conversation was over. Lynn went down the antenna first and looked up to see Mother pausing at the edge of the roof, her gaze directed south.

"A log splitter," she muttered. "Asshole."

Two

The storm that blew in that afternoon was a mixed blessing. The water Lynn had set out to purify on the tin wouldn't be getting the full eight hours of sun, but life was falling from the sky. All the containers they had, from plastic measuring cups to five-gallon buckets to old glass bottles, were strewn throughout the yard. Mother and Lynn ran back and forth during the rain, emptying full containers into the barn tanks and dashing back outside to catch every possible drop with the empties.

"It's a good rain," Lynn said as they took a breath together in the barn. "The tank we're on is nearly full. Only one empty left."

"There's never enough," Mother said. "Don't forget that."

The animals came out after the storm, like clockwork. The worms and moles came up for air as their tunnel homes flooded.

The worms brought the birds, the moles brought the cats, and birds and cats brought the top of the food chain—the coyotes. Mother said back when she was a teenager it was rare to see one, usually only a brief flicker in the headlights in the dead of night. Now they hunted in the light of day, and curiosity brought them right into the shadow of the house in the afternoons.

"There he is," Mother muttered under her breath as they paced the yard together, gathering the last of their rainwater. "That big bastard," she said, handing the binoculars over to Lynn. "Look."

Lynn adjusted them and raised them to her eyes. "I'd say sixty, maybe sixty-five pounds, you think?"

"Maybe more."

Lynn watched him through the binoculars. He was leading a small pack of foragers, two other scraggly creatures that nipped at each other in play as they went. Their leader's nose was to the ground, his focus intent. A flash on the horizon caught her attention, and Lynn swept her gaze southwest.

"Stebbs has got a bead on him," she said.

"What?" Mother squinted into the distance.

Lynn adjusted the binoculars again, took a longer look. "He's got the .30-30 out, the one with the scope."

"Probably just looking then. I doubt he fires on a coyote, no matter how big."

Lynn looked back at the pack. The leader turned, irritated at his comrades' lack of commitment, and pinned one to the ground by its neck. He let it up slowly, and both the smaller ones rolled over, exposing their submissive bellies. "Think he should?"

"Normally, I'd say no, don't waste a bullet on a coyote, especially a thirty-thirty. Meat's too tough. You burn up more energy chewing it than you get from eating it." She outstretched one hand for the binoculars, and Lynn gave them over. "Big Bastard though . . . he needs shooting."

Lynn saw the flash from the sun glinting off Stebbs' rifle as he put it down.

"Asshole," Mother muttered. "He fires that gun so little he probably never has to clean it. Which reminds me: bring our cleaning kits up to the roof when you come."

Lynn dumped the last of the rainwater into the barn tank, shaking every last drop from each bottle, cup, and bowl. The rain still clung to the long grass as she made her way to the antenna, soaking her jeans and driving a chill into her skin that would stay with her all evening.

"I was thinking about hunting," Mother said as they cleaned their rifles. Her tone was casual, but the remark brought Lynn's hands to a stop.

"So early? There hasn't even been a good frost yet. The meat will never keep."

"I thought we might as well smoke the meat this year instead of freezing. A smokehouse won't draw any attention we don't already have. The meat will taste better cured, store better, and it's something we can do now to worry about less later."

"But what about firewood? How much will it take to cure the meat?"

"Shouldn't be a problem," Mother answered as she rammed the pipe down the barrel of her gun. "You only want green wood for a smokehouse fire, most of what we burn in the basement stove is—"

"Seasoned," Lynn interrupted. "How much green wood?"

"Four to five days' worth, depending on how big of a deer I bag."

Lynn jammed the ramrod down her own rifle barrel unnecessarily hard.

"You're not happy about it," Mother observed.

"No, I'm not. It's stupid to use wood for smoking meat we won't be alive to eat because we froze to death."

"Stupid to store up the wood to die warm and starving."

Lynn finished cleaning her gun in silence, loaded and cocked it, set the safety, and placed it on the roof. "I just don't understand why we can't do things the way we've always done. Wait for winter, kill a deer, freeze the meat."

"Because we can't eat frozen meat if we're on the run. Smoked meat, we can. Things have changed," Mother answered, her gaze drawn to the southern horizon. "So we change with them."

◆ ◆ ◆

14

Lynn rested by the sheet of tin, mesmerized by the sun glinting off the hundred plastic bottles. The batch hadn't had the full eight hours of sun the day before because of the rain, but today the sun was out in force, raising the temperature of the tin enough that Lynn could feel heat rolling off the bottles. Mother's scope flashed as she moved about on the roof, keeping an eye on everything.

To have an afternoon of rest was rare. Usually Lynn would cut wood while the bottles heated, but Mother wasn't comfortable letting her out of sight with the threat from the south still fresh in her mind. Instead, she sat on an upside-down bucket and tapped the wire handle against the side to keep herself from sliding into a doze.

She'd lost a bucket once, before she could swim. She hadn't stood that much taller than the bucket, and the weight of the water flowing into it had pulled her forward. The fear of losing a bucket had forced her to hold on well past her last breath, the wire handle had sliced into her tiny fingers as she kicked for the surface but refused to give up her grip. Red dots had filled her vision before Mother was able to get down from the roof and dive in after her, unfastening her clenched fingers from the handle. They'd sat on the bank, dripping together, Mother so shaken that she didn't reprimand Lynn about the lost bucket or the wasted water dripping off their clothes.

Her lost bucket rested on the bottom now, not far from the edge. Lynn used it as a marker, a sign that they hadn't had enough rain in the dry summers. The year before she'd been able to see the white plastic grip on the top of the handle, floating only a foot below the surface as the level dropped. Each day brought it into clearer focus, driving a spike of fear into her heart and inviting the flood of certainty that this would be the year they didn't make it. This would be the year they died. She could have grabbed it then, saved from the shame of losing it so many years ago. But getting it back meant a slow death by thirst loomed nearer.

The rustling of grass snapped Lynn into the present, though she didn't move. A snort exploded nearby, an unmistakably animal noise. Slowly she reached for the rifle at her feet. As she did, the grass on the other side of the tin parted and a long dark snout emerged.

At close quarters, Big Bastard was larger than she'd expected. Domestic dogs had fallen in with the wild coyotes and their bloodlines had lent their feral cousins a larger stature. They regarded each other carefully for a moment, his eyes flickering toward her hand as it curled around the rifle strap. Another snort and he was gone, bounding back into the tall grass.

Lynn exhaled slowly. Even though he hadn't threatened her overtly, she had seen the intelligence in his eyes. He'd been watching her as she daydreamed, had even snorted and alerted her to his presence. Only going for the rifle had been enough to scare him off. He knew what guns were and what they could do, she guessed. And he'd also known she was no threat to him without hers.

Lynn raced through the grass as soon as he was gone, not even trying to ignore the primitive urge to run to the antenna. "You see that?" she asked the second her foot hit the shingles. "You see Big Bastard come right up into the yard?"

"I saw him wander through the back acre a while ago," Mother said. The pruning shears in her hands snapped down onto a maple branch that had come too close to the roof. She waited for the crash from below to finish her thought. "But I figured he was going to go rustle up some of the groundhogs out from the barn."

Lynn snorted. "What he rustled up was me."

Mother glanced over her shoulder. "He wasn't scared of you?"

"Not until I went for my gun, then he backed off."

Mother turned back to the maple, hands on her hips as she surveyed her work. "We've got bigger concerns than coyotes right now."

"Unless nobody's coming," Lynn said, voicing the hope that had surfaced as the days passed uneventfully. "Unless they're gone and you're just being—" She stopped abruptly, aware of what she'd been about to say.

Mother glanced away from the trees, eyebrow raised. "Paranoid? You wouldn't be the first to think it."

Lynn glanced away, and Mother looked to the south again. "You'd best rest now," she said. "I'll wake you up in a bit. We'll stay on the roof tonight, sleep in shifts."

"Why tonight?"

"Same buck and his two does have been taking that fencerow

path all season, but this afternoon he turned them away from grazing there. They ran off with their tails up screaming 'danger' for anyone smart enough to see it. Whoever's coming for us, they're in the fencerow, waiting for us to be stupid."

They took turns dozing until the sun set, and they sat together in a silent companionship, rifles across their knees, listening to the crickets singing.

"Crickets got a lot to say tonight," Lynn said absently.

Mother grunted in assent. "Always do, before the first hard frost," she said. "Like they know they better get it out, because soon they won't be able to sing."

Dusk fell and a low fog crept in from the fields, obscuring their vision sixty yards out in all directions.

"What do we do if it's full dark?" Lynn whispered. "When they come?"

"Shoot at what you hear. I trimmed the trees so there's brush around the house. They can't possibly be silent. Couple shots might be enough to scare them off."

"If it's not?"

"If it's not, don't be frightened when I turn my gun on you."

"What?" The idea of being on the end of a gun Mother held made Lynn's voice spike in panic.

"There's things I haven't told you," Mother said quietly, eyes averted from Lynn's face. "Now isn't the time; I don't want you distracted. Just know that there's bad men in the world, and dying fast by your mother is a better way than theirs."

Lynn swallowed hard, fighting the rise in her throat. "Yes, Mother."

Darkness fell and they sat together quietly, shoulder to shoulder, facing south.

Three

Hours later Mother's voice jerked Lynn out of sleep.

"Remember what you asked earlier? About what will we do if they come after dark?" She gestured toward the south field. "The idiots are bringing flashlights."

They flattened themselves onto the shingles, cocked their rifles, and sighted toward the fan of lights coming for them. Mother counted slowly under her breath.

"I see seven," she said. "I'm going to drop the one on the far left, supposing the others will break right when he falls." She raised the rifle to her shoulder. "You might want to lead in that direction."

"Yes, Mother," Lynn said, raising her own gun.

The crack of Mother's rifle made Lynn startle, even though she'd been expecting it. The lights immediately scattered, except for the farthest left, which fell to the ground and stayed there. Lynn's first shot went too far right in her excitement, causing the running men to scatter in all directions. Mother's rifle fired again, and another light fell to the ground, motionless. Irritated, Lynn fired again, this time dropping a light.

"Take a second to listen," Mother said.

Lynn cocked her gun, ignoring the warm shell that rested against her arm. While they'd initially panicked and scattered, she couldn't hear any shouting, or cries of alarm. The four remaining lights gathered together in a group, motionless, and stayed that way.

"What are they—"

"Shush," Mother said. "Listen."

The lights didn't move, and the utter silence of the night overwhelmed Lynn. Even though it was cool, she swiped a bead of sweat that rolled down her nose. A stunned cricket tentatively renewed its song, to be answered by another a second later. Soon a chorus had begun. The lights still didn't move.

"Think they gave up?"

"No," Mother said tightly. "Be quiet."

The lights remained still, but the crickets stopped.

"Here they come," Mother said confidently, cocking her weapon. "Aim at what you hear. They dropped their lights."

The rustling sounds of field grass followed moments later, and Lynn fired toward it. The scuffling stopped, but another sound followed, a low moan that could only mean she'd hit her target. More silence ensued. A male voice cut through the night, a sound so alien to Lynn that she cringed.

"Come on down now, girlies. We know you're up there," he shouted, his voice much nearer than expected.

"And now I know where you are, you stupid son of a—" Mother used a word that Lynn had never heard before, and fired her weapon once. The sound of a body slumping to the ground followed. Minutes passed with nothing but the continuous low groan of the man Lynn had wounded.

"What's that word you said?" Lynn asked, curiosity getting the best of her.

"Never mind that now."

A cricket chirped and the wounded man cried out again, silencing it. Lynn thought she heard movement farther out from the house, and Mother's taut body reflected that she heard it too. It faded, and they sat tensely together for nearly an hour, hearing nothing but the occasional complaint from the wounded man.

"I think they're gone," Lynn said.

"Yeah," Mother agreed, her eyes still scanning the darkness futilely. "We'll stay up on the roof, go down in the morning, get those flashlights. They'll come in handy."

Another low moan rose from the grass. "That was a good shot," Mother said, nodding toward it.

"Not good enough."

Mother shrugged. "It was dark." She rose and stretched out her stiff body, a sign that she truly felt safe. "You'll get better."

Another cry. Mother licked her finger, tested the wind, and fired once into the night.

Silence fell.

The morning sun revealed five bodies. Lynn spotted the one she had clipped; he had been standing on the west bank of the pond. The man Mother had spoken to was startlingly close to the house. The thought of him picking his way up the antenna while they sat together facing south gave Lynn goose bumps. She wrapped her arms around herself and rubbed them for warmth. Mother rose from where she'd been sleeping during Lynn's final shift, unmoved by the sight of the carnage.

"They didn't take the bodies," Lynn said. "Not even the ones farthest out." She nodded in the direction of three who had dropped while still holding their flashlights, nearly a hundred yards from the house.

Mother made an unpleasant noise in the back of her throat. "Type of men who gather up seven of themselves to attack two women in the middle of the night generally won't go back for dead friends." She scanned the horizon with her naked eye, nerves still on edge. "Anything?"

"Nothing." Lynn shook her head. "Think they'll be back?"

"Depends."

They descended together, rifles in hand. Mother took a few moments to look over the body of the first man they came upon, the one she had spoken to. "Seems well fed enough," she commented, after struggling to turn him over. She stripped him of his gun and ammo, leaning them against the side of the house to collect later. Together they dragged his body out to the field for the coyotes.

The other bodies revealed nothing else. None of the men had been in any danger of starving to death. Lynn and Mother relieved the bodies of their weapons, and were lucky enough to find a pack of matches in the pocket of the man lying near the pond. Lynn noticed that her shot had taken him in the kneecap and she winced at the thought. Mother's tidy, round hole in the middle of his chest had ended it soon enough. He was not a large man, and Lynn looked at him longer than she had the others, trying to figure out what made him seem different.

"I'd say he's not much older than you," Mother said when she noticed.

"Really?" Lynn peered closer at his face. "How can you tell?"

"Well," Mother peered up at the gray sky as she considered how to answer, "I guess it's in the way his skin isn't so tough, he's still got the little bit of baby soft on him."

Lynn leaned forward, trying to see what Mother meant.

"Also, he doesn't have much in the way of whiskers." Mother touched her own face to illustrate. "Kinda built small too. You oughta put your foot up next to his, see if you think his boots would fit."

Even the appearance of the other men had screamed "enemy" to Lynn. But this one, with his small hands and eyes that were clear even in death wormed at her. "No," she said. "I don't think I will."

Mother watched her cautiously. "It's probably time for me to—"

A flash of light along the corner of the woods to the southwest brought both of them flat on their bellies, rifles to the ready. Through her scope Lynn saw Stebbs, his own rifle at his shoulder, peering in their direction. To her surprise, Mother stood up and hailed him with one arm. "Yeah, we're all right," she said under her breath. "Asshole."

Mother looked down to where Lynn still lay prone in the grass, her rifle barrel resting across the torso of the dead boy. "You don't have to help me with this one, if you don't want to."

"I'm fine." Lynn said, proving it by grabbing him under the arms and dragging him away before Mother could move to help. When she came back from the field, his boots were knotted together, dangling from her neck. They were nicer than her own, newer, with steel toes.

The guns and ammo from the men went into the old steamer trunk Mother had tucked away beside the root cellar. Years of dropping anyone who came close to the house had given them a ready supply of weapons and ammo, but both women stuck to the rifles they had learned on, the stocks worn smooth from years of resting their cheeks against them.

Lynn glanced at the shelves of the root cellar while Mother packed away the guns. The dim light that filtered in didn't show her anything reassuring. The glass jars from last year's canning were almost gone. The few carrots and celery Lynn had pulled from the ground earlier in the harvest were covered in sawdust, their green tops wilted.

"We need to get out to the garden," Lynn said. "The second planting is out there waiting."

"I know it," Mother muttered into the gun trunk. "But I don't like being so far from the house with those men from the south about."

"I don't like the idea of starving."

Mother's answer was to give her a handgun. "I'll come with you. We work fast and get back to the house. You should be purifying today too."

Lynn stuck the handgun into her belt. "I can't take a day sitting next to the tin when we should be harvesting. For all you know it's wasted time anyway, the water could be just fine."

"That's how people in Africa cleaned their water, back when we still knew what people on other continents were up to."

"Hell of a lot hotter in Africa," Lynn argued. "Their water probably just about boiled on sheets of tin."

Mother snapped the lid of the gun trunk shut. "You ever had cholera?"

"No."

"Then it must be working," Mother said.

"Either that or the water's always been fine," Lynn said, hating the idea of useless hours spent watching over bottles of water that didn't need purifying.

"Only one way to find out, and if you're wrong we're both dead. Now let's get out to the garden before I change my mind about that."

Mother's mouth stayed down in its normal position, not inviting conversation as she stripped husks off sweet corn. Lynn was shelling the last peas while debating the pros and cons of breaking the silence. Though they spent most of their days working side by side, they hardly spoke to each other if they weren't on the roof. Voices could attract people or cover the sound of someone approaching. Mother kept her rifle within reach, the safety off. Only the right words could be used to break the silence.

"We had four cords of wood, this time last year."

Mother stopped shucking, her hands still for once. There was a small grunting noise that Lynn took for agreement.

"We've got two." Lynn ventured. "It's not enough."

"No," Mother agreed. "It's not." Her hands kept working, building up their store even in the face of futility.

"So why bother?" Lynn's voice shook as she tossed the last pea pod into the bucket. "Why gather water? Why pick the vegetables?"

Mother smiled thinly, hands still working. "If I'd thought like that sixteen years ago, I'd have drowned you the second you were born, then shot myself."

"But you didn't."

Mother snapped another ear of corn from the stalk. "Plenty did. *'I took the road less traveled by—and that has made all the difference.'*"

Familiar with the glance Mother gave her, Lynn asked the question. "Who wrote that one?"

"Robert Frost."

Lynn tossed another handful of peas into her bucket, where they barely covered the bottom. "Why do you always quote poetry at me when all I want is a straight answer?"

"Because I need to use my English degree," Mother said, then cracked a smile when Lynn's brow furrowed in confusion. "Yes, I've thought about quitting once or twice. Then I remember how they looked when they died—others who quit. It's not an easy death."

"I've seen people die."

"Not slow, you haven't. Not people who know they're dying and have got the worst of it ahead of them still." Mother kept working, calm hands unfazed by the images in her mind. "No, I've never really considered quitting. Not after seeing them."

Lynn began plucking tomatoes off the vines, the spicy scent of the broken plants making her belly rumble. She talked over it quickly so that Mother wouldn't notice.

"So what are we gonna do?"

"Tomorrow I'm going to start turning the little outbuilding into a smokehouse. Shouldn't be too hard. I'll pull up some flooring and put stones for a fire pit between the joists, cut a hole in the roof for ventilation. It won't be airtight around the door, but it's better than nothing. Like I said before, I can kill a deer sooner if we smoke the meat instead of freezing it. You'll do the canning over an outside fire and we'll keep a lookout while we work. With luck, we'll have everything we need for the winter squirreled away sooner rather than later, then spend most of our time on the roof and wait for them to try again for us. Meantime we hope they starve or freeze to death."

"And what about us? What's to stop us from freezing to death if we don't have enough wood for the winter?"

"There's always ways to get warm, Lynn. We've got blankets, our own body heat. We can go back to sharing a cot like we did when you were a kid if we have to."

"Or you can let me take the truck and go cut wood on my own."

Mother shucked the last piece of corn, her mouth back down in its usual position. "I could," she said. "But I'd worry the whole time you were gone. You haven't been running a chain saw that long, and you can't cut wood and hold a gun at the same time. The noise would bring people to you like bees to honey."

"What if I took the ax and looked for smaller trees?"

"Smaller trees mean smaller pieces of wood."

"Smaller pieces burn better than nothing," Lynn shot back.

Mother didn't answer; instead, she looked at the pile of tomatoes beside Lynn and the heap of potatoes between the two of them. "It's not a bad harvest. You get all the root crop down into the cellar, and the canning done here before the day's out, and I'll let you take the truck and ax out tomorrow."

Four

It was a bittersweet victory, Lynn had to admit by her sixth trip out to the garden and back down to the root cellar. She raised the woolen blanket they kept dropped over the entrance to their pantry, sidestepping past the huge plastic drum that held the purified water supply. Even though her arms were shaking, she was careful not to drop the buckets loaded with potatoes for fear of bruising them. They went into a pile beside the crooked shelves made out of stacked cement blocks and mismatched lengths of wood. Canning was a hot job whether done indoors or out, but Lynn didn't complain since Mother had taken the water-gathering duties for the day in return. She dragged the cast-iron pot up the basement stairs with the last of her energy and started a fire with one of the matches taken from the dead man. The tomatoes came to a red boil as Lynn started a second, smaller fire to sterilize the glass jars.

Work calmed her fears as usual. The feeling of doing something always overcame the fear of nothing. There would be vegetables for the winter, and if Mother let her have her way, plenty of wood as well. The purified water still had to be moved down to the basement tank, but they weren't lacking. Soon the days would be short, and the breezes would bite.

Lynn had never minded the cold. Winter meant diving back into the much-coveted books that lay untouched on the shelf the rest of the year. Mother had used the encyclopedias to teach her something of the world beyond their small borders, but Lynn had no interest in what surrounded them. Not after seeing the globe.

Mother had rummaged in the attic for it when she was making an argument for heading south, hoping that an illustration might sway Lynn. The vast expanse of blue that covered it had fascinated Lynn, and she'd asked Mother why they didn't seek out this unending expanse of water called "ocean." Mother had knelt down to her height and held her face in her hands.

"I know it's hard to understand, but that water would make you sick."

Lynn remembered arguing, her childish hope refusing to admit that so much blue could be a bad thing.

"There's a famous line from a poem about the ocean," Mother

had finally said to end the discussion. "'*Water water every where, but not a drop to drink.*'"

Lynn had broken the globe afterward, smashing its false promises to bits on the chopping block with her hatchet. The tears that had fallen while she worked were as salty as the ocean, but she had sucked them greedily off her lips.

The canning was done by the evening, and Mother had emerged from converting the outbuilding into a smokehouse to help her carry the hot glass jars down into the pantry. They had fresh corn over the fire and the kernels burst juicily in Lynn's mouth as she crunched down on them, relishing even the feel of the bits that stuck in her teeth.

That night, Lynn tried on the steel-toed boots. They fit well, and she giggled when Mother dropped the biggest encyclopedia (*M*) on her foot to illustrate what a good choice it had been to go ahead and take them. She tried not to let on how much it bothered her to feel the outlines of the dead boy's feet inside the boots.

"You chop your hand off and the shock'll kill you before you can make it back to the house."

"Yes, Mother." Lynn hefted the ax into the back of the truck.

Mother glanced nervously at the steering wheel as Lynn climbed into the cab. "Stay in sight of the house."

"I will."

"I'll keep my eye on you as much as possible," Mother said, slinging her rifle over her shoulder. "But I can't be always watching."

That finally caught Lynn's attention. "Smoke to the south?"

"Again, yes," Mother answered, shifting her eyes in that direction as she spoke, nervously scanning the skyline for any hint of other people. "This morning, while you slept."

"What do you make of it?"

"Don't know. You have a handgun too?"

Lynn nodded.

"Just remember to squeeze the trigger, don't pull it. And go to the west, not south. Stay—"

"Stay in sight, right. I know. Mother, it'll be okay."

"Right." Mother gave Lynn a long look before she stepped away from the truck. "Okay then. Go."

Mother had taught Lynn how to drive as soon as her feet could reach the pedals, but it had been years since she'd been behind a wheel. Gravel sprayed when she tapped on the gas, and Lynn tried to reassure Mother with a smile and a wave as she pulled away. Even from the road she could see the concern stamped on Mother's features, but there was no help for it. They needed heat. They needed wood.

Lynn surveyed the countryside as she drove, making sure to keep the house in the rearview mirror while dodging the huge potholes that pockmarked the road. She spotted two or three downed trees that looked as if they'd fallen years ago. A strong wind a week earlier had knocked most of the grass down so that Lynn could see woods in the back acres of the fields, untilled even during Mother's time.

The ride back to the woods was bumpy, the shocks on the truck having given out long ago. Lynn smacked her head on the ceiling of the cab, but it was exhilarating. The smell of the crushed grass under her tires, the two tracks following her in the rearview mirror, even the panicked grasshoppers that accidentally jumped through the window were a cause for amusement, a break from the norm.

She parked parallel with the woods, putting the truck bed near a huge cracked trunk of a maple. Lynn got out of the cab and looked toward home, barely visible on the horizon. She waved, not knowing if Mother was watching her at that moment or not, but it felt better to pretend she was. She grabbed the ax and headed toward the tree.

She recognized the warning shot for what it was the second it sliced through the mud at her feet. Lynn instantly froze and put her arms into the air as far as the weight of the ax allowed. The *crack* of the shot faded away into the distance, but no one called out to her. Slowly she lowered her arms and studied the woods. The shooter was undercover there, and she was in no position to return fire. There was a handgun tucked into her belt, but her hands were full and she was in the open.

She was near enough to the fallen tree now to see cuts in the trunk and bright piles of fresh sawdust strewn around. Lynn turned back toward the truck and walked slowly, very aware of what her back would look like in the crosshairs of a rifle. Whoever it was, they didn't mean her harm. The courtesy of a warning shot was more than most people extended these days, and the fact that she'd left the field with her truck said a lot.

The thought of returning to Mother with nothing after having to beg to be allowed to leave in the first place made Lynn's cheeks burn brightly as she drove home. She slammed her palm against the steering wheel, borrowing the new phrase she'd learned from Mother the night the men from the south had come.

"Son of a bitch!"

Mother seemed more amused than anything, once she saw that Lynn was perfectly fine, minus a bruised ego. Lynn stamped across the floor of the basement, her fuming anger more than sufficient to heat the room.

"At least it was someone nice enough to fire a warning shot," Mother said.

"Doesn't matter," Lynn snapped. "That's the farthest out you're going to let me go. I won't be able to see the house much past that and I didn't see anything else that was down and big enough to be worth cutting."

Lynn went to the pantry for an apple, her anger not enough to quell her appetite. "You hungry?"

"Oh, pretty much always," Mother said, and Lynn brought her an apple as well. When she handed it to her, Mother grabbed her wrist.

"What's that?" She pointed to a cut across the palm of Lynn's hand, bruised and red from a slight infection.

"Nothing," Lynn said. "I got scraped the other day moving wood over for the canning fire and forgot to clean it out right away."

"Always clean," Mother said stiffly. "Always. You know what to look for?"

"Red streaks for blood poisoning, going up toward my elbow."

"And gangrene?"

Lynn snorted. "I'm sure if I develop gangrene you would notice the smell pretty quick."

"I won't always be here to double-check you," Mother said.

"Don't say things like that." To even hint at a future time when Mother wouldn't be around sent her heart soaring into her throat, a worried pulse of adrenaline shooting through her veins.

"How do you know what gangrene smells like anyway?" Mother changed the subject.

Lynn pulled the stem from her apple before answering. "Because of Stebbs," she said quietly. "Because of his leg."

Mother looked down quickly and cleared her throat. "I didn't know you remembered that."

"Kind of tough to forget."

When Mother didn't offer anything else to the conversation, Lynn barreled on. "How old was I? I'm guessing seven?"

"Six," she was corrected. "You were six." But nothing further.

It seemed young, Lynn thought, to have been sent to get the tomatoes from the garden alone. But at the time the coyotes had not been so numerous as they were now.

The smell was distinctive. Even in her youth she had known that meant danger. She had stopped, sniffing the air like an unsure fawn in the spring. The hand had come as a shock, starkly white against the new green grass of the tromped path. White and flecked with freckles, something she'd looked at curiously for a moment; neither she nor Mother—the only people in the world, for all she knew—had them.

"Hey there, little one." His voice had been thin and weak. But still it set her back and she'd tripped in alarm, landing on her bottom. "It's all right," he said. "I need help. Get Lauren."

The last word had meant nothing to her, a foreign mixture of two syllables she'd never heard before.

"Your mother," he added patiently. "Get your mother."

That word she knew, and she had bolted home, a panicked message on her lips that Mother had deciphered after a few moments. Lynn remembered the shock that had passed over Mother's face; it was the first time she'd ever seen that Mother could feel fear. And then she had turned and run, leaving Lynn to follow as best she could. The strange man was propped on his good leg and leaning against Mother by the time she caught up. The sight of a metal trap, its jaws embedded firmly into swollen, stinking flesh just above the man's ankle, had brought Lynn to a screaming halt.

The two adults had shuffled awkwardly back to the house, Lynn carrying both their weapons and following behind. The man's foot had banged against the cinder-block wall of the cellar as they clumsily helped him down the stairs, and he'd howled so loudly that Lynn had run back to the landing, peering down into the basement as Mother eased him onto her own cot and looked critically at his ruined foot.

Mother had ordered Lynn back downstairs, and she had been put to work ripping a rag into shreds for binding, boiling water, and then to the upstairs kitchen for their sharpest knife. After that, she'd been banished to the upstairs bedrooms, somewhere she'd hardly ever been before. A thick coat of dust covered the room that Mother called "Lynn's room," even though she'd spent most of her life on the roof or in the basement, where the only windows were inches above ground level and easy to defend. She'd sat on the dusty frame of her unused bed and tried not to listen to the screams coming up through the vents.

The memory still had the power to chill her. The stranger had passed out under Mother's ministrations, and a shaken, pale version of her mother had come upstairs and sat next to her on the bed for a few moments before speaking.

"That man is named Stebbs, and he'll have to stay with us for a little while until he gets better," she had said calmly.

It was the first and only time Lynn could remember speaking to anyone other than Mother. She had very little memory of him, only that she'd had a fascination with his stubble that seemed to amuse him, once he was healthy enough to be amused by anything. And then he was gone, someone she would only see for years afterward through the lenses of binoculars or the crosshairs of a scope.

Five

The constant grating of Mother's handsaw came from within the outbuilding as Lynn cut maple saplings out of the fencerow with her hatchet. Mother needed green wood to smoke the meat, and Lynn's hands were soon slick from working with the living trees. The hard bulk of the handgun tucked into her waistband chafed against her ribs as she worked.

Making brine for the meat before smoking it was the next job, which required an unheard-of sin: pouring salt into water. Lynn balked at the thought, even after Mother had explained that it would kill the bacteria in the meat. The logic wasn't enough to stop her from bristling as she watched Mother pour twenty gallons of water into buckets loaded with salt.

"Gotta keep the brine cool," Mother said idly while she stirred.

"We'll leave it down here in the basement once I've shot a deer, and it's curing. Should take about a week."

Lynn only muttered in response. Gallons of the purified water she'd hauled into the basement bottle by bottle were ruined. Salted. As useless as ocean water.

Mother glanced up at her. "I know you don't like this, but it's for the best. It's worked in the past to shoot a small deer and freeze the meat, but this way I can take something bigger down. We salt it, we smoke it. We can take it with us without having to worry about spoiling."

"Take it where?" Lynn asked, her tone dark.

Mother kept stirring the brine, even though Lynn could see that all the salt had dissolved. "We got lucky the other night, Lynn. Real lucky. They weren't expecting us to be anything less than an easy target. We put them down, and they're not going to be happy about it."

"But you said they're set up in that little town that the stream runs through. Why would they want the pond?"

"Because the stream isn't dependable," Mother answered. "Those people to the east will learn it soon enough, I'm guessing the men from the south suspect it. But also they'll come because we beat them. Because they're men."

Lynn ground a naked toe against the stone floor of the basement, ignoring the pain as it bent backward. *Men.* Mother always spoke that word with such malevolence that Lynn could not imagine what they must be like. The dangers they posed to her survival she was aware of. Other threats, only hinted at by Mother, remained a mystery.

"So what do we do?"

"We go south with canned food and enough meat to take us as far as we need."

"You go on and make all the brine you want," Lynn said, pushing hard enough on her toe to bust the nail. "You can salt up a damn bear and pack him into nice little bundles. I'm not going."

Mother glanced at Lynn, her mouth twitching in a flash of humor. "Then I guess we'll have to kill the assholes."

Butchering was work. Mother had shot a much larger deer than usual, and the stripping of muscle from bone was exhausting. Once all the meat was immersed in brine, they looked at each other critically. The basement had a drain, but most of the blood was on them rather than down it. Even Lynn's face had splotches on it where she swiped at her hair while working. Her arms were slick with blood, and it squelched between her bare toes.

"I'll bring in some unpurified water," Lynn suggested. "We can use the tub."

Using the upstairs of the house was typically off-limits. When it was warm, they rinsed themselves in the pond, and during cold months there was a claw-foot tub in the basement that could be used for bathing. But that would mean dragging it out from the back-room, and neither of the women had the strength. Mother nodded in agreement, and Lynn began gathering buckets.

"You go ahead," Mother said when Lynn came back with water. "I'll keep a watch."

"You sure?"

Mother nodded. Rivulets of sweat ran down her face, cutting salty tracks in the deer blood. "I could use a break. I'll be up on the roof."

Lynn went inside, turning right on the landing instead of going straight to the basement. Five steps led up to a door that opened onto the kitchen, a door she'd walked through only a handful of times in her life.

She'd been taught to call out upon entering any house, something that had saved her skin once or twice when scavenging for food. "Hello? Anyone here?"

Nothing answered. Her voice echoed off the empty wooden cupboards. Even so, she felt a strange sort of comfort as she walked through the kitchen into the dining room. It was still her house, even if she lived underneath it. In a different life, she would've known the creak of these wooden floors as intimately as she did the hatchet marks in the wooden beams that held them up.

Lynn made her way to the bathroom, leaving footprints in the dust behind her as she went. The bathroom was a minor miracle in her eyes, to think that water had once come out of the faucet at the turn of a knob. Mother had even said that it was hot or cold depending on how you turned the knob, not on what season it was outside.

She twisted her finger around the faucet, imagining how amazing it would be to turn it and hear the splash of water in the porcelain tub. Mother had seen such things, had lived in a time when taking a hot bath was a relaxing thing, not a job that required hauling and heating water. Mother had used this room when she was Lynn's age, soaking in the heat and not worrying whether someone would kill her that night.

Lynn wondered what that would feel like as she stepped into her chilly bath and the blood slid from her skin, turning the water pink.

Four days after butchering, Mother said it was time to smoke the meat, and they spent most of the morning hanging the large chunks of venison from the rafters with hooks. Cold salt water dripped onto Lynn's shoulders and back as she dumped the last bucket of pinkish brine down the drain. Lynn was pouring fresh water over the bloodstains when Mother began unhooking chunks of venison from the ceiling.

"I'm carrying a load out to the smokehouse," she said. "I don't see anyone nearby, but come out and cover me with the rifle when I get ready to start the fire."

Lynn nodded, ducking under a dripping hunk of shoulder meat. She hurried to finish cleaning the floor as Mother's feet disappeared up the steps.

Lynn shivered once she made it outside and the cold air struck her wet shirt. The days had ceased to be pleasantly cool and were now downright cold, with a breeze that made Lynn wish she'd thought to grab a coat before rushing outside. She climbed the antenna before Mother made it out for her second trip, giving her the all-clear signal. An hour later, Lynn had set her rifle down and was lifting her shirt away from her skin.

Mother signaled that she was on her last trip, and Lynn waved back that she understood. Lynn flexed her fingers against the chill. Mother would be starting the smoke fire soon, which could attract attention. She was reaching for the rifle when she saw the tall grass swaying in a pattern that could not be caused by the wind. Three straight lines took shape, moving fast and headed toward Mother.

"MOTHER!" Lynn screamed. She was on her feet in an instant, the rifle aimed at the largest of the coyotes as he broke through the grass. She fired as she screamed, and Mother spun toward the sound.

The bullet caught Mother in the thigh, and the spurting blood drove the coyotes into a frenzy. They leapt at Mother, knocking her on her back and sending venison to the ground all around them. The salted meat was ignored—they were onto something fresh.

Lynn sprinted across the roof and flew down the antenna, skipping the last four rungs. She fell to the ground, her left foot folding underneath her. The cracking sound from her ankle drowned out her cry and she propped herself upright with the rifle. The triumphant high-pitched hunting song of the coyotes rang in her ears as she pulled herself to her feet and lurched around the corner of the house.

Big Bastard had Mother by the throat, while the other two tore at the wound that Lynn's bullet had opened. She fired again, from the hip, catching one of the smaller ones in the shoulder. The force of the shot threw the smaller coyote off Mother, and its partner backed away, head close to the ground and eyes glued on Lynn. Blood was no longer spraying from Mother's wound in an arc, but gushing as her heart slowed.

Lynn fell forward, her injured ankle refusing to support her. She landed on her stomach, knocking the wind out of her lungs and losing her grip on the rifle. Big Bastard still had a firm grip on Mother's neck. His ears flattened as his eyes met Lynn's, and he growled deep in his throat, claiming his prey.

"Bastard," she screamed, her throat clenched tight with tears.

The injured coyote struggled to her left, its leg dangling uselessly from the ruined shoulder. Its partner circled Lynn, sensing her weakness. She lunged for the rifle and it bolted away, dragging a piece of venison behind it. She swung the barrel and fired, but Big

Bastard was gone, leaving deep footprints in the ground that were steadily filling with Mother's blood.

Lynn dragged herself on her elbows to Mother's side. "Mother? I'm sorry," Lynn sputtered. "I'm so sorry, I didn't see them, I wasn't fast enough—"

"Shhhh," Mother muttered weakly, causing blood to bubble from the tooth marks in her neck. "Shh . . ."

Lynn leaned over her, plugging the holes with her fingers. When Mother spoke she could feel the air pulsing underneath them.

"When they . . . do that. Best thing in a . . . dog fight—" Mother inhaled sharply. "Try to . . . shove your arm . . . down its throat. Can't bite then."

Lynn nodded, tears dropping down onto Mother's upturned face. "Okay, Mother. I'll remember that."

"Didn't know if I . . . had told you that . . . should work . . . but my hands . . . were full." Her last words faded away, and Lynn hunched closer, desperate for more.

But all she heard was the death rattle.

Six

Twilight had fallen by the time Lynn had made a binding for her ankle out of Mother's shirt. She felt like a vulture as she stripped Mother's body of anything useful—knife, matches, even the hair tie she'd been using. Nothing should be wasted. Scavenging from bodies was nothing new to Lynn, but taking Mother's shirt from her as a cold sleet began brought her to her knees. She cried in long, gasping breaths that ripped through her body. Her knees slipped in the blood-soaked mud, and she fell face forward into the muck, where she saw her rifle.

She crawled toward it, wiping it as clean as she could on her shirt. The wind was gusting now, spitting freezing rain into her face and forming her hair into dark icicles around her face. She braced herself against the barrel of the gun and rose to her feet. Agony shot up her leg the second she tried to put any weight on her ankle. Bulging, swollen flesh puffed out from between the strips that she'd used to bind it.

Lynn heard muffled sounds in the grass between the gusts of the wind, and she looked at the pieces of venison still strewn around them. They were drawing predators. She grabbed Mother by the armpits and dragged her away from the circle of blood and meat. Her legs were useless; she settled for crawling, dragging Mother's corpse behind her. It took an hour for her to get to the driveway. The gravel bit into her flesh as she struggled to pull her own weight and Mother's.

She pulled Mother's body under the shelter of a pine tree and rested. The pine offered a little cover from the sleet, and she hoped that the smell might help mask their human scent. She was covered in blood and to an animal nose, Mother would already smell like death. The scavengers came and went through the night, fighting over the pieces of salted venison. At one point she heard two raccoons screaming at each other and then the shattering of glass. The smokehouse door had been open. She cracked her head against the trunk of the tree in frustration. All their meat was gone.

Shock had its way with her once the adrenaline was spent, and Lynn dozed. When something tried to drag Mother away by her foot Lynn snapped awake and fired blindly. She stared futilely into the black night, launching pinecones and curses at any noises she heard once she'd run out of bullets. When pink stained the sky, she saw that Mother's eyes were frozen open.

It was two days before she admitted that she would not be able to dig the grave. Her hobbled efforts had yielded a hole barely a foot deep in the frozen ground. She'd never be able to get Mother deep enough to keep the coyotes from digging her up. The skin around her ankle was green with bruising, the hollow pounding of it echoed in her ears as she dragged herself around on her elbows hour after hour, checking on Mother's body and attempting to claw away at the ground.

Leaving Mother to the coyotes was unthinkable, burying her impossible. After a long debate, Lynn pulled Mother into what was left of the smokehouse. The left window was broken, the door hung open. Clumps of dried mud formed a path where animals had tromped through the soaked yard to get their share. The few hooks left hanging from the beams had errant strips of meat clinging to them, peppered with teeth marks. Some were large and clearly canine. Tiny mice teeth had nibbled the pieces near the rafters.

Lynn laid Mother on the floor, looking upward through the hole she'd been cutting in the ceiling the day before. Thanks to Mother, Lynn knew what poetic justice was, and a sad smile tugged at her mouth as she used a match taken from the body of a man Mother had shot. The old wood of the outbuilding caught without hesitation, and the plume of smoke that reached into the sky would be visible to the south, Lynn knew. She sat in the tall grass with her injured ankle folded beneath her, and the rifle across her knees, almost hoping that someone would come.

The fire burned hot and fast, bringing down the building in a shower of sparks and leaving behind a pile of coals with no hint of bone among them. Once the last red ember had winked out, Lynn lurched down the stairs and to her cot in misery. She curled into the fetal position and faced the wall, her throbbing ankle resting on top of her healthy foot. The puffy flesh that rose from the top of her makeshift bandage pulsed against the fabric, fighting for the freedom to swell further. She would find no peace in sleep while it throbbed, but she pulled her pillow over her face to muffle her sobs.

She did not gather water for ten days.

Fear drove her from the tomb of the basement. A nightmare, rampant with images of men filing out of the fields and dipping their buckets into her pond had brought her up from her well of grief and pain. Her ankle was not broken; she could put more weight on it. She fashioned a splint for herself by snapping a wooden yardstick in half and binding the two strips to either side of her foot. It wasn't a cure, but she could hobble well enough to take care of herself.

She needed to get wood downstairs, the tiny pile next to the stove that had kept her alive while she mourned was gone, the level of water in the purified basement tank lower than what she cared for. The mental list of chores assembled in her head made Lynn feel better. The weight of purpose and responsibility helped to erase the feel of Mother's frozen hand glancing against her hair as Lynn pulled her into the smokehouse.

"*Work without Hope draws nectar in a sieve, And Hope without an object cannot live.*' Samuel Taylor Coleridge," Lynn said to herself as she tightened her bootlaces around the homemade splint.

The sight of trampled ground around the perimeter of the pond brought her rifle to the ready, safety off. Large coyote prints criss-crossed freely, brave and confident. Smaller tracks littered the shallower bank, where raccoons had been. Among them all, standing out sharply, was a pair of boot prints. Lynn stared at them, fear rising in her throat. By the depth of the print, he'd stood there a while.

Anger joined the fear as she imagined him surveying the property, dragging his eyes over her house while she lay injured and grieving in the basement. She heard something behind her and whirled, frightening a rabbit that had come to drink. The wildlife had become bold with no one to defend the pond, no shots ringing out over its placid surface.

Lynn made the trek to the barn and retrieved her buckets. Pain shot through her foot at the extra weight of ten gallons of water, but she struggled up the bank in spite of it, teeth gritted. There was no one to cover her, so she strapped her rifle to her back and hoped that she could be quick if the man returned.

Water seen to, she went back to the basement, unhooked the hinged window, and tossed wood through the hole until her arms couldn't take it anymore. With two people, the job had never felt hard. But Lynn was alone and injured.

She gathered blankets, extra ammunition, and a pillow. While the weather was warm, she would stay on the roof. Keeping a continuous watch would be impossible, but she could at least make her presence known. The man had been alone, of that she was sure. Whether he was only a traveler come to fill his bucket, or a scout sent by the party that had tried to overwhelm her and Mother, she did not know. Whoever he was, she would be ready if he returned.

Instead of men she saw dogs, and she blew the head off the first coyote that came to the pond for a drink. Boredom had taken a toll as she waited for the return of the mysterious man, but the still-kicking corpse of the coyote filled her with satisfaction. The second coyote came to investigate hours later, and she took him in the rear leg. He made it nearly a mile from the house before collapsing, which brought others out to him. She made short work of two and picked off the slowest ones as the pack bolted away.

It became an obsession, a twisted revenge for the needless death of Mother. The body that had fallen near the pond she dragged out into the field. None ventured any closer. The stink of surprise and death that it had sprayed in its dying throes was too powerful for animals to ignore. When the coyotes learned to skirt the western field, she picked them off in the east, and the buzzards swarmed.

Gathering water became a function she performed out of habit, not the task that used to fill her with a sense of urgency. She ate quickly and tasted nothing, but her real prey never showed his face. Lynn killed fifty coyotes in a few days, but never saw Big Bastard. Her bullets flew without thought for size or guilt, or even the ammunition that Mother had always warned was precious. By the fifth day, the smell of rot filled the air. The only thing that cut through it was the tang of gunpowder when she took another down.

Lynn's eyelids were growing heavy, her cheek resting against the warm rifle stock when a dark cloud of buzzards rose from the field, cackling anxiously about their disturbed meal. A man was coming across the field from the southwest, a handkerchief across his face to ward off the smell of the dead. Lynn squinted into the scope, watching as he skirted the corpses scattered in his path. His left leg dragged, the foot turned awkwardly inward.

Recognition startled Lynn. The loss of Mother had struck her so deeply she'd forgotten there was one other person she could name in the world—Stebbs. His halting pace slowed as he came toward a boulder that rested in the middle of the field. He leaned on it, mopping his neck from the strain of walking the distance from his cabin.

Lynn studied him through the scope. The twisted foot she

remembered from years of watching him lope back and forth on his daily routine in the woods. The red handkerchief she'd seen before too, often tied around his head if he was sweating, which seemed to be always.

He pulled something out of his pocket and held it up in the air. A piece of paper fluttered brightly in the wind. Lynn turned her barrel slightly into the setting sun so that rays flashed off it. He saw her signal and set the paper on the boulder, using another stone to weigh it down. Then he turned and slowly made his way back to his shack in the woods.

Lynn debated. Going out would be difficult. Without Mother, even trips to the pond were a test of nerves. With no one to cover her back, every step felt like a reprieve from death, each silent second without a sniper's bullet an unprayed-for miracle. The walk itself wouldn't be easy. Her ankle was much better, but the boulder was a half mile out. She tightened the laces on her boot as she thought through her options. Anyone watching the house would take it now, while she was gone. There would be no chance for her to sprint back and defend it, in her condition.

She slid behind the wheel of the truck cautiously, careful not to bang her ankle against the running board. The old engine fired to life and she backed out of the pole barn, sick at the thought of leaving the house even for a moment. She drove through the field without bothering to swerve around offal, oblivious to the riddled coyote bodies underneath her tires. When she reached the rock she left the engine running, moving as quickly as possible to get the note and drive back home.

She didn't open the folded paper until she was back on the roof. When she did, she snorted with unexpected laughter.

"Can you read?" it asked.

Lynn wrote her response. "Yes, I can."

She thought a second, then added another line.

"Asshole."

Seven

Lynn's war against the coyotes had caused a complication. Deer wouldn't venture within her range. After dropping her response to Stebbs at the rock, she tried to ignore the blooming hunger in her belly. Long months of vegetables for breakfast, lunch, and dinner lay before her. There was still a chance that she could hunt, take down a small deer sufficient for herself. If she wanted meat for the winter she'd have to leave the roof.

She lay prone, silently watching everything around her. Stebbs had not come for her note yet. Lynn bit her lip as she watched his red handkerchief moving through the woods as he went about his evening routine, as familiar to her as her own. Smoke bloomed to the east and the south, and Lynn looked at both pillars with suspicion.

She had come to think of the people to the east as the Streamers, which was a nicer name than Mother had used when they kept burning green wood. The lone boot print at the edge of the pond strayed through her mind. It could have been a Streamer, but what use would they have for her water? If it had been one of the men from the southern camp she doubted he would've overlooked the chance to take the house while it was unguarded. Stebbs was not in doubt; never in all her life had he approached her pond.

The white smoke of the Streamers dispersed into the evening sky, sending out a gray pall over the fields. There was no breeze; the smoke hung densely in the air. An evening fog rolled in from the west to join the haze, making the boulder stand out in stark contrast. As Lynn watched, a figure appeared beside it. She raised her binoculars to watch Stebbs.

She thought she detected a laugh go through his shoulders as he read her note. He scribbled an answer on the same piece of paper. Lynn didn't dare venture out until morning. The fog that had formed was becoming thick, and she might get turned around in the night. She pulled the quilt tighter around her shoulders. There was a chill in the air, enough that she gathered up her rifle and descended the antenna.

A night's uninterrupted rest would be welcome. If she couldn't see, they couldn't either. Lynn settled into her cot, oblivious to the complete darkness of the basement. When Mother had been alive, they would light the oil lamps and stay awake to talk, planning the next day's activities. Lynn needed no light to lie alone, wondering what the note waiting at the rock would say.

Lynn could live on her own. The daily duties of survival were well within her capabilities, but she couldn't defend herself constantly. The pond was foremost in her mind, and she couldn't keep a watch over it while cutting wood in the fencerow. Trips to the forest for larger loads of firewood were out of the question, as was any foraging of neighboring houses for the little things she would inevitably need.

Stebbs suffered the opposite problem; his daily chores were a trial because of his lame leg. They would benefit each other; he could watch the pond while she cut wood, and she would give him half in return. Water she would not part with. It seemed Stebbs wasn't in need of any, even though she never saw him hauling water to his shack from some unknown source.

Her ankle was taking weight more easily, though she still wore the makeshift brace under her boot. She was able to walk, but the stench of the coyotes choked her throat nearly shut as she made her way out to the boulder. Her shirt was tucked over her nose and she had her nostrils pinched shut through it by the time she opened the note. It read:

There are people at the stream.

She stared at it. She'd been expecting an offer of help, questions about Mother, or the burning of her outbuilding. Instead, it was a statement so obvious as to be nearly insulting. She was chewing on the end of the pen that she had brought, debating on an appropriate response when the man stood up from behind the boulder.

Lynn's instincts were too finely honed to allow for screaming. The rifle that had been lashed across her back snapped to the front so quickly that she would find a burn between her shoulder blades from the strap that evening.

He looked much different than she remembered. Years of watching Stebbs through the binoculars had not prepared Lynn for the reality of his person, the fine lines around his mouth, the brightness of his eyes, or the silver-streaked hair that peeked out from underneath his hat. She backpedaled, even though his arms were in the air and he had no weapon. The closeness of anyone other than Mother was so alien to Lynn that she had to smother the need to run away from his strangeness.

"Lynn," he said calmly, "it's all right."

She had never heard her name spoken by a man before. Even when he'd recuperated at their house, Mother had not allowed Lynn to be near him much. But his voice brought long-dead memories to the surface, the pleasant sound of his tones seeping through the floorboards above her head, murmured conversations not meant for her ears. His voice hadn't changed, but there was a calming note to it now, which her addled brain had a difficult time placing.

There was a brief time as a child when a fever put Lynn in her cot for a week, and Mother's entire demeanor changed. She had barely ventured to the roof, even neglecting to collect water as the fever spiked. The lines around her eyes, harsh from years of squinting into the sun, had softened during those few days in the basement. And her voice changed. The factual, clipped manner of her speech had dropped, to be replaced by a softer, more comforting tone.

Lynn recognized the same elements in Stebbs' voice. Her muscles relaxed slightly, and she brought the barrel of the gun down but ready to spring back to his center mass if necessary. Her throat, still constricted from the smell of rot, tightened further as she wondered what to say. Mother was the only person she could remember ever speaking to.

"Why'd you surprise me like that?" Lynn asked.

"I'm sorry." He came around to the front of the rock and sat on it, pulling his hat off his head and running his hands through his hair. "Didn't think you'd come if you saw me here, and I didn't want to waste days writin' if we could have a talk."

"Uh-huh?"

He reached for his inner jacket pocket, and Lynn's rifle snapped upward. "Whoa," he said in the same calming voice. "Just getting my hankie." She nodded for him to go ahead and he did so, slowly, keeping an eye on her trigger finger. The red handkerchief appeared and Lynn resisted the urge to reach out and touch it.

It was the only element of the outside world that had ever spoken of hope: a flash of red in the woods that had assured her they were not the last people left. Stebbs was proof that not everyone would attack them for the sake of drinkable water while they slept. For sixteen years, that splash of color had been her only proof of decency in the world.

Up close, details sprang out at her. The hankie wasn't solid red but decorated with a black-and-white paisley pattern. One edge was frayed away, and she could see awkward stitches in the splitting, brittle fabric where he had tried to prevent it from unraveling.

She'd seen many exactly like it, in the farmhouses she raided across the countryside. In one house, there'd been an entire drawer filled with red like his, and also navy blue ones. No doubt he'd come across them too, yet he stuck stubbornly to this one, with its patched holes and dangling strands. The handkerchief—familiar and yet foreign—drove a spike of emotion through her heart so unexpected her legs buckled underneath and she crumbled to the ground.

"I shot her." The words tore from her throat, a confession she'd not made aloud even in the solitude of the basement. "I killed Mother."

He was beside her in a second, strong hands on each of her shoulders. His touch was not the shock she had expected. Her skin did not recoil instantly, though years of being warned of the danger posed by all men had been ingrained in her. Instead, she leaned forward and put her head on his shoulder, relishing the feel of his jacket against her face.

"I heard shots." His hand patted her back, awkward but soothing. "What happened?"

"She's dead." Lynn pulled back from him, suddenly embarrassed at their closeness. "There were coyotes, and I . . . I missed."

He nodded that he understood and patted her shoulder with one hand. A flicker of deep emotion passed beneath his eyes, but with a single blink it was gone. He swallowed once, hard, and rose to his feet. She wiped her eyes quickly dry and he did the same. Stebbs cleared his throat and faced east.

"There are people over to the stream," he said.

"I know." Lynn clumsily rose, her ankle throbbing inside the tight boot. "Mother thought the Streamers wouldn't last the winter. They're burning green wood."

He grunted his agreement. "No shots from that direction. They don't have guns. They've stayed next to the water even though it's cold. I think they've got someone sick who can't be moved."

"Or they've got no way of hauling water," Lynn added, glad to be able to play a familiar game, even if it was with a new player. "So they weren't smart enough to bring a bucket."

They shook their heads at the same time. "City people," they said in unison, and Lynn caught herself smiling, her face creasing into the familiar pattern before she was aware of it.

Lynn jerked her head to the south. "Those men, they're bad news." Mother had used that phrase to describe the worst possible things in life: the haze of a hot summer morning that meant storm clouds but no rain; black, fuzzy caterpillars warning that the winter would be especially harsh; the tiny black droppings of mice scattered in their makeshift basement pantry.

"Bad news for sure," Stebbs said, shifting his weight off his twisted foot. "I heard them try to take you girls down."

"Didn't work," Lynn said stiffly.

"No . . ." he said, his voice trailing off in a wave of nuance that Lynn wasn't practiced enough to understand. The sound of his voice was unfamiliar to her ears, and only Mother's small actions, mimicked and perfected forms of communication, were translatable.

They stood in awkward silence for a few moments, sharing their dread of the black column of smoke to the south. "I don't know what to do about them," Stebbs said, and Lynn nodded her agreement.

"They've got a decent-sized group," she said. "Mother picked quite a few off in the dark that one night."

"Did she?" A smile skimmed across Stebbs' face as he continued to watch the south. He lowered himself slowly to the rock, resting his crooked foot at an odd angle. "What will you do if they come now?"

"Shoot them for as long as I can."

Stebbs nodded. Lynn's eyes trailed to his foot, her plan—labor in exchange for his guarding of the pond—seemed insulting with his mangled limb stretched out in front of her. He didn't appear to be in need of anything, from what she could see. His skin was tan, his color healthy, his arms heavily muscled. Making the offer would only make her seem weak, the deal balanced in her favor.

After a few moments rest, Stebbs propped himself on his good leg, jerking the other one underneath him as he rose. "You gonna be okay, kid?"

Lynn kept her sight trained in the distance. "Yup," she said dismissively, "I'm fine. Mother didn't raise any idiots."

"Didn't expect she would." Stebbs motioned toward the smoke of the Streamers' pitiable fire. "After their smoke's gone for a few days, I'm going over there, see if they had anything useful."

"Okay," Lynn said, surprised at his freedom to wander without worry. His little shack must hold nothing of value, and his source of water well hidden. She took a sideways glance at his injured foot. "It's a decent hike."

"Yup."

"I could go," she offered hesitantly. "If you'd stay and watch over the pond."

Stebbs rotated his twisted foot for a moment, considering. "You trust me to do that?"

"You could have killed us at any time." Whether Mother had liked him or not, Stebbs had been a constant presence who never threatened them, even when their defenses were down. "You don't need our water."

"No," he said. "I don't."

Lynn nodded, letting the conversation drop there. To ask where he got his own would be the highest of betrayals in their world. "So two days, do you think?"

"Two days of no smoke from the stream, and I'll come."

"All right."

They nodded stiffly and parted ways, each picking their path carefully through the bloated, rotting bodies of the coyotes.

Eight

"I can't go right now," Lynn argued, her arms bloody from the elbow down. A small deer carcass hung from the tree, a pile of organs and intestines underneath it. Stebbs looked critically at the jagged cut she'd made from clavicle to pubic bone. Mother's stronger, more confident slashes had looked much neater.

Stebbs ignored her protest while he looked at the tarp she'd rigged around some green saplings, tepee style. "You going to smoke it?"

"That's the plan. The shed's gone, but that tarp should do the trick for now."

"It'll draw attention."

"They know I'm here."

"Don't know you're alone," he countered. "If they send someone for a look and they don't see Lau—your mother, you'll be in a world of hurt."

She ignored him while she skinned subcutaneous fat off the carcass. He had a good point, but she didn't want to admit that she'd made a mistake in shooting the deer too early to freeze the meat.

"There's another way, you know," Stebbs said. "You can salt it, hang it in the trees to cure."

"I don't have enough salt."

"I do. I'll butcher this while you're gone; you split with me whatever the Streamers had."

Lynn didn't ask how he had enough salt that he could offer to preserve a whole deer for a neighbor. The process of rotting had begun the moment the heart stopped pumping, and already the flies were gathering at the folds of the wound she'd opened.

"Go get your salt then," she said stiffly.

Walking away from the house felt like a crime, even though she trusted Stebbs. The familiar roof looked distinctly odd from a distance, the tilted angles of the second story at odds with the lightly sloping section over the kitchen where she and Mother had always camped. When it was blocked from view by trees, Lynn clamped down on the surge of betrayal that filled her gut. She pushed the ever-present worry of whether Mother would approve to the back of her mind, as she crossed the clover field she'd seen every day of her life but not set foot in once.

She had tucked her hair under the stocking cap, a simple gender disguise that Mother had taught her, and the cool breeze brought goose bumps to her exposed neck. They prickled down her chest and the length of her arms. Autumn was gorgeous, with the leaves changing and falling, spinning to the ground to be crushed under her boots. But their death and downfall served as warning echoes to the other living things around them: the cold is coming, be prepared.

Lynn was confident the Streamers were dead. Their meager green fires had sputtered, then stopped entirely. Anything in a weakened state would not have survived the past two nights without a fire. She kept her rifle in the crook of her elbow as she picked her way through the long grasses toward the stream. There was no doubt that the camp of men had also noticed the passing of the Streamers. Buzzards wouldn't be the only scavengers picking over their campsite.

In other circumstances, it would have been a pleasant walk. The countryside was resplendent with color, the sky a bright blue. The breeze shifted the grass around her, wafting into her face the faintly spicy scent of green leaves turning brown. But Lynn's eyes saw only usefulness in these small miracles. The fading greens and yellows allowed her brown coveralls to blend nicely with the surroundings; the unclouded sky gave a little more warmth to the earth. The breeze shifting the grass covered the sounds of her movement, the slight fragrance from broken stalks masked her scent as she neared the stream.

She approached the camp from downwind, studying the area around her for other intruders. A squirrel chattered angrily and she dropped closer to the earth, aware that it was signaling distress. Lynn crept forward, ignoring the brambles that tugged at her as she moved.

The squirrel was perched warily on the opposite bank, rocked back on its haunches and regarding a straight line of acorns with suspicion. It chattered again, letting the whole woods know he was uneasy with the situation and unsure what to do about it. At the other end of the line of acorns squatted a little girl.

Her arm was outstretched, palm up, beckoning the squirrel to come closer. She was filthy, her face streaked with grime except for two clean rivulets streaking from her mouth where she'd drank from the stream. Her tattered shoes sucked at the mud as she tried to lure the squirrel closer. The sharp corner of her elbow poked through the worn crease of her sleeve.

The squirrel continued to chatter at the girl, while taking hesitant steps closer, stuffing acorns into its mouth. Lynn spotted the Streamers' campsite thirty yards downstream. Someone had dragged a fallen tree over to a live tree with a fork growing in it, propped the dead one into the notch and stacked branches along the sides to provide some cover. It wasn't a bad idea, but they'd neglected to put any mud or leaves over the branches. It might provide the barest shelter from the wind, but rain would drip in constantly, and it would hold no heat. A pile of half-burnt sticks lay in front of the opening.

No matter how badly it was made, the person who built it would've been much bigger than the child kneeling in the mud. Lynn kept her eyes on the shelter as she moved closer to the bank. Left on her own, the child would die, and soon. Even if she were successful luring squirrels, she had no way to cook meat and no source of heat. Even a stocked pantry wouldn't save her once the snow fell. She would die of exposure, leaving a small white skeleton to be carried away by the swollen spring river.

That image caused Lynn to fire her rifle before she was aware she'd made a decision. The squirrel's chatter stopped instantly, its body blown sideways. The girl jerked to her feet, oblivious to the fine spray of blood that flecked her pale face. Lynn crossed the stream with the gun pointing downward, hoping the girl would realize she meant no harm.

But the harm had already been done. When Lynn picked up her kill by the tail and presented it to the girl, her bottom lip shook.

"Cha-Cha." Her tiny voice barely escaped her mouth before evaporating in the cold afternoon air. "You killed Cha-Cha." The resounding wail that followed was much stronger, and Lynn dropped to her knees beside the child as tears started to spill forth.

"Stop!" Lynn spun left and right, nervous that they would draw attention. "Stop, please stop." She put her hands on the tiny, sharp shoulders, alarmed at how near to the surface her bones were. "I'm sor—"

The blow came from above and to the right, knocking Lynn into the stream, her rifle spinning out of reach. She flailed wildly, gasping for air before she'd cleared the surface. A rush of cold water filled her lungs and she scrambled for the bank, where she retched it back out. She'd lost her hat; cold, wet coils of hair hung in her face and she swiped them away, searching for her attacker.

"Christ," said a male voice. "It's a girl."

He was standing in front of the child, his arms spread wide to shield her, a thick branch in one hand. Lynn clutched her midsection, still queasy from the feeling of water rushing into the dark internal corners of her body. Her gun was lying in between them on the bank, but she made no move for it.

"Yes," she said, "I'm a girl." She struggled to her feet, alarmed at the unsteadiness in her legs.

He dropped his makeshift weapon and grabbed the child, pulling her in front of him. "Take her," he pleaded. "Take her with you."

"What?" Lynn crossed her arms over her chest, shivering in her soaked clothing.

The little girl recoiled, clutching at the boy and wailing incoherently. He pushed her toward Lynn, leaving small muddy ditches in the wake of her feet.

"Take her," he repeated. "I can't . . . I don't know how."

Lynn backpedaled away from his reaching arms and their strug-gling burden. Her unsteady legs folded underneath her, and she landed in a clumsy tangle of limbs and wet clothing. The child was shoved into her lap and instantly kicked her in the jaw. Lynn went over sideways, clutching her face.

The boy lifted the girl bodily in the air, shaking her with frustra-tion. "You'll die," he screamed into her face. "You stay here with us and we'll all die!"

A slow, building groan filled the forest, a sound so odd that hack-les rose on Lynn's neck and she dove for her gun. The boy didn't try to stop her. His arms went slack at the noise, and the little girl puddled to the ground at his feet.

"Mama," she wailed, fresh tears cutting paths in the grime of her face. "Mama."

"Everything's okay," the boy shouted toward the makeshift shel-ter, and Lynn's grip on the rifle relaxed. "It's all right," he said again, voice quivering with the effort of yelling. "Lucy's fine, she's right here with me."

The noise subsided, replaced by the small whimpering of the child kneeling in the mud. "Mama," she said again, peering anx-iously at the tent.

"Don't," the boy warned her. "You can't go over there."

Lynn glanced at the little girl. "Is your mama sick?"

She nodded vigorously in reply, but didn't speak.

"I put her in there," the boy said. "I didn't know what else to do."

"Is she yours?" Lynn asked, gesturing toward Lucy.

"What? No! I'm only sixteen," he said by way of explanation. "She's like, seven years old."

"I'm five," came the disgruntled retort.

"Is she *yours*?" Lynn tried again. "Your responsibility?"

"Oh. Well, I guess they both are, now," he said, fatigue filling every syllable. The little girl scuttled to his feet and perched there, eyeing Lynn distrustfully.

Lynn gingerly probed her head where the boy had hit her. A good-sized bump was forming there; it nearly filled the palm of her hand.

"Sorry," he said. "I thought you were one of them, coming back."

"You've been attacked before?"

He nodded. "Yeah, just the once though. Not an attack really, they just walked into my camp and took our food."

Lynn's jaded gaze swept what he referred to as his camp, and she saw him bristle even though she held her tongue.

"There wasn't anything I could do," he said. "They said they wouldn't hurt Lucy or Neva if I gave them our food."

"Neva?" Lynn asked, curiosity spiked by the unfamiliar name.

"Mama," came the answer, from the boy's feet. The girl, grown bored with the conversation, was drawing in the mud. "Mama's sick," she repeated when Lynn looked down at her. "I can't go in there, Eli said."

"Eli's probably right," Lynn answered. "Those men—when was this?"

He shrugged. "Neva wasn't in the tent yet, so maybe three weeks?"

"What have you been eating since?"

"Not much. I caught a fish with my hands one day. We found some berries, and Lucy's been catching grasshoppers—" His voice broke on the last word, tears that she hadn't expected began streaming down his face, but he was past the point of embarrassment. "I told her they were to cheer up her mom, but—"

He lost control again, a sob that shook his emaciated shoulders racked his body and buckled his knees. His arms folded around the little girl protectively, but when he looked up at Lynn there was steel in his voice. "You've got to take her."

Lucy trudged along by her side, tripping when the long grasses snared her knees. She refused Lynn's offers of help, stolidly asserting that anyone who had shot Cha-Cha didn't need to hold her hand. As the girl had gone to bid her mother good-bye, Lynn had quickly spitted the dead animal and hidden it behind a tree, explaining the process to Eli as she did so. He'd turned even paler at the sight of the sharpened stick emerging from Cha-Cha's throat, but didn't argue against eating him.

As they approached the house, Lynn hailed the roof with one arm. She didn't want Stebbs to mistake her for someone else. There was an acknowledging movement from the house, then she saw his dark form clumsily descending the antenna. Lynn glanced down at the little girl plodding alongside her. Weak as she was, a grim determination made her keep pace.

Lucy had argued, fought, pleaded, and eventually thrown rocks at Eli when he insisted that she was leaving the stream. He'd taken her aside and assured her that she could return once her mom was better, although the fleeting glance he'd shot at Lynn told her how long those odds were. Eli wasn't trained to survive and had even less experience in tending the sick.

The grasses shifted in the wind as Stebbs made his way toward them, rifle slung across his shoulder. Any surprise he felt at seeing Lucy was well masked. "Hi there, little one," he said. He bent down on one knee to talk to her, even though the posture was difficult for him with his twisted leg. "How are we supposed to split you, I wonder?"

Whatever animal magnetism the man had used on Lynn worked on Lucy as well. She ran forward and pitched herself into his arms, nuzzling her face against his old coat as if she'd known him forever. She pulled back, pointing a stiff finger at Lynn.

"She's a bad girl. She shot Cha-Cha."

Stebbs brow furrowed in confusion. "She shot who now?"

"There wasn't anything there for me to bring back," Lynn said for the third time as the trio huddled close to the cookstove, eating their supper.

"So you've said," Stebbs said, shoving a forkful of beans in his mouth.

"I just don't want you to think, you know—"

"That you stashed stuff in the woods and will get it later, when you don't have to split it?"

"Yeah, that exactly," Lynn said into her plate, face blazing. "I wouldn't do that."

Stebbs nodded and turned his attention to Lucy, who was eating from two jars at the same time. "Cut her off. She wasn't starving, but was close. She eats too much right away, it'll kill her."

"I know," Lynn said, stabbing a green bean with undue force.

"So the others, at the stream? You said there was a boy and a woman?"

"Yeah, Eli he said his name was, and the woman . . . I forget. Something weird."

"Neva," the little girl piped up. "Mama's name is Neva. It's pretty, not weird."

Stebbs and Lynn shared a glance. After that, they ate in silence, the sound of their forks dinging against the sides of their jars the only sound in the basement. The fire in the little cookstove was crackling pleasantly, and Lucy began to nod off. Her head tipped to one side and came to rest on Stebbs' shoulder.

"She's done in," he said, gently taking her food and fork away. "Wouldn't have lasted much longer."

"Yeah, I know," Lynn grunted, pretending to search for the last bits of bean stuck to the sides of her jar.

"You done the right thing, bringing her back."

"What else was I going to do?"

Stebbs' face became serious as he looked down at the little head nestled against him. "There's always options."

"The mother won't be lasting long."

"What is it, do you think?"

"Don't know," Lynn answered. "The boy wouldn't let the little one here close to the tent. They both drank straight from the stream, so I wouldn't be surprised if it was cholera. I never got a look at her, and I wasn't interested."

"Mama's sick," Lucy mumbled. "Baby won't come out."

Lynn and Stebbs exchanged glances. "Baby?" he asked. "Your mom is pregnant?"

Lucy nodded sleepily. "Eli wouldn't let me see her, he said the baby might come out, and it would be yucky."

"That's one word for it," Stebbs said, gently urging Lucy's head off his shoulder. "Come on now, little one, time for bed."

"A real bed?" Lucy asked as Stebbs cradled her tiny frame in his arms. "With a pillow and everything?"

"A pillow and everything," he promised, and laid her down on Lynn's cot. She burrowed under the blankets, curling her knees up to her chest. Lynn tried not to grimace at the sight of her filthy head resting on the clean pillowcase.

"Think she's got lice?"

"Lice, and fleas too, I wouldn't doubt," Stebbs said, motioning to Lynn to follow him up the stairs. "You'll want to boil those sheets in the morning. And get her a hot bath, first thing."

They emerged into the cold night, the stark brilliance of the stars shining down on them. The air was so cold, the stars so clear, that Lynn could make out the shapes of the last leaves clinging to the maple branches. Larger shapes hung among the limbs as well.

"The venison?" she asked, jerking her chin toward them.

Stebbs nodded. "Leave it there 'bout a month or so. I'll come help when it's time to get it down, take my share. Nothing much should bother it up there, a squirrel or two maybe. I understand you're not too partial to those?"

"I didn't know it was her pet," Lynn shot back.

Stebbs sighed and looked up at the brilliance of the night sky. "Your mom taught you a lot, but she couldn't've taught you what she didn't know, like how to take a joke."

"I'll laugh when something's funny," she retorted, sinking down to sit on the ground. "And right now, that's not a lot. My provisions are back to feeding two."

"I'll help, and I owe you for my supper tonight."

"No," Lynn said. "Bringing her back was my decision, and our deal was to split whatever I got from the camp in return for you butchering my deer. You did your half, and all I brought back was more work."

"Maybe," Stebbs answered. "But the deal *was* to split what you found. I'll help with the girl."

There was silence between them for a moment while a strange feeling bloomed inside Lynn's chest, something else Mother had never taught her. Gratitude.

"Now," Stebbs said. "What to do about the boy and the mother?"

"I've got my share of work," Lynn said. "And then some."

Stebbs lowered himself to sit beside her, an action both clumsy and endearing. "Maybe so, but if they get back on their feet, the girl won't be your problem anymore."

Lynn shook her head. "They're sunk. The boy was in worse shape than the little girl. I'm guessing he's been giving most of the food to her and the woman."

"Who is eating for two," Stebbs reminded her.

"Like I said—sunk."

Another silence settled over them, this one permeated with the knowledge that an argument was about to begin.

"I won't leave them there to die," Stebbs said.

"You were happy enough to last week."

"It's different now. That little girl has a family; we're able to stop her from being orphaned. Wouldn't you want someone to take a chance if it meant you could have your mother back?"

A long pause followed. Lynn dug her fingers into the cold ground at her feet and watched Stebbs from the corner of her eye. He was absolutely still, but she could feel his steely blue gaze.

"Those people wandered out here unprepared, they invited their own fate. The only person to blame for what happened to Mother is me." She stood up, wiping the cold dirt from her hands. She offered him a palm. He took it, and she jerked him to his feet roughly, forcing all of his weight onto his bad leg. Stebbs grabbed at her for support and she dug her free hand into his upper arm.

"We'll help them," she said. "But you don't ever talk to me about Mother again unless I ask."

He nodded his agreement and she released his arm. He stumbled away from her, rubbing where her iron grip had been. "It's the right thing to do. Just like bringing Lucy back here was."

"I'll go with you tomorrow night, after she's asleep," Lynn continued as if Stebbs hadn't spoken. "The boy knows me, at least. If you walk in there, he might hit you over the head with a rock. Wouldn't want that."

"Tomorrow night," Stebbs agreed, and melted into the darkness. "I think we're in danger of becoming friends," his voice echoed back.

The girl was deeply asleep when Lynn returned to the basement, and she didn't have the heart to wake her. Stebbs had unknowingly put Lucy in Lynn's own bed, and so she laid down in Mother's cot, surprised at the waft of scent that enveloped her as she slid under the blankets. Mother's smell was there, the outline of her body still imprinted on the mattress. Lynn fit into it nicely, and watched over Lucy while she slept.

Nine

The girl slept through the morning, and Lynn took the opportunity to confirm the fact that she did have lice. And fleas. She heaved a long sigh as she rocked back on her heels, contemplating the work to be done. The girl could bathe in water straight from the pond. It would have to be warmed on the cookstove, then carried upstairs to the bathroom. She took one of Mother's huge canning pots down from a hook in the ceiling. It would take a very hot fire and a lot of time to boil the amount of water necessary for cleaning the bedding.

She made her first trip to the pond as a ribbon of pink was appearing on the horizon. A pistol was tucked into her belt, but Lynn was satisfied that nothing—and no one—was roaming in the grass. The onset of fall and lack of rain had dried everything to a crisp, making any movement a crackling announcement of your presence. The sight of the pond's gravelly bank didn't improve her mood. A fresh, new ribbon of shiny broken mussel shells and small rocks showed where the pond had recently receded. The white grip of her bucket handle loomed ever closer to the surface.

Lynn toyed with the idea of leaning in to grab it, removing forever the implied threat at the sight of it. But without it she was lost. All ponds have a bottom; she could only hope that hers was still well beneath the surface. If Mother had known exactly how deep the pond was, she had never told Lynn. The bucket handle was the only frame of reference she had.

Her boot stuck in the fresh mire near the pond's edge as she struggled up the bank. It came free with a sucking sound and sent her reeling forward, dumping half a bucket of freezing water down her leg. "Son of a bitch!" She screamed the worst thing she'd ever heard Mother say, then kicked the bucket in anger, which only resulted in splashing her with more cold water.

Miserable and wet, she filled two more buckets and struggled toward the house with them. The basement air was warm and welcoming after the biting cold of the fall morning. Lynn peeled her wet clothes off and hung them from the rafters, put on fresh clothes and filled the stove pot with cold water. More wood went into the stove, and she checked her indoor supply. Low. Nearly out. She'd have to haul more before the end of the day if she was going to get the girl clean, her sheets sanitized, and a large enough fire to keep them warm through the night.

She considered waking the girl up and making her help, but the tiny little wrist hanging over the edge of her cot stopped her. It wasn't much thicker than the kindling she used to start fires. If she asked her to haul wood, it might snap. Once she started throwing wood in through the window it would wake her. Lynn decided to give her a few more moments' rest.

It was cold enough for her to slide mittens on to shield her fingers from the frigid metal of the antenna as she climbed to the roof. There was nothing to the south. Lynn rested her binoculars on her chest. She hadn't heard gunshots lately; the men were not hunting, though three weeks ago they'd been desperate enough to steal a few cans of food from a young girl and a pregnant woman.

There was nothing from the Streamers' camp. They were the Streamers again, nicely impersonal. Lynn chose not to think of them as Eli and Neva. Especially with no smoke rising after such a cold night.

She raised the binoculars again and searched for Stebbs, not finding him. If he was off gathering water at his mysterious source, she might be able to spot him on the return trip. Half an hour passed with no movement. Disappointed, she laid the binoculars on the shingles beside her. Twenty minutes later, a thread of worry had traced its way through her heart. Was he injured? Had she been too forceful with him last night when she threw him off balance? Had she hurt his leg?

A flash of red caught her attention and she flipped the binoculars back up. Stebbs emerged from inside, yawning and stretching. He patted his midsection a few times before sitting down on a large stump near his door. Lynn checked the sun. It was nearly ten in the morning. "Lazy asshole," she muttered.

A rustling sound and the flight of several disturbed grasshoppers caught her attention and Lynn dropped the binoculars, snapping the rifle up to her shoulder. Below, Lucy burst out of a clump of grass, empty palms desperately smacking at the grasshoppers. A lump formed in Lynn's throat.

"Hey," she yelled toward the ground. "You don't have to do that anymore."

Lucy looked around, trying to find her.

"Up here," Lynn called. "I'm on the roof."

The little girl shaded her eyes and waved when she saw Lynn. "I don't have to do what?"

"Eat grasshoppers," Lynn explained as she climbed down the antenna. "I've got real food here."

The girl made a face. "I wasn't going to eat them. Who eats grasshoppers?"

"Uh, nobody I guess," Lynn fumbled, forgetting that the boy had never fessed up to Lucy about what he was feeding her.

"I was catching them for you," Lucy continued. "Eli always was saying that they made Mama happy, so I should catch as many as I could. I thought maybe they'd make you happy too."

"It would make me happy if you didn't come busting out of the grass like that," Lynn said. "Don't surprise me when I've got a gun. I don't want to—"

She broke off, unable to speak around the lump that had gotten bigger.

"You don't wanna what?"

"I don't want to shoot you by accident."

It began to rain. A lovely blessing for many reasons. Years ago, Mother had the insight to run a drainpipe from the roof down into the bathroom. The jagged edge of the rusty pipe was jammed with a piece of flannel that Lynn jerked free. A tide of rusted water and leaf debris came first, spilling into the bucket she'd brought. Once the rainwater ran clear she let it fall down into the tub to supplement the hot water she'd dragged up from the basement.

"Wuzzat?" Lucy's nose wrinkled at the smell of the rotted leaves in the bucket.

"Just rotting stuff," Lynn said, swirling her hand through the water to test the temperature. "This'll even out in a second, and I'll plug the pipe so it's not dripping rainwater on your head."

The girl shrugged her indifference and continued to pick at a scab on her knee. "Why don't you turn on the faucet?"

Lynn sighed and rested her head on the side of the tub. "I told you, I don't have running water. That's why I was dragging buckets up from the basement."

The mundane task of boiling water had brought quizzical Lucy to the edge of the cookstove, climbing onto a chair to pinpoint the exact moment the bubbles started forming on the surface. "How do I know when it's boiling?"

The question had brought Lynn to an abrupt halt. "I don't know, 'cause it's . . . boiling." The answer hadn't satisfied Lucy, so Lynn had explained the concept of bubbles and steam. "Haven't you ever boiled water?"

"No," Lucy had said defensively. "Why would I?"

That response combined with the request to turn on the faucets caused Lynn's own curiosity to flutter. "Where are you from anyway? What were you doing out in the woods?"

"Entargo," the girl answered, testing the water with her fingertips.

Lynn stopped stirring the water. "Entargo," she repeated. "The big city?"

"Yeah," Lucy said, blissfully unaware of the effect her answer had. "We lived there my whole life, 'til we had to leave."

"Why? What happened?"

"Don't know. We just did."

Lynn hadn't known many people in her life, but the flat line of the girl's mouth was familiar enough to her. There would be no more conversation along that line.

Lynn stuffed the flannel rag back into the end of the drainpipe, ignoring the spray that spattered her as she fought against the flow. She dug into the linen cupboard for a thin washcloth and a bar of flat white soap, handing them to the girl.

Lucy looked at the bar in her hand. "What's this for?"

"It's soap. To wash with."

The girl looked dubiously at the bar, then sniffed it. "It doesn't smell like the soap from home."

"It smells like clean," Lynn said brusquely. "Mother and I made that ourselves. That's hard work, so don't you be wasting it."

Lucy closed her grip around the soap. "Where's your mama?"

"Dead."

The little girl nodded and stopped asking questions. Young as she was, she understood that the conversation ended there.

Lynn cleared her throat. "All right then. You clean up good. Wash your hair with this." She handed Lucy a bottle filled with a green gel. "Let it sit for a bit before your rinse off."

The girl bit down an objection when she saw the picture of a dog on the bottle, but took it meekly enough.

"Toss your clothes out in the hall," Lynn continued. "I'll be burning them." There was no response so she slid out the door.

"Wait!" The anxious call brought her back.

"What is it?"

"I can't do these," the girl said, pointing to her shoelaces.

Lynn sighed and plopped onto the floor next to the girl. "It's not so hard," she said. "You just pull on the loose end. Didn't your mama teach you that?"

"I can untie my shoe," Lucy objected haughtily. "They just won't come off."

Without asking for an explanation, Lynn tugged on the laces. The rotten ends fell off in her hands. "Sit still," she ordered, and went to the kitchen for a knife. The rest of the laces split easily under the blade. She gripped the shoe and was about to tug it off when the girl cried out, digging her fingernails into the bar of soap.

"What's the problem?"

The girl only shook her head, biting down on her lip as Lynn slid the sneaker off her tiny foot. The bloody, pus-encrusted sock answered her question.

"Kid," she said, covering her nose against the smell, "how long have you been out there?"

The attic brought back memories that Lynn would have preferred to leave buried. It wasn't a place they had used often, only when putting away the clothes Lynn had outgrown and finding the box that held her next size. Mother had always called it "going shopping," and encouraged Lynn to try on everything as soon as she found the right box. It had been a game of sorts, one of the few times Mother would rest, reclining on an old chair propped in the corner as Lynn tossed clothes everywhere in her excitement. Clothes. Clothes and shoes.

Lynn was guessing as she made her way through the antique trunks Mother had used for storage. Lucy couldn't be nearly the size she had been when she was five. It might be best to go for a size lower. She popped the lid on the right trunk, glancing through the contents for something for the girl to put on when she was out of the tub.

"Something warm, something warm," Lynn muttered to herself as she tossed aside clothes. The rain continued to fall, pounding out a staccato beat on the roof of the attic. What little light there was came from a small circular window. A pair of shoes rolled out of the pile of clothes she was holding and rattled to the floor. She considered them briefly, but tossed them aside. Lucy's feet had practically become a part of her shoes, the sides had burst long ago and water had seeped into them. Judging by the state of her feet, the little girl hadn't complained, so no one had told her to take her socks off and dry them.

She made a pile of warm clothes, choosing only two or three outfits. Lucy wasn't moving in, she reminded herself firmly, she was only staying until . . . until when? The look the boy had shot her yesterday had said Lucy's mother wasn't going to make it. Once he was free, would the boy move on or stay to care for the little girl? Lynn hadn't thought past the initial action of taking Lucy with her, when Eli's gray eyes had begged her to. Suddenly angry with herself, Lynn snagged two pairs of warm socks out of the trunk and slammed the lid shut.

A high-pitched singing filled the downstairs, along with splashing noises. Lynn paused before opening the door; the unencumbered sound of happiness was so odd to her that she allowed Lucy's off-pitch, unfamiliar tune to fill her ears, like the rising sound of the filling water tanks. A massive splash and wasted water cresting over the edge of the tub made her crack the door to the bathroom.

"Hey in there, you need to be getting out soon. Water'll get cold and I don't need you sick on top of everything. I gotta see to your feet as it is."

There was a long pause. "Will it hurt? My feet?"

"Probably," Lynn answered, thinking of the flaps of skin that had peeled off along with the socks.

"I think I'll stay in a little bit more."

"C'mon now," Lynn said, pushing her way into the bathroom. "You've been in there long enough."

Lucy's frail body floated on the surface of the tepid water. Her ribs stuck out so far that water had rushed into the valleys in between them. More dead skin had sloughed off her feet in the water; strips of it trailed from her heel. Lynn wrapped her in a towel, astonished at the lack of weight in her arms. The girl burrowed into her cotton fortress and admired her new outfits while Lynn picked through her hair for dead lice and nits. There had been a thriving civilization on Lucy's head, and it took the better part of the afternoon to rid her of them.

Lynn saved the feet for last, once Lucy was happily snuggled into her basement cot and eating corn. The warm bath combined with food and the heat from the fire lulled her. Lynn waited until she had fallen asleep, her small hand still tightly gripping the spoon. Her feet were a mess. Dead skin hung in flaps from blisters long since burst, a fungal infection covered most of her left sole, and all her toenails had grown inward in response to the shoes that hadn't left her feet. It was a miracle that the girl could still walk.

The dead skin came off first, Lucy's feet twitched in response but there was no real pain. The baking soda paste Lynn used on the fungus caused her to whimper a little, but she soon quieted. The toenails presented a real problem. Cutting them out was going to be painful. Three of her toes were inflamed with the pressure, two of them had pus-filled cysts under the skin. It would have to wait until Stebbs was there to hold her down.

There was a small supply of painkillers hidden away with the guns, but Lynn could never remember using them. When she was about Lucy's age one of her eardrums had burst from an infection. It had swollen so tightly that the eventual rupture had spewed pus, blood, and small pieces of her eardrum. She'd held her tongue tightly against the pain, knowing that Mother had been splinting her own broken ankle a week before without so much as a Tylenol.

Lynn's hand snuck to her ear as she remembered. Mother had been furious with her, even as she had sponged the stinking mess of pus from her face. "You should have told me," she'd seethed. "I would have given you something."

But Lynn was partly deaf at the time, and Mother's words had been muffled. They were both saving the pain medications for another day, a different, more horrible wound. The fever had passed, her eardrum had grown back, and the painkillers remained untouched. Lynn pressed one of Lucy's infected toes experimentally, and the girl whimpered in her sleep. Lucy had done the same, hidden her pain to save others the worry.

Lynn pulled the covers down over the small white feet, tucking them under her heels. "When it's time, we'll use the medicine, little one," she said softly. "You don't need to suffer more than you have."

Ten

Stebbs appeared a few hours later, at dusk. The reverberations of his awkward footfall on the basement steps caused Lucy to stir but not wake. Lynn lifted the edge of the sheet that hung drying from the rafters. "Shhh," she admonished, gesturing toward the small form humped underneath the blankets. "Don't wake her."

"Sorry," Stebbs whispered, then gestured for her to follow him.

Lynn grabbed her rifle and tucked a pistol into her belt. Aboveground, the sun was leaving the last hint of a pink stripe in the sky. Stebbs considered it while talking to Lynn. "Think she'll sleep long?"

"Don't know. Not around kids much."

He grunted in response.

"She fell asleep right after her bath," Lynn added. "I don't imagine we'll be long down at the stream anyway."

The implied question was not answered, and she glanced at him out of the corner of her eye. "Sorry about last night," she finally muttered. "I shouldn't have pushed you."

"I shouldn't have pushed you either," he said.

It was her turn to grunt. They both watched the horizon for a few minutes, their gazes drawn to the south. "All right then." She hoisted her rifle across her shoulder. "Let's go and be done with it."

They made their way to the creek, conscious of the rustling of nocturnal wildlife all around them. A raccoon lumbered across their path. He stood on his hind feet and studied them closely, his black nose wiggling while he tried to place their scent.

"Scat," Stebbs hissed at him. The coon lowered himself and tumbled into the night, unconcerned by their presence. "Used to be we shot them that acted like that," Stebbs said. "Meant they were sick with the distemper."

"And he's not?"

Stebbs shook his head. "Doubt it. Just doesn't know what to think of people, is all. We're not as common as we used to be." They trudged on a few more minutes in silence.

"Almost there," Lynn said when she spotted her own boot prints in the wet bank. They stood out black and hollow even in the dying light of dusk. "This is where I spotted the girl."

"You should be the one to call to him," Stebbs said. "Beings as he'll know your voice."

"We didn't talk all that much," Lynn said, then cupped her hands to her mouth. "Hello, the camp!"

The only answer was the rustle of falling beech leaves, and a frantic scurrying sound in the underbrush nearby. "Try again," said Stebbs.

She shouted again, this time adding a high-pitched whistle on the end of her call. No response.

"How bad of shape were they in?" Stebbs asked.

Lynn's eyebrows drew together in concern. "Not as bad as all that," she said. "Unless someone—"

A piercing scream split the night air, dropping Stebbs and Lynn to the ground in an instant, their hands going to the pistols at their belts. It broke on a high note, followed by a screech and a howl of pain that dwindled into a racking sob.

"The woman," Stebbs said soberly. "That'd be labor."

"Labor?"

"The baby's being born."

Lynn's hand tightened on her gun, for all the good that it would do her in that situation. "What do we do?"

Stebbs got to his feet awkwardly and brushed the dead leaves from his flannel shirt. "I know a thing or two about it," he said. "If that boy is as green as you say, I doubt he's much help."

Lynn stayed on the ground, peering through the bracken as if for an enemy. "What do you want me to do?"

"Get up, for one." He hauled her to her feet.

Lynn hallooed the camp when they were close enough to make out the feeble gray wisps of smoke climbing skyward from the fire. Eli burst out of the shelter, looking wildly in every direction. "Girl? Is that you?" He held a branch above his head in case it wasn't her, but it didn't look like he posed much of a threat. His weapon was thicker than his arm.

"Christ, he's skinny," Stebbs muttered.

"I'm coming in with a friend," Lynn yelled toward the camp, pausing only slightly before using the word *friend* to describe Stebbs. They splashed across the stream to Eli, who lowered his club and squinted into the night.

"Hello, son," Stebbs said as he emerged from the darkness. "Name's Stebbs." He held out a hand, and Eli shook it.

"Eli," he said shortly.

"The girl here is Lynn, somehow I doubt she introduced herself properly when you met." Lynn nodded to Eli across the fire.

"How's Lucy?"

"The girl's fine," she said. "That her mother screaming?"

Eli nodded and gestured toward the shelter but came up with no words.

"She trying to be mother to another?" Stebbs asked gently.

99

"All day it's been like this," Eli said. "I don't know what to do. The baby won't come out, and Neva is exhausted."

A cautious silence had emanated from the shelter since they'd converged onto the camp. Lynn had stalked a bobcat through the woods once. Mother had sent her out to find a turkey, but the unfamiliar flash of a feline coat had caught her attention and she'd taken it as a challenge. Bobcats weren't common, and Lynn had known she was out of her league when she'd emerged into a clearing where she knew the cat should have been, but was out of sight. The same feeling was with her on the bank, the idea that she was being watched by unfriendly eyes attached to a body that was ready to pounce if it made up its mind to do so.

"We're not here to bother," she said loudly, hoping her voice carried to those perked ears. "Just wanted to let you know Lucy's all right."

Eli's face fell. "You're not leaving, are you?"

"Hold up now," Stebbs said to Lynn. "If they need our help, we're here to give it." Lynn's eyes cut uneasily to the shelter Eli had constructed, but she kept her mouth shut. "First off, why are you down here on the stream? There's plenty of empty houses to put her up in to bear the child."

"Neva says she won't go. She's heard too many stories, people's faces turning black without water, their bodies shriveling up as they die slow."

"It happens."

"She won't come away from the water. I set this up for a temporary camp, but she wouldn't move from it."

"It's not so bad," Stebbs reassured him. "Probably leaks like a bastard though."

"It's not waterproof, no," Eli admitted.

"Can't hold any heat either, I reckon."

In the firelight, Lynn could make out a blush creeping up Eli's sharp-boned cheeks. "No, it can't."

"So here you've got a pregnant woman and a child living under a bunch of dead twigs next to a stream when winter's coming on?"

"I didn't know what else to do," Eli said tightly, desperation making him bite off each word.

"How about not letting the most paranoid person in your bunch call the shots?" Lynn suggested, then fought down her own blush when Eli turned his angry glare on her.

Stebbs cleared his throat. "Water can be hauled. You get her set up in some real shelter with some heat in it and bring the water to her. Staying next to the stream in the summer and fall's fine. But in the spring, it'll drown ya, in the summer it could disappear altogether. You stay by it in the winter, one morning you'll wander out to your precious water source to find out you froze to death in the night."

Eli's jawline was set tightly, and Lynn had lived long enough with a person who had a temper to know that the fuse was getting short.

"I'm afraid your suggestions come a little late," he said as another wrenching moan rose from the shelter behind him.

She'd been fighting it. Lynn could tell by the stifled sound of the cry that the sufferer did not want them made party to her pain. Stebbs flicked on a flashlight and moved to the mouth of the shelter. "I'm here to help you. I'm no doctor, but I've seen my share of goats born and helped a few of them along."

He'd made it about a foot into the shelter when he came flying backward, landing in the mud.

"Keep away from me, you fucking perverted cripple!" The scream that followed Stebbs' exit was shrill, laced with fear and pain. "Eli! Eli, where are you?"

Lynn helped Stebbs up as she listened to Eli trying to calm the panicked woman inside. She approached the entrance to have a clod of dirt smack her in the face.

"I'm done here," she said to Stebbs. He grabbed her arm as she turned for home.

"She's in labor—you don't know what that's like."

"Don't much care either," Lynn said, rubbing the spot on her jaw where the dirt had hit her. But she stayed.

Eli emerged. "She said you can go in." He pointed to Lynn. "But not Stebbs."

"Stupid choice," Lynn said. "I don't know the first thing about this. At least he's seen it."

"With goats," Eli countered.

"More than I got," Lynn answered, but ducked her head and shuffled into the shelter.

The woman lay under a pile of clothes, writhing with pain. When she realized Lynn was there, she made a conscious effort to control it, but her hands dug deeply into the dirt on both sides of her hips. The repeated action had dug holes there as deep as her wrists.

"You don't have to hide it," Lynn said. "Pain is nothing to be ashamed of."

Black eyes regarded her with contempt. "Pain isn't the word," she seethed, her perfectly symmetric white teeth biting off each syllable. Another contraction struck and she balled her fists into the earth. Cords stood out on her neck as she struggled against it, and her lips peeled back in a grimace. Lynn could only watch until it passed.

"Do something," the woman spat at her. Sweat streaked her face even though the night was cold, her black hair was tangled in dark coils from tossing.

"I can't," Lynn said calmly. "I know nothing about it. Better off to let Stebbs in."

"He won't be touching me."

The undeserved hatred directed at Stebbs made no sense to Lynn, so she sat quietly through another contraction that left Neva panting. "I'm wasting my time here with you," Lynn informed her. "I've gotta get back." She rose to leave.

"Wait! I'll let him in," Neva said as if granting a favor. "Just get it out of me."

Lynn emerged into the darkness, handing the flashlight off to Stebbs. "Your turn." He ducked into the shelter, and a murmured conversation followed, pausing whenever Neva suffered a contraction too painful to speak through.

"What do you think?" Eli asked, his gaze bouncing off Lynn's when they met over the flickering fire. She lowered herself to the ground before answering.

"Don't know. She's worn out though, and that's not good with the baby still on the way."

Eli nodded and they sat in silence. He flinched when Neva's cries came again, louder this time and more desperate. Lynn stared impassively into the fire, noticing that Stebbs had placed dead wood on it.

"You got to use the dead," she said. Eli snapped out of his trance.

"What was that?"

"Dead wood." She pointed to the fire. "You use the green, living stuff and you get more smoke than heat."

"Okay."

The silence fell again, but it felt awkward now that she had tried to break it unsuccessfully. "They take your blankets? Those men?"

"Yeah." Eli's voice caught in his throat from disuse. "Yeah," he repeated more clearly. "Blankets and our food. I went to a house looking for more, but they'd all been stripped. Most of the clothes were gone too, except for some that were way too big for anybody I've ever seen. I took them to use for blankets for Neva and Lucy."

Stebbs voice cut through the night. "Lynn, come here."

She approached the entrance warily. "What is it?"

"Take this," he handed her a bundle. "Bury it."

Lynn gingerly took the dirty shirt, alarmed at the heat soaking through it. She shot Stebbs a questioning glance.

"Born dead." He drew an arm around her shoulders, bringing her closer to him. "Take the little thing a bit aways and bury it. Mother's not doing so well."

"She going to make it?"

"Not doing so well up here." Stebbs pointed to his temple, then his heart. "And here."

Lynn tucked the small bundle under her arm. Eli followed her downstream, dazed and silent. She had no idea how she was supposed to dig a grave in frozen ground with no shovel, but Stebbs had his hands full with the mother. She climbed the bank when it rose to shoulder height and chose a small clearing enclosed by mountain ashes.

"This should be easy enough to find again, if she wants to come and see it," she said to Eli, who only nodded. His fingers were clenched tightly around the flashlight Stebbs had handed off to him. "Plus the bank is high enough here, spring floods won't wash it away."

There was no response. Lynn sat the little bundle on the ground, ignoring the wetness that had soaked through the wrappings onto her clothes. "Find me a good-sized stick, pretty sharp." Eli seemed grateful for direction; he disappeared into the darkness.

Lynn waited for her eyes to adjust to the moonlight, then went back to the streambed in search of rocks. They met again in the clearing and he began hacking at the ground with the stick, opening raw wounds in the earth. Once he had a furrow dug Lynn scraped away with a flat rock. "We won't be able to get very deep," she said. "But we'll cover him with some good-sized rocks so nothing will bother him."

"Him?"

"What's that?"

"It was a boy?"

"Oh." Lynn thought for a second. "I don't really know. Stebbs didn't say."

Eli hesitated before unwinding the motionless bundle. Lynn looked away, intent on her task. "You were right," he said after a moment. "It was a boy."

She grunted in response, unsure what to say. Eli rewrapped the tiny body. "He's cold already." His hands hovered over the little bundle that had held warmth before the night wind had ripped it away. "My brother always wanted a son."

"He can have more. Come help me."

An hour later, Eli laid his nephew into the small hole they'd managed to scratch out, and they piled rocks on top of it.

"He can't," Eli said out of nowhere.

"Can't what?"

"My brother, he can't have more sons. He's dead."

"Oh," Lynn said. "Sorry."

They regarded the rocks together in silence. "I feel like we should say a prayer to God, or something," Eli said after a moment.

"A what to who?"

"Never mind," he said. "I just feel like I should say something, you know, over the grave."

Lynn stood next to him in the dark, aware of the heat rolling off his body in contrast to the chill around them. "I can," she said. "If you want."

He nodded, and Lynn took a breath of cold air before the words spilled out.

"'*I balanced all, brought all to mind,*
The years to come seemed waste of breath,
A waste of breath the years behind
In balance with this life, this death.'"

Even in the dark of night she could feel him staring at her as she finished. "That's William Butler Yeats," Eli said. "How the hell do you know Yeats?"

"I can read, and I have books," she said stiffly.

When they got back to the camp, Stebbs was sitting by the fire, warming some soup he had brought with him. "She's all right," he told Eli. "But you've got to get her some decent shelter. You two will die down here in a month."

"What do you suggest?" Eli asked. "She won't leave the stream, especially now." The image of the small, lonely grave in the moonlight remained unspoken.

"Well, it's not a bad site, really. You've got fresh water, and the bank is high enough that you should be safe from the spring thaw flow. It's not something you'd know, but the stream does go dry from time to time, so a dry summer could put you in a pinch. But there's plenty of game here, once you learn to hunt, and gathering wood'll be a snap now you know to get the right kind."

Lynn wondered who was going to teach Eli to hunt. She certainly didn't have time, especially now that Lucy was her responsibility. She opened her mouth to say as much but the sight of Eli's face—exhausted and blank—stopped her.

"Shelter's the priority," Stebbs continued. "As of now. She won't move, and you won't make her, which means bringing the shelter to you. We can throw up something quickly in a few days, get something better and more permanent for you later, if she still won't see sense."

Lynn shifted uneasily at Stebbs' use of the word *we*, and the encompassing wave of his arm that included her.

"I'm already in your debt, both of you—deeply." Eli looked intently across the fire at Lynn. "Anything you do for me, I can't—there's no way for me to return the favor."

"You don't worry about that right now," Stebbs said, intervening easily when he saw Lynn about to open her mouth. "We'll work things out as we go, right now keeping you and your woman alive is the priority."

"She's not my woman."

Lynn felt an inexpressible bubble pop in her stomach. His inability should have filled her with contempt, but instead it made her want to help him. And the woman in the shelter was so sharp-tongued, it didn't take much imagination to picture him sliced to ribbons at her feet. For some reason, she didn't think she wanted to see that.

Stebbs watched Eli closely for a moment before speaking. "She's a good-looking woman, yours or not, you've got a duty to protect her now."

"It's been my job since Bradley died, my brother."

"That was his baby?"

"Yeah, his son. Neva was his wife. He died as we were leaving

Entargo. One of the guards shoved Neva. Usually she's pretty light on her feet, but she was so big with the baby she lost her balance. Bradley lunged to catch her, and the guard shot him, said he was going for his gun."

"Just like that?" Stebbs asked.

"Just like that. He bled out in the square with his kid and wife right there. Lucy had crawled up into my lap, bawling for someone to help her daddy, and Neva was on her hands and knees cradling his head against the baby. There was a crowd around us, and a few that I knew to be doctors, but nobody could help."

"Why not?" Lynn's question brought Eli's attention back to her.

"Population schedules," he said. "You're only allowed one child per couple, and they already had Lucy."

Stebbs sighed and tossed a stick into the fire. "I thought they would've lifted that ban by now. So that's the deal still? You screw up and the entire family is out of the city?"

"They won't waste water on lawbreakers. Sometimes they'll keep older kids, males mostly, to help protect the city. Lucy not being a boy helped her out in that respect."

"Won't help her out here," Stebbs said shortly, giving Eli a hard stare.

"Yeah, I know," Eli said. "I guess we were lucky when those men came for our food, Neva being pregnant and Lucy being . . . well, none of them seemed to be of that persuasion."

Lynn glanced from Stebbs to Eli, completely lost.

"Maybe so, but your lady isn't pregnant anymore," Stebbs said. "And like I said, she's your responsibility."

"Being good-looking doesn't seem to drop the survival rate out here." Eli darted a glance at Lynn, but she was still trying to puzzle out their earlier exchange.

"Being good-looking and a sharpshooter doesn't hurt," Stebbs said with a wry smile.

The mention of shooting brought Lynn to her feet. "I gotta get back, been here too long already."

"True enough," Stebbs said, struggling to rise. "We'll get you squared away, son. There's no point you dying here when we've got the means to help."

Lynn chewed on her lip as she and Stebbs struck for home. His parting words to Eli had been meant to console him but also to let her know where Stebbs stood on the issue. She'd been reluctant to offer her help for the evening, and Stebbs had promised more without asking her. She wasn't rooting for Eli and Neva to die of exposure, but she wasn't against them figuring out the basics of survival on their own either.

Stebbs seemed to understand her mood and held his tongue. Early morning dew had fallen on the long grass, soaking their pants as they walked and chilling them to the bone. Lynn clicked off the flashlight to save batteries once a strip of gray appeared on the horizon. They were halfway to her house when Stebbs took a misstep that turned his good ankle and brought him to the ground with a crash.

Lynn helped him to his feet and he tested his good leg. He winced when he put weight on it. "You go on without me if you want," he said. "I know you're in a hurry to get back to—"

"Lucy," Lynn said, snaking an arm under his. "Yeah, I am."

Stebbs leaned against her for support. "I was going to say 'the pond.'"

"Yeah, that too." She ignored the curious look he shot her as she stepped back to give him some room. "Can you manage?"

"I just need to walk it off."

Lynn was already backpedaling toward her house. "I'll check on you," she called over her shoulder and dove through the grass, suddenly anxious.

She'd been seven when Mother had gone on an overnight hunt, too young to help carry the large chunks of meat Mother would be bringing home. Mother had promised she would be back the next day, and she had appeared by mid evening, dragging a travois loaded with meat behind her. Lynn had put on a brave face and claimed everything had gone well, not wanting to admit to her rock of a mother that the nighttime hours had taught her the meaning of fear.

The basement was the only home she'd ever known, but

waking in the middle of the night without hearing Mother's rhythmic breathing had taken away her feeling of safety. Every dark corner held an unfamiliar noise, each soft rustling an unidentified threat. How would Lucy, a stranger to the darkness of their underground shelter react if she woke and found Lynn gone?

Lynn cracked the basement door and held her breath for a moment in order to make out the softer sounds of Lucy's rhythmic breathing rising up from below. She was safe and sleeping. Lynn snatched her rifle and climbed to the roof to check on Stebbs.

A pang of guilt struck her when she saw him fumbling across the fields, a walking stick in hand. She should have helped him back to his shelter. She lowered the rifle once Stebbs made it to the rock, rested a moment, and continued toward home, picking his way through the field of coyotes that had been reduced to skeletons and drying sinews.

There was time for a few hours of sleep, at least. Lynn crept to her cot silently so as not to disturb Lucy and rolled to face the wall. Nightmares were nothing new to Lynn; her waking life was full of enough disturbing images, she didn't think it was fair that some could snake into her dreams as well. Mother's death plagued her every night, replayed in such detail that she could count Big Bastard's teeth as they sunk into Mother's neck.

Lynn closed her eyes, fully expecting to see blood spilling onto grass, or even the lonely little mound of mud she'd left behind her at the stream. Instead, it was Eli's face, flickering in the light of his badly made fire. She studied him as she drifted off to sleep, in a way that she never would have allowed herself in daylight.

She could see what Mother had meant about the dead boy whose boots she'd taken. Even starving, Eli had a sparkle of youth about him, though he lacked the paunchy cheeks of the boy she'd shot. Lynn balanced the two faces in her mind, trying to tack down what exactly made them so different. In the end, she decided Eli was just easier to look at.

For the first time since her death, Lynn dreamt of a face other than Mother's.

Responsibility brought Lynn out of the light nap, and she went about her morning chores. Lack of sleep combined with unfamiliar emotions had her mind at a rolling boil, occupying every corner of thought. Which was a good way to get killed. Her empty buckets banged against her knees as she trudged to the pond, determined to nail down the slippery feelings so that she could concentrate on reality.

Guilt she'd known before, when she'd failed Mother in a simple task or taken an extra sip from the purified water. The crushing weight of her own role in Mother's death was constant, a dark cloud that followed her waking thoughts that she knew would billow into a storm of a nightmare if she slept.

Smaller shards of guilt were starting to prick away at her. The image of Stebbs resting at the boulder in the field floated across her vision and she shook it off. His square trade of curing her venison in exchange for her scoping out the Streamers' camp had turned into a mess that landed her with more work than she'd had before. She ended up on the sharp end of that stick, so why did she feel bad about him struggling home?

And she should be angry with him for volunteering both of them to help Eli and Neva, Lynn thought bitterly as she plunged her first bucket into the frigid morning water. Stebbs seemed to think that the Streamers had become their responsibility, and she wasn't sure she disagreed. Their complete inability to care for themselves would leave them dead before winter. She and Stebbs had the chance to prevent that.

Lynn's stomach clenched as the first flickers of doubt swept through her. The dark, sacred confines of the barn calmed her, and she breathed it in deeply; must and moisture, spilled oil and the ghost of gasoline. Above it all, she could smell the water, straight through the plastic tanks her nose found the scent of survival. She knew what Mother would have done. Nothing. And there would be two large graves next to the small one under the ash trees.

Lynn quickly dumped her second bucket into the tank to chase that picture away. She stood motionless above the tank for so long that the ripples settled, and she regarded her own reflection in the water.

◆ ◆ ◆

Lucy woke to find her new protector sitting in the other cot with her arms crossed defensively, her gaze unfocused. The little girl stretched luxuriously, reveling in the smell of her clean hair and the feel of the warm blankets on her back. The trapped warmth from her body lulled her back down into sleep, but not before her hands brushed against something unfamiliar. A stuffed red dog, worn from years of love, had been tucked under the blankets with her.

"What's this?"

"Just something I got for you out of the attic," Lynn said. "It's no big deal."

Lucy ran her fingers over the soft, red fur, the hard nubs of plastic that formed his little black nose and eyes. "Was he yours? What's his name?"

"I just called him Dog."

"Dog," Lucy repeated, pinning back his floppy ears and releasing them to fall down into her face. "You're not good at naming things."

"I had a real dog once," Lynn said. "He answered to 'Dog' just fine, and didn't seem to mind it."

Lucy tossed the stuffed animal into the air. "What happened to him?"

"That," Lynn said, snapping her hand out neatly to snatch the dog before he landed, "is not a good story."

Lucy stretched her thin arms out, fingers wiggling for her gift. "Can I call him Red Dog?"

"Call him what you want," Lynn said, letting him fall to the little girl's chest, where she grabbed him in a bear hug. "He's yours now."

Lucy snuggled back under the covers, taking the newly rechristened Red Dog with her. Two fingers pinched onto one ear and rubbed in an ever-slowing circle as she drifted back down into sleep.

"Can I ask you something?"

Lucy jerked awake. "Mmph?"

"Am I good-looking?"

The child nodded, her gold curls bobbing up and down on the pillow. "Verry purty," she mumbled.

Minutes of silence filled the basement, broken only by the sound of Lucy's even breathing. "Huh," Lynn finally said to herself. "Who'd've guessed?"

Eleven

A killing frost had fallen, turning the morning dew into a deadly covering of ice that stilled the insect voices. The sharp morning air ripped into Lynn's lungs as she zipped her coveralls up to her neck. Beside her, an unrecognizable Lucy trotted loyally along, an oversized hat pulled down to her eyebrows, a scarf wrapped up to her nostrils.

"What're we doing today?" Her voice was muffled by the layers of fabric Lynn had covered her with before trusting her frail skin to the outdoors.

"Gotta get wood inside. You sit if your feet start hurting you."

Lucy had proven less a hindrance and more a help as the days went by. Her endless energy and curiosity could be put to good use, Lynn had soon realized. Small jobs, like gathering little bits of kindling and checking the supply of sanitized water, had soon bored her, and Lynn began trusting her with more work. Her feet were still healing from cutting out the overgrown toenails, something that had been less of struggle than Lynn had anticipated.

She'd asked Stebbs to assist, expecting crying, pleading, and a general struggle from Lucy. Her request that he hold the child down while she did the cutting had been met with a raised eyebrow and the suggestion that they try a less violent route first. After his patient, carefully worded explanation to Lucy, she had submitted gracefully to his touch, wincing and burying her head in Lynn's lap for the worst moments. There had been tears, but no wailing. The throb after the surgery Lynn had dulled with some aspirin, after struggling with the cap. It hadn't been removed in years.

Lynn had debated allowing Lucy to help her haul wood in. One dropped log could send the child into a world of pain. But Lucy insisted that boredom was worse than a bloody toe, finally consenting to wearing three pairs of socks inside of an old pair of Lynn's boots. She plodded along beside Lynn as they made their way to the pole barn, curious and comfortable.

"All right," Lynn said as she shoved the rolling door open. "I've got a wagon in here you can drag around the yard, gather all the little sticks, things we can use for kindling if our coals go out downstairs."

Lucy's brows knitted and she stopped in her tracks. "That's not a new job. You said you had a new job for me."

"You get to use the wagon now." The flash of inspiration had struck Lynn on her water-gathering chores the evening before when she'd spotted her old red wagon, rusting in the dark corner.

"That's an old job, just with a new wagon. I wanna help you with the wood."

"You *are* helping with the wood," Lynn insisted as she tugged on the handle to dislodge the wagon from its ancient resting place. "Kindling is wood."

Lucy muttered something under her breath, but it was lost inside the scarf covering her mouth. She took the handle of the wagon and trudged glumly out the door with the wagon wheels squeaking their protest. Lynn followed, warned Lucy to stay in the yard, then made her way to the wood cords on the east side of the house.

They would make it through the winter. The basement retained heat well, especially once she dropped the woolen blanket that covered the entrance to the pantry room. There wouldn't be much excess firewood to rely on for the next fall, which made cutting in the summer a must. How she would manage to leave the house to cut was a question she didn't have a good answer to. The pond could not be left unguarded. She'd probably have to trade labor with Stebbs again, and even though she didn't like the idea of needing him, the feeling of shame that usually erupted at having to ask for help had subsided a bit.

Self-reliance had been Mother's mantra. Nothing was more

important than themselves and their belongings. Allowing Lucy into their home had gone against everything she'd learned, but leaving the little girl to die beside the stream went against something that was simply known and had never been taught. She'd shared the thought with Stebbs after they worked on Lucy's feet. He told her it was her conscience, guiding her to the right decision.

Having a conscience was a new experience, and one Lynn was starting to question as she regarded the sullen child tossing twigs into the rusty red wagon. Lucy would have to go back. Eli and Neva had shelter now; a few days ago, Lucy had come running down to the pond, the armload of sticks threatening to take an eye out if she fell.

"Lynn—there's a truck coming down the road!"

Such a nonsensical comment had brought Lynn to her feet, sidearm in hand. They'd rushed to the roof together, Lynn impatiently smacking the little girl's backside when she'd balked twenty feet up. The sound of an engine had been noticeable on the cold morning air, and Lynn chided herself for not hearing it sooner. She'd been distracted by the looming handle of the water bucket that should be ebbing and flowing peacefully far beneath the surface of the pond, not mere inches from it.

The hum of the engine grew louder and Lynn saw that Lucy was right. There was a truck coming, Stebbs behind the wheel. As he passed, she saw that the bed held a chain saw and raw lumber. He waved happily, throwing his arms up in mock surrender when he saw Lynn's gun. Lucy jumped up and down, waving back ecstatically.

"What's he doin'?" Lucy asked.

"Looks like he's going to build your mama a house."

Lucy stood on her tiptoes to watch as Stebbs disappeared down the road. "He's kinda like magic, isn't he?"

"Yeah." Lynn had smiled a little in spite of herself. "Kinda."

No amount of coercing would convince Lynn to visit the new home by the stream. "I'm sure it's great," she assured Stebbs as he regarded her over a shared supper in the basement. He'd brought beans with him and offered to help Lynn cut down the cured venison from the trees. It seemed rude to let him walk off into the cold evening without a warm supper. The venison had been frozen, but a few chunks cooked up nicely on the stove with the beans. Lucy sat on her cot, running her finger along the inside of the bean jar to get the last bits of sauce.

Stebbs watched her for a second before continuing. "It's better than great. Tiny, on account of we tossed it up so fast, but Eli had a good idea. There's a loft where they can sleep so they don't have to roll up their bedding every morning. Wasn't the easiest thing in the world to build, but there was some sense in it, 'cause there's not much floor space."

Lynn stared moodily down at her supper. The idea of Neva and

Eli snuggled together in the loft made her stomach feel funny in a way that wasn't related to hunger.

"That Eli, he's a worker. Give him some food and it gets turned into pure muscle. I'm telling you, Lynn, you wouldn't recognize the boy from the first time you saw him."

She grunted and studied her food.

"Then I got lucky and found an old woodstove over at the junk-yard. Nothing pretty, but it's not too big." He took a bite of venison, and Lynn welcomed the moment of silence while he chewed.

Stebbs swallowed. "Cut a hole in the roof and run some pip-ing up there and they were home, neat as pins. Doesn't have a door though. The stove, not the house. I told them they'll have to watch for sparks flying out of there 'til I can fix it."

"Until *you* can fix it?"

"Sure, why not?" He took another bite of meat and spoke with his mouth full. "I got nothing else to do. You're not exactly begging for help."

"I don't need any."

"I see that." He motioned toward the well-stocked pantry and the full clean water tank beyond that. "You'll be setting even better once the little missy is off your hands."

"Off my hands?"

"Sure." Stebbs wiped his mouth on his sleeve. "Now that there's a real home over there, with her mother in it."

"Right, her mother. Who hasn't asked about her once." The swelling anger in her belly took her by surprise, and she fought hard to keep her mouth tight, her tone even.

"Now, how would you know that? You're not exactly the visiting type. For all you know, Neva is over there crying her eyes out over her little girl."

Lynn gave him a cold stare over their empty plates. "But I bet she's not."

Stebbs shot a glance over at Lucy, who was busy hitting the bean can with a stick. "No, she's not crying. But I can tell you she's not doing so well either. Women don't always show their emotions clearly, and that one is hurting. She lost her home, husband, and brand-new baby all at once. If she deals with it by sticking by the stream and sitting quiet, that's her business."

Lynn's eyes narrowed. "You like her."

"She's pretty," he said defensively.

"Pretty useless."

They glared at each other in silence long enough for Lucy to notice the change. She kicked the can over to where they were sitting cross-legged on the floor. "What's wrong?"

"Just this young lady here and I having a difference of opinion, is all," Stebbs said, rising awkwardly to his feet. "Time for me to be going, I suppose. Thanks for supper."

"You brought it," Lynn said grudgingly. Happy with him or not, she wouldn't have him thanking her for his own food.

Stebbs sighed and winked at Lucy. "Thanks anyway. And if you get it in your head to go over that direction, there's at least one person by the stream who I think wouldn't mind seeing you."

"I can't leave the pond." Lynn ignored the reference to Eli, although a flush crept up her cheeks that she hoped wasn't obvious in the dimly lit basement.

"That the problem, is it?"

"I was lucky the one time. Can't count on luck." Even days after their trip to the stream to deliver Neva's baby, Lynn was haunted by what could have happened in her absence. "I won't do it again."

Stebbs considered that for a moment. "All right then, what if I got them to come over here? Kind of like a homecoming party for the little one, when it's time?"

"Yeah sure, when it's time."

Time passed slowly. The days were shorter now, the sun making its arc from one horizon to the other so quickly that Lynn was hard pressed to accomplish her outdoor work in the daylight hours. Lucy was a welcome helper, and their pile of kindling near the basement window was sufficient enough for two winters, but Lynn didn't tell her to stop. Boredom would be the new enemy, she was well aware. The freezing air would drive them permanently indoors soon, where long hours would stretch.

She stopped gathering water. Every bucketful she removed from the pond brought the handle closer to the surface. Lynn managed to convince herself that if it remained submerged, they would be fine. They were safe for the moment; the clean tank in the basement was full, as were the huge tanks in the pole barn, safe from freezing by their sheer volume. It was the future Lynn stored up against; the possibility of a snowless winter followed by a dry spring. No snow-melt meant no runoff. Since their pond wasn't ground fed, it relied on rain and runoff for refilling. There had been no rain for weeks.

Lynn shut the barn door behind her, drinking in the smells for the last time in a long time. The basement tank held a thousand gallons. With her daily routine at an end, she might not be back to the barn for refresher fills on the basement tank for a month. Lynn snapped the double padlocks onto the pole barn door, typically Mother's last act before giving in to the relentless push of winter. A spasm of grief twisted her gut and she missed Mother desperately. It was so much easier when someone was there to tell her what to do, how to survive. Now she was on her own, with responsibilities she hadn't asked for.

Lucy responded well to the cold weather, bundling up in layers of Lynn's old clothes and running for hours through the tall grass, enjoying the sound of the brittle stalks breaking under her feet. Soon she had a meandering maze of a trail pounded down through the unkempt yard, which Lynn could see clearly from the roof. Lucy played for hours with Red Dog, building him little houses out of sticks and destroying them with imaginary natural disasters. She wanted to simulate a flood but Lynn wouldn't loan her the water. She settled for tornadoes and blew herself red in the face.

She was destroying his third home of the week when a flash of movement to the east caught Lynn's eye.

"Lucy! To the house!" The little girl jumped to her feet and ran for cover without question.

Lynn peered through her scope, but saw nothing. Wildlife had begun to return to the field where she had slaughtered the coyotes, but she hadn't seen any more of the wild dogs lately. She followed the path of the road with her scope, willing the tall grass to part and give her a clear view. A breeze snuck through the weeds and spread them far enough for her to see an unnatural shade of blue moving toward the house.

Lynn's heart skipped a beat; her rifle barrel jumped. Strangers who walked the open road were dangerous. Mother had taught her that those who didn't hide themselves believed they were the ones to be feared and were best dropped at a distance. Her finger clutched the trigger impulsively, but she let out a slow breath. The man had moved out of her sight behind the overgrowth of the ditch, but the breeze brought an alien sound to her ears.

Whistling.

"Can I come out now?" Lucy's hesitant voice rose up from under the eaves. Lynn started and lost her grip on the rifle. The sweaty barrel struck the shingles and she reflexively covered her ears, but it did not go off.

"Lucy," she hissed, "go in the house." Lynn wiped her hands on her coat and repositioned the rifle. She didn't hear the back door opening. "Lucy," she growled, a little louder. "Inside. Now."

Silence met her demand and a dark dread billowed in her stomach. "Lucy?"

"Who is making a song?" The little voice sounded curious, yet cowed. "You don't do that."

Lynn was off her elbows and down the antenna in a moment, rifle clutched in the crook of her arm. Keeping the man in her sights and her aim steady was impossible with Lucy standing in the open, every step bringing the stranger closer to spotting her. She grabbed the little girl by the elbow and yanked her inside, Red Dog trailing from her other hand. When she turned right at the landing instead of heading down the stairs, Lucy quit protesting and clutched Lynn in return, the strangeness of going into the upper levels of the house quieting her.

Lynn headed for the living room, where the two front windows looked out onto the road only ten feet away. She silently raised the window enough to slide her rifle barrel under. Lucy crouched beside her, eyes wide.

The whistling was much louder now. He came into view slowly, hobbling on bare feet over the patchy gravel road, hands jammed into his pockets against the slight chill of the breeze. Lynn could see the stark outlines of his meager muscles under the thin covering of his goose-bumped skin. Still he whistled, each shuffling step falling in time with the tune he forced between his teeth, though it seemed it was a struggle even to breathe.

Lynn took her own breath, exhaled partway and stilled her chest, eye to the scope. Suddenly she was very conscious of Lucy's hand on her arm, the warmth of each tiny finger seeping into her skin.

"He looks lonely," the little girl said, and Lynn let out the rest of her breath in a rush, pulling away from the scope.

"Of course he's lonely," she snapped. "He's alone. Now I need you to be quiet and not touch me for a minute."

Lucy's grip on Lynn's arm tightened. "You're not gonna shoot him, are you?"

"I . . ." Lynn looked down at Lucy, her blue eyes wide and questioning, Red Dog tucked protectively under her elbow. "This is what I do, Lucy," she said softly. "This is how I keep us safe."

"But he didn't hurt us," Lucy said, bewilderment bringing her fine eyebrows together over her tiny nose. "He hasn't done anything wrong."

"We don't know that."

Lucy's lower lip stuck out in an expression Lynn knew all too well. "Then ask him."

"What?"

"I'm not letting you shoot him 'til you know he's a bad man."

"You're kidding."

Lucy crossed her arms and raised one eyebrow imperiously at Lynn, the strongest echo of Neva she'd seen in the child yet.

The whistling had stopped. Lynn glanced out the window and saw that the stranger was standing directly in front of the house, his gaze riveted on the freshly cut woodpile. "Looks like he knows we're in here already," she said. "You stay inside." Lynn tapped her finger on the end of Lucy's nose with every syllable for emphasis.

The front door hadn't been opened in years, and the hinges groaned as she pulled it inward, heart in her throat. The porch was covered with piles of rotting leaves, years of debris left to decay. Lynn stepped around them, her attention hooked on the stranger's face. He had jumped at the sound of the door but now stood hunched against the chill, eyes wary and trained on her rifle.

Her stomach clenched in apprehension before she spoke, every muscle in her body straining to stop her tongue from breaking Mother's rules. "Where you headed?"

He looked away from the gun and up to her face, then jerked his head to the west. "That way, I suppose," he said.

Lynn licked her lips to hide her irritation. "Why that way, is what I'm asking, and I think you know it."

A small smile played with the man's lips and she noticed that though his face had fine lines on it like Stebbs, his hair was solid brown with no traces of gray. "I'm headed that way because it's the opposite of the direction I come from," he said. "And I'm in a hurry to get away from there."

Lynn checked her grip on the rifle and took a step closer. "Where are your shoes?"

"They took 'em," he said briefly, and Lynn saw his eyes dart over her shoulder, drawn to the window by some movement of Lucy's. "You alone here, girl?"

"No," she said. "My father lives here with me."

"But he sends you out to investigate strange men?"

"I'm the better shot."

The man's eyes went to her hands on the gun, sure and confident. "I believe ya." They watched each other warily for a moment and the wind gusted, making him jam his hands farther into his pockets and turn away from the breeze.

"Who was it took your shoes? Another wanderer?"

"I'm no wanderer; least, I wasn't 'til a few days ago. I was set up nice, just like you."

Lynn's eyes cut to the bloody gashes on his feet, the dirt packed in between his toes. "So what happened?"

"It was all taken from me, in the night." He looked back to the east as he spoke, as if the words could conjure those who had harmed him. "A truckload of men come up on me, took my gun, coat, shoes, anything in the house they thought they could use and some stuff there's not been a need for since I don't know when. They loaded it all up and left me smelling their exhaust."

"You couldn't stay and make a go of it?"

He shook his head and looked at the ground. "All's I had left was the roof over my head, and there's plenty of those still standing. Thought I'd find something else, maybe a house with some wood already cut and left behind, a few tin cans hanging around in the cupboards."

"Don't be thinking because I asked your story I'm interested in being a part of it," Lynn said coldly.

The man put his hands in the air. "Didn't mean nothing by it. You can see I'm in no shape to be taking anything from anybody."

"All right then," Lynn said, backing away from him with her gun slightly raised. "I'm gonna walk back inside the house here, and I want you to sit tight—"

"Stand tight, you mean?"

She saw another flicker of a smile and she fought down the urge to smile back at her own mistake. "Whichever," she said, no trace of her stifled humor showing in her voice. "I'll be back shortly." Lynn ducked inside the house and shoved the door closed. "Lucy," she whispered, "run down to the basement and get my mother's boots and coat."

"The ones by my cot?"

"Yeah, go grab 'em. Hurry now, while I keep an eye on him."

Lucy scrambled off, evidently believing that Lynn's good humor could evaporate at any moment. She returned slightly breathless and buried underneath the quilted dark blue coat that Mother had always worn, the boots dangling from one hand. Lynn took them from her without a word, ignoring the quick puff of air that still smelled of Mother. When she pulled the door open, the stranger was cowering against the chill, the veins in his arms flat blue lines. Lynn walked to the edge of the porch and tossed Mother's boots and coat into the wind, the right boot pinwheeling over the left and landing at his feet. "My mother wasn't a large woman, but you're not that big of a guy. It might be a fit," she said, her mouth clamped tightly against the emotions that welled in her throat, threatening to break through and send her running after the coat, an object that was so entwined with the thought of Mother she could hardly picture her without seeing it.

The man bent down cautiously, watching Lynn as if waiting for some trick to be played. She remained still, gun pointed downward, and he grunted appreciatively when a pair of balled-up socks rolled out of one of the boots. The coat was snug through the shoulders, but the sleeves were the right length. He sat down to lace up the boots, and Lynn felt a pang of protectiveness shoot through her at the sight of an adult going through Lucy's morning ritual, although his hands were numb from the cold and somewhat less sure than her nimble fingers.

Lynn cleared her throat when he stood up experimentally. "They fit?"

"They do, and I thank you," he said, clear eyes connecting with hers and holding her gaze for the first time. "You probably saved my life."

"I owe a few."

He nodded once as if he understood and looked back to the east. "Whether you're alone or not, you be careful now, girl, you hear? Those men took everything from me, and they'll take that and a bit more from you, understand?"

"I can take care of myself," Lynn said. "You best be on your way now."

"Good luck to you then," he said, and gave her a two-fingered wave and went west, his boots making a scuffing noise against the gravel as he adjusted to walking in shoes again.

Lynn went inside and crouched by the window with Lucy, who wordlessly tucked herself into the curve of Lynn's body. Lynn wrapped her arms around the little girl, allowed her warmth to flow up her arms and into her chest, where her heart still ached for the loss of Mother. Lucy tilted her head against the window to watch the stranger go, her breath making a fog against the cold glass, until they could see him no more.

"Good luck, mister," she said, her words filled with the hope of a child.

Twelve

A few days later, the grim specter of the traveler still haunted Lynn. If there were truly people hunting possessions down, her house would be a prime target. The stranger had faded from Lucy's mind though, her quick, happy thoughts soon overwhelming any reminder of the despair of their world. Lynn's long sojourns on the roof held no interest for the girl, and the games she'd been playing with Red Dog had lost their appeal.

"Lyyyyyynnnn..." Her high-pitched voice carried up to the roof easily in the cool fall air. "I'm booooooorrrred."

Lynn pulled her eye away from the scope. "Read a book or something."

"I can't read on my own, dummy. And all you have is big, stinky poetry books. No pictures."

"There's a set of encyclopedias. They've got pictures," Lynn argued, but was answered with what could only be categorized as a butt noise, followed by giggling.

"Can I go see Stebbs?"

"No, you're not crossing the field alone."

"Then you come with me."

Lynn sighed and put the rifle down. Lucy had walked out into the yard far enough that she could see her from the roof. She looked down into the petulant face. "I've told you—I can't leave the pond, especially with what that guy said the other day. There's people out looking and taking."

Lynn heard Lucy whacking at some of the dead weeds for a few minutes before heaving a deep sigh. "But I miss Stebbs," she argued as if they'd never stopped talking. "We haven't seem him in a looooong time."

Even though she was exaggerating, Lynn's brow furrowed. She'd spent most of the last few days on the roof looking out for Lucy while she played, watching the smoke rise from the Streamers' new home, on alert for threats from the south. She hadn't been watching for Stebbs, but she hadn't noticed movement in his direction either. Lynn scoured her memory to see if the familiar red flash of his hand-kerchief had become so commonplace that she'd ceased to notice it, or if she truly hadn't seen it in days.

She brought her eye back down to the scope, focusing on Stebbs' small shelter tucked away in the woods. It was much easier to spot now that the leaves were off the trees, the undergrowth of the woods stripped bare by foraging animals. There was no smoke rising from his building. Lynn set down the rifle and grabbed the binoculars, feeling intrusive as she zeroed in on his house. The binoculars brought it into closer detail and movement grabbed her attention. His front door was banging open and shut in the wind. The wrongness of the image made her stomach drop. Stebbs was so far removed from the road she hadn't thought to warn him about the stranger's news of men in trucks.

"Lucy, do you have your good boots on?"

"Yeah."

Lynn strapped the rifle across her back. "We're going for a walk."

The field was difficult to navigate; the frozen clumps of dirt kept tripping Lucy up, and the bleached white skeletons of the coyotes fascinated her. Her endless curiosity brought the expected flow of questions, but Lynn remained silent about the piles of bones. She kept one hand on Lucy, the other resting on the butt of the handgun stuffed in her waistband. She didn't like being away from the pond, but she couldn't ignore the fact that Stebbs would never have left his front door open in the winter. Something was wrong, and her newly found conscience wouldn't let her ignore it.

"All right," she said to Lucy once they were on the edge of the woods. "I want you to stay here until I say you can come in."

"Why?"

"Because I don't know what happened. There could be bad people in there, or . . . or something you shouldn't see."

Fear made the little hand clench hers tighter. "Bad people like the ones that took that guy's shoes?"

"Just like those."

"Don't leave me here alone."

Lynn wrenched her hand away from the girl's, ignoring the stab of guilt when her lower lip trembled. "You're safer here. Sit tight. You'll be able to see me the whole time, and I'll be able to see you. Once I know it's safe, you can come on in."

"Okay," Lucy said doubtfully, but she sat on the ground.

Lynn approached Stebbs' shelter warily. She'd never been in his woods. The only houses she'd ever walked into were ones she already knew were empty. Stebbs' shelter was a converted shed that had still been standing when the ancient brick house that accompanied it had crumbled. Lynn skirted the pile of crumbled bricks as she approached the shed, gun in hand.

She stuck her foot out to stop the door from banging against the side of the building and peered around the door frame. There was no one inside. A small stove rested in the corner, cold and empty. There was a window facing east with a small shelf above it that held one plate, one fork, one spoon, and one cup. That was all. The only luxury Stebbs had was a real bed pressed up against the west wall. It was small, but with a true mattress. Lined up beside the door were three pairs of boots, the right heel worn much lower than the left on all of them. His coat hung limply from a nail by the door.

But Stebbs was not there.

Lynn stuck her head out the door and called for Lucy, who came crashing through the undergrowth. "Where's he at? Where's the magic man?"

Lynn sat on the bed, relishing the comfort of the mattress even though her mind was enveloped in worry. "I don't know," she said.

"Maybe he went to see my momma and Eli."

"Maybe," Lynn said, only to comfort the girl. Dead leaves were skittering around the floor of the shed in the breeze. The door had been open for a few days at least.

Lucy stood on tiptoe to glance onto the shelf above the window. "So where's his food? Where's his water?"

"What's that?"

"We've got all our food and water right where we can get it. Where's his?"

Lynn jumped to her feet and kissed the little girl on the head. "Thanks," she said. "You're a genius."

Lucy's nose scrunched up. "Huh?"

Lynn swept back the braided rug beside the bed to find a carefully cut trapdoor that opened on well-oiled, silent hinges. A weak voice rose up from the dark depths below.

"I'm flattered you came to check on me."

The ladder that led down into Stebbs' underground storage space had broken under his weight when he'd gone to retrieve his supper two days before. His ankle had twisted underneath him badly enough that he couldn't walk, but he'd been in no real danger. The walls of the little bunker held canned food, vegetables, even a camp toilet. His plan had been to wait until his good ankle supported him well enough to pull himself up through the trapdoor, but Lynn and Lucy were a welcome rescue party. He handed pieces of the broken ladder up to Lynn, who tossed them aside.

"I've got plenty of ladders back in the pole barn," she called into the darkness of the hole. "I'll go back and get one. We can get you out easy. How long of one do you need?"

Stebbs flicked on the flashlight he'd been carrying with him when he'd fallen. The light swept up the earthen wall so that Lynn could see for herself.

"I'd say what, ten feet?" she called down.

"Should do it," came the agreement.

"You sure you're okay?"

"I'm fine, it was just a fall."

"I'll be right back with the ladder," she called to reassure him.

Lucy tugged on her sleeve.

"Can I stay here?"

Lynn looked at her for a second, considering. Lucy's little nose was red from the frigid air that had bitten at their skin as they crossed the field, her lips chapped.

"Yeah sure, I guess." Her eyes swept to the cold stove. "Go out into the woods and get kindling, just like at home, okay? When I get back we'll get a fire started so that it's warm for Stebbs once we get him up. Don't go far while you're looking, though, and don't do anything stupid like sing."

Lucy took her instructions seriously; Lynn could hear the little girl moving through the dead brush as she walked away, but just barely. She stifled a flash of pride. "It's not like she's yours or anything," she reminded herself out loud as she crossed the field toward home.

Lynn chose one of her shorter wooden ladders and headed back over the field with it across her shoulders, both arms draped through the rungs. She felt awkward and vulnerable. If there was a threat, animal or otherwise, she'd never be able to disentangle her arms from it in time to defend herself. She cast a glance back toward her house and the pond as she crossed the field. Already they'd been away longer than she was comfortable with.

She called out to Lucy when she approached the house, and the door was opened for her. They slid the ladder down into the hole and

Stebbs flicked the light on so they could see as they descended. Lucy insisted on coming down with Lynn, exhilarated at the thought of exploring Stebbs' hiding place. Stebbs was sitting on the earthen floor, one leg folded under him, the other stretched out straight, with the foot propped on top of a bucket.

"That looks comfortable," Lynn said, brushing dirt from her front.

He grimaced. "It's not the best, but it keeps the swelling down."

"Pretty nice setup you've got here," she said as her gaze swept the room. She could only see within the range of his flashlight, but even in that small area, there was enough canned food to last two winters. She heard a scurrying in one of the dark corners.

"Lucy? That you?"

"Check this out," the little voice answered, followed by a metallic click, the sound of rushing water and a yelp.

"Lucy! Stop!"

Stebbs shushed her with a hand. "It's okay," he said. "Push that handle back down, Lucy."

Lynn heard the metallic noise again and the sound of running water stopped. Stebbs' light jumped to the corner where Lucy stood next to a spigot, looking sheepish. Lynn grabbed the light from Stebbs and walked over to it, cupping her hand under the mouth to catch a few drips that fell from it. She raised it to her lips. Fresh water. Cold and clear.

"How the hell did you get lucky enough to find a well?"

Stebbs was quiet for a moment, and Lynn switched the light back in his direction. "I witched it," he finally said.

"Bullshit." Lynn's voice came out strong, but the beam of the flashlight shook.

"What's 'witched' mean?" Lucy asked. "Like he really *is* a magic man?"

Lynn and Stebbs regarded each other quietly before she answered the little girl. "He might as well be."

They got Stebbs up the ladder and into his bed, with his foot propped under his balled-up coat. Lucy was thirsty, so he gave her the flashlight and his cup off the shelf, and showed her how to close the trapdoor from the inside, as well as how to pull the rug back over it using a string he'd tied to one end that dangled down into the underground room. They could hear her banging around happily underneath them while they looked at each other.

"I always wondered where you got your water," Lynn said eventually. "I never saw you gathering any."

"No need to," he answered. "It's always right there, fresh and for the taking."

"How deep is it?"

"I only dug down fifteen feet or so before hitting it. I reinforced the sides before dropping the pipeline but, really, there was no work to it."

"It ever run dry?"

Stebbs shook his head. "Not once. You know how these veins are though, persnickety as hell. With only one man drawing off it, I do okay. But these same little sources feed places like the creek. You and I both know exactly how dependable that is."

Still, it was wonderful. His water source was always at arm's reach and deep enough he had no need to purify for fear of human contamination. Anyone looking at his tiny shelter wouldn't think he had anything worth taking, unaware that a gold mine lay underneath. Lynn's large house, outbuildings, and obvious pond made her a constant target.

There was a thump as the trapdoor opened and Lucy's head emerged. Her face was filthy, her hair covered in cobwebs. "That's the coolest place ever."

"That place is a supersecret special place, do you understand?" Lynn said. Lucy nodded solemnly. "If the bad people knew that Stebbs had that place under his house, they would come and take it from him."

"They're mean," Lucy said, making a face.

"Very mean," Stebbs agreed. "It's important that you not talk about it, okay? Especially the part about how I can find water."

"You mean that you're a witch?"

"Yes, that is a very, very big secret," Stebbs said, and Lucy looked from him to Lynn, frightened.

"He's not a witch the way you're thinking of it, Lucy," Lynn explained. "He can find water under the ground. It's called 'water witching.'"

"There's water under the ground?"

"Yeah, c'mere." Stebbs motioned to Lucy and she approached his bed. He held out his chapped hand. Dark blue veins rose prominently over his knucklebones. "See that?" he asked, pointing to them. "There's veins down under the ground like these that are in our bodies, 'cept they're full of water, not blood. The ground is like the skin here on our bones, keeps the water down inside. I can find that water without seeing it, and then I dig where it's at to make a well."

"How do you do it?"

"Lynn, go outside to that witch hazel and cut me a forked switch."

"You're not serious," she said. "You're giving a demonstration?"

"The least I can do is provide some entertainment for my rescue party."

Lynn bit down on her retort and went out in the waning light to cut the switch with her pocketknife. When she came back in, Lucy had three piles of blankets on the floor beside the bed and Stebbs was sitting up. She handed him the forked switch.

"All right now, close your eyes," Lucy said. "No cheating."

Stebbs obeyed and Lucy slid the cup of water under the middle blanket. "Ready," she said, and scurried over beside Lynn to watch.

Stebbs pulled himself to the edge of the bed, held the forked ends of the switch loosely in his hands with his palms up, and swept the other end over the blankets slowly, starting on the right. He'd barely passed over the middle blanket when the stick turned in his hands, jabbing downward at the cup of water hidden underneath.

"Am I right?" Stebbs asked Lucy, even though Lynn could tell from his eyes that he knew he was.

Lucy bolted up from the ground. "That is sooo cool," she shouted, then pulled the cup of water out from under the blanket to look at it suspiciously. "Can I still drink it?"

"Sure," Stebbs laughed.

"How do you do that, really? Is it magic?"

"No, nothing like that," he said. "It's just something I'm able to do. Sometimes it's genetic—my grandfather could do it. Some people can just feel water."

"Lucy, pick up this mess," Lynn said, pointing to the blankets. She took the switch from Stebbs, forced him to lie back down on the bed and re-propped his foot. "That was stupid," she said to him. "She was excited enough already, now she's going to chatter about it forever."

"Who's she going to talk to? You? Eli? Her mother? Them

knowing doesn't bother me."

"But the others? What if they're watching? What if they overhear her saying something to one of us? What if she slips in front of a stranger one day?"

"I just wanted to make her happy. The kid's got little enough to smile about."

"It's not worth it," Lynn shot back. "You know what would happen to you if the wrong people found out you can douse? You'd—"

"Hey, guys, look!" Lucy's cry of joy reverberated inside the small shelter. They turned to see her holding the dousing stick expertly in her upturned palms, the long end pointing emphatically at a bundle of blankets.

Lynn jumped to her feet and yanked the covering away. The little cup of water that had been underneath spilled across the floor. Her gaze met Stebbs'.

"Shit," he said.

"So I'm a water witch too?" Lucy asked as they crossed the field by the light of the newly risen moon.

"Shut up about that!" Lynn turned in her tracks and thrust a finger in Lucy's face. "Remember that man on the road, and those men that took his shoes?"

Lucy's lip quivered as she looked into Lynn's angry face. "The bad men?"

"Yeah, the bad men. What he had that was worth anything to them, they took. His wood, his food, his gun—right down to his socks—they took everything that meant anything. What you've got isn't something they can just pull out of your hands, and it's worth more than shoes. You can find water, Lucy. If anyone knew, they'd take—"

"They'd take me," the little girl said. "Because it's like I got the water inside me, and they can't just take it out."

"Yeah," Lynn said softly, shoving down the hard spike of fear that had risen in her chest. "They'd take you. Or Stebbs. Either one of you would be worth more than gold, but I don't think the life you'd be living would be worth shit." Lynn glanced around the field and readjusted the rifle on her back. "C'mon," she said tersely, jerking the little girl by the arm. "We've been gone too long already. And stop talking."

Lucy was silent the rest of the way home, and Lynn regretted speaking so harshly to her. Fear had fueled her tone, but there was no way to explain to Lucy the wave of panic that swept over her even in daylight when seconds passed between Lynn calling out and Lucy answering. In the dark field, it felt to Lynn like predators would see Lucy not only as the easiest target but also as Lynn's weakness as well. She hoped Lucy could feel the affection coursing through her fingers, even though the grip on her tiny wrist was iron.

Lucy gathered courage to speak again once they were both tucked into the warm safety of their own cots. "How bad's his ankle?"

"What's that?"

"Stebbs' foot? He going to be okay?"

"He'll be fine," Lynn answered. "It was just a bad sprain. He couldn't stand to pull himself up out of the bunker because his other foot is lame."

"He'll be okay though? Like to come over and see us again sometime?"

Lynn found herself smiling in the dark; she wasn't the only one who found Stebbs' company comforting. "I doubt we can keep him away."

Lucy was quiet for a moment, but it was a heavy silence. "I bet my grandma coulda fixed his foot up nice."

Lynn turned in her cot. She could barely make out the pale moon of the little girl's face on the other side of the basement. "Your grandma?"

"She's a doctor back in the city. Said she'd come and find us, when she could get away. I thought maybe she could fix Stebbs' foot, make my mommy better too."

"Your grandma is a doctor?"

"Yeah, she's important in the city. Has a big office in the hospital and all that. I got to visit her there once, and I wanted to see the babies but they don't even let her into that part of the hospital."

"So she's not a baby doctor?"

"No, just a sick people doctor."

"Be nice to have one of those around here."

"She said she's coming," Lucy said quickly as if her saying so would make it true. "Soon as she could get away, she said she'd follow us. She said Neva's her little girl and she won't be away from her, no matter what."

"Follow you how, Lucy? It didn't seem like you guys even knew where you were going."

A long silence followed, and when she spoke Lucy's voice shook. "My dad saw you on the water map."

"What?" Lynn sat up in her cot, alarm spreading through her body. "What do you mean, a water map? He saw *me*?"

"I'm not supposed to talk about it." Lucy folded up into the fetal position on her cot. "It's a bigger secret even than Stebbs and me being witches."

"No, Lucy," Lynn said as calmly as possible. "I think you should tell me. I need to know what you're saying about a water map. This is important."

"I know it's important. All the secrets are."

"Jeez, little girl, how many do you have?"

"A lot!" Lucy's voice cracked, and she started to cry. "I've got a lot of secrets."

Lynn got out of her cot and headed over to Lucy's to cradle the little head in her lap, a feral wave of protective instinct overwhelming her at the touch of the tiny skull. "It's okay, kiddo," she said. "You don't have to tell me all of them. But I want to know about this water map."

"It's . . ." Lucy wiped the tears from her face while she looked for a way to explain. "Do you know what a computer is?"

"I've seen dead ones in some of the houses I've been in, never been around one that worked though."

"Well, all the ones in the city work, and there's these things up in the sky called stalactites. They take pictures and give them to the computers, so people can see all the land all around. People use the pictures to find water."

"Like my pond," Lynn said, a cold finger of fear running down her spine.

"Yeah," Lucy said, her voice still thick with tears. "They don't let everybody see those maps though, even in the city. Only soldiers get to look, and even then only the superspecial ones. 'Cause the people who run the city, they don't want everybody who lives there coming out here to get water for themselves."

"Why not?"

"'Cause then they won't pay for it," Lucy said simply. "But my dad, he said even if they did let all the people know where the water was, nobody would be able to get to it out here because of the crazy hillbillies. He said people were better off paying for it than being shot."

Lynn ignored the rush of anger. "So how did your dad know about these maps? Was he one of the soldiers allowed to see them?"

"Yeah. Mommy and Daddy got real nervous a while back, right before her belly got big. They started talking a lot after I was supposed to go to sleep. I could hear them through their door. Daddy started sneaking looks at the water maps, to find somewhere for us to go. Then he'd come home and draw it out as best he could, and Uncle Eli would watch. They memorized them, then burned them up."

"You said your dad saw me?"

There was another reluctant silence. Lynn got up and opened the door to the stove and threw some wood on the glowing coals. Lucy's wet face gleamed in the firelight.

"We were supposed to take your house."

"Excuse me?"

"Daddy said it was a good place."

"It is a good place," Lynn said stiffly. "It's also mine."

"He didn't know you were here," Lucy said, her face scrunching up to cry again. "Daddy didn't know there were people here."

"Okay, okay, I'm sorry." Lynn crawled back onto the cot with Lucy, and cradled her head once more. "So why didn't you?"

"We got caught. Daddy got killed, then me and Mommy and Eli got kicked out. Uncle Eli followed the map in his head but when he saw there was someone living at your house, he said he was too weak to take it by farce—"

"Force."

"Yeah, force. And Mommy just sat down and wouldn't go anymore."

Lynn stroked Lucy's hair and thought for a moment. "Did your grandma see these maps that your dad and Eli memorized?"

"Yeah, she learned them too."

"It's possible then, she could find us."

"You think so?"

"Don't get your hopes up too far, kid, but maybe."

Lucy's eyes were fluttering down toward sleep when Lynn asked her last question. "You said your grandma could fix Stebbs' foot, and maybe your mother too. What did you mean? What's wrong with Neva?"

"I don't know," Lucy answered slowly. "But when we got arrested, me and Mommy and Daddy, we were sitting in jail and some of the soldiers came and took her away. When they brought her back she looked okay but she was walking funny, like they hurt her somehow. Then she just curled up like I am now and wouldn't talk to me or Daddy."

Lucy looked at the fire while she talked, and the flames illuminated her fresh tears. "Mommy would have days like that, before the jail, even. Sometimes she would just say it was a 'bad day' and she would have to lie down or not get out of bed at all. Daddy tried to make it a 'good day,' but usually Grandma was the only one that could help. It was worse after the soldiers came to the jail. I think maybe whatever those men did to her it's still hurting. Maybe Grandma can make it better?"

Lynn tightened her grip on the frail little body. "I don't know, kiddo. Maybe."

Thirteen

A week later, snow fell. And continued to fall. Lynn sent Lucy indoors once visibility had reached zero. The girl could easily become disoriented in the blinding white snowfall and wander to a lonely death in the snow. Lynn climbed down from the roof moments after sending her inside. She could see nothing. If anyone were stupid enough to wander out in a snowstorm to attack her, she could shoot them just as easily coming down the basement stairs. Easier, even.

They spent two days indoors, with Lucy mocking the reading selection, and Lynn pumping her for more information about Entargo. Once the conversation steered in the direction of Neva's mom though, Lynn became less enthusiastic. A lone woman wandering in the blizzard wouldn't make it far, especially a city dweller.

She kept the harsh thoughts to herself and tried to distract Lucy by pulling out a tin of cocoa, something that had been reserved for Christmas when Mother was alive.

On the third day, Lynn ventured back onto the roof and spied the meandering black snake of a trail that Stebbs was making as he lurched toward the house. She hailed him, and Lucy ran out to meet him, her own progress hampered by the snow that nearly reached her thighs. She fell flat on her face twice before she reached Stebbs, but resolutely got up and pounded her way through the drifts. Even though Lynn knew it cost him, he swung Lucy up and onto his shoulders.

He warmed himself by the fire and gave Lucy a present he'd made during his own time indoors; a wooden flute that he'd whittled. She began tooting it immediately and stomping around the basement in a chaotic parody of a parade.

"Thanks for that," Lynn said drily.

"At least now we don't have to walk outside to have a conversation," he said over the din.

Lynn's eyes narrowed. "What's up?"

"I want you to go over to check on Eli and Neva. My foot won't hold up to the trip, so I thought I'd stay here and watch over things for you."

Lynn tried to ignore the little skip in her heartbeat. "Something wrong?"

"I don't think so, no. But it's their first real blizzard so it wouldn't hurt to check."

Bleak winters could drive even the most seasoned country dwellers to the brink. Mother had told her of a married couple who'd survived the violence immediately following the Shortage, only to have the wife go after her husband with a hatchet during the winter that followed. Being shut indoors could do funny things to people, Mother had said.

"I can do that," Lynn said carefully, certain there was more.

Stebbs unshouldered his backpack. "Take 'em this. It's got vegetables enough to get them through for a little while. Bring the pack back, and we'll stock 'em up again in a bit."

"And what are they giving you in return?"

"They've got nothing to give."

Lynn took the pack reluctantly. "I don't like you just giving them things. When does it stop?"

"When they're able to look after themselves."

"And when will that be, with you always treating them like they're babies fresh out of their mothers?"

Stebbs gave Lynn a hard look. "I know you're just saying what you think your mother would've wanted. Seems to me you're starting to grow a heart on your own, but every now and then you think of her and it kills it dead like the frost to a seedling. You weren't taught any different, but it used to be that people helped each other."

"Used to be a lot of things different."

"But people are still the same," Stebbs said, an edge on his voice that usually wasn't there. "And all everyone is trying to do is survive."

"That's what I'm doing."

"You're not exactly in bad shape, kiddo. Those poor bastards your mom blew away over the years? They was just trying to get a drink, to get by one more day. Shit, one time the widow of this fella came back to my place, out of her head 'cause she saw one of your mom's bullets peel off part of her husband's skull. Died the next day, she did, and I'm not so sure it wasn't the shock that killed her."

Lynn fiddled with the strap on the bag he'd handed her. "When was this?"

"Seven years or so back."

"That wasn't necessarily Mother that shot him. That might have been me."

"Jesus." Stebbs put his head in his hands and left it there. "You woulda been just a kid."

Lynn glanced over to where Lucy was playing the flute, happily plugging different holes to change the notes. "Killing people was easier when the only face I ever saw was Mother's. Back then, anyone else was the enemy and shooting at an outline in a scope wasn't any different than taking down a deer, just in a different shape."

"And now?"

"Now I've seen other faces," Lynn said, thinking of the traveler on the road, who Lucy had begged her not to shoot. "And I can't help but wonder what the people I shot looked like."

Stebbs patted her knee. "We'll leave it there."

"There was a man on the road the other day," Lynn said. "I meant to tell you when we came to your place, but what with you falling and . . ." She trailed off, unable to say "water witch" even in the privacy of her basement. ". . . uh, all the excitement, I forgot to tell you."

"This man, did he pass by?" Stebbs watched her carefully.

"He did, and Lucy talked me out of killing him."

"She's a good influence."

Lynn shoved his shoulder. "He said—"

"He *said*?" Stebbs eyebrows flew up in surprise. "You *talked* to this guy?"

"I did, and I'll be done talking with you if I can't get a word in edgewise," Lynn said, pointing her finger at him while she spoke. Stebbs threw his hands up in surrender and she went on. "He said that he was turned out of his place, that men had come and taken what was his, right down to his shoes."

Stebbs digested that information for a minute, eyes on Lucy and her innocent play. "He say whereabouts this happened?"

"To the east, but the men were in trucks. They could've come from anywhere."

"So they're rifling for supplies but have enough gasoline to travel to find them . . . that doesn't feel quite right."

Lynn shrugged. "It doesn't, but I'm not trying to wrap my brain around it. I'm just going to shoot them, they come this way."

"In their case, fire away," Stebbs said, gaze still on Lucy, mouth grim.

Lynn looked at the little girl happily piping on her flute, oblivious to the threats that seemed to surround them. Dread bloomed in Lynn's stomach, along with a fierce streak of protective rage that usually only surfaced when she thought of the pond. She shoved it down with effort and opened the pack Stebbs had handed her. There were two cans of green beans, a Mason jar of dried sweet corn, and a can of peaches.

"Peaches," she said awkwardly. "I bet Neva'll like that."

"She's doing better, that girl. Talking about starting a garden in the spring. I gave Eli a bow of mine and he's a better shot than you'd have guessed. We won't be carrying their weight for long."

"Lucy says Neva's mom is coming to find them."

"Eli said as much, last time I was over to the stream."

"He tell you *how* she was going to find them?"

"You mean the satellite maps?" Stebbs shrugged. "I figured people were still using those, yeah."

"Stalactite maps, you mean," Lynn said, using the word Lucy had so carefully pronounced whenever they talked about it.

"Uh . . ." Stebbs struggled to keep a straight face. "No, Lynn. Those are called 'satellites,' not 'stalactites.' Trust me on that one, kiddo. The little one must've gotten her head a bit muddled."

Lynn flushed at her mistake and her irritation seeped into her words. "So you never thought to tell me something was watching us from the sky?"

"Well, now you know. And what are you going to do about it?"

"Nothing."

"That's right. There's nothing you can do except worry about it and get yourself all worked up."

"Still would've liked to have known," she said sullenly. "If people in the city can see my pond without me being able to see them, I don't much like it."

Stebbs rolled his eyes. "Use your head for something other than aiming a rifle, Lynn. I know it's hard for you to grasp how many people are in Entargo, but it's thousands. Your pond could help maybe a hundred of them for a week and then it'd be all over. You're only one person—two now, I guess—so to you it's a lifeline. To them it'd be a swallow. Same with my little well, if they could see it. We're small fish, kiddo, and I'm glad of it."

"Then why are they even looking?"

"Eli said his brother Bradley was part of a special team that did a little work on the side for private citizens. Only very few people know that the satellites are still running, or what they're looking at. I'm bettin' those people were important enough to have money, and a backup plan in case things in the city went bad. 'Cept in

Bradley's case he took what he was paid to find out and used it for himself once they knew Neva had an illegal baby growing inside her."

"Eli tell you Neva's mom is a doctor?"

"Yup. I wouldn't mind meeting her." Stebbs winced as he raised his still-swollen ankle and rested it on Lucy's cot. "It's better," he said, "but I probably shouldn't have tried walking over here yet."

"So I think . . ." Lynn's voice trailed off as she searched for words. "I think maybe I know part of what's wrong with Neva. With her hurting, like you talked about."

Stebbs laced his fingers behind his head and leaned back, watching Lynn closely. "Uh-huh?"

"Lucy said that some of the soldiers came and got Neva out of their cell after they arrested them, and when they brought her back she wouldn't talk."

"Uh-huh?"

"So I think they hurt her."

"I'm sure they did," Stebbs said, still watching Lynn's face.

"So . . . what'd they do?"

"Your mom never told you much about men, did she?"

"Not much that was nice."

Stebbs leaned forward and put his face in his hands. "Oh, Lord, that I should be the one having this conversation. Thanks a lot, Lauren."

162

Minutes later, a red-faced Lynn was fighting through snow on her way to the stream. "Thanks a lot, Mother," she muttered to herself. "That wasn't embarrassing or anything."

Her anger fueled her progress, and Lynn reached the little house by the stream before she'd fully recovered from Stebbs' revelations. Eli was outside, awkwardly attempting to hang a deer by himself. He heard her approach before she hailed him, and turned with the deer still slung over his shoulder, giving her an awkward wave.

He was wearing an old pair of coveralls from Stebbs that would have been much too big for him at their first meeting, weeks ago. Now he filled them out, and the color in his face was as much from healthy exertion as the frigid air. She felt a rush in her veins that had nothing to do with the walk, but she stamped on it, the memory of what Stebbs had just told her too fresh in her mind to even meet Eli's gaze.

"You're doing that wrong," Lynn greeted him.

"Hello to you too."

She walked past him to the tree, inspecting the rope that he had slung over one of the lower branches. "This isn't high enough, your deer isn't going to be off the ground. You can field dress it on the ground and hang it after."

"Field dress?"

"Just put it down," Lynn said, and Eli gratefully dropped the animal. They knelt beside the body together. Lynn pulled out the arrow carefully, to avoid breaking the tip. "Nice shot," she said.

"Thanks." Eli took her first kind word as encouragement. "Stebbs has been working with me. It's my first deer."

"She's a decent size. With just the two of you eating off her, you're set for the winter." Lynn rolled the doe onto her side. "Got a good knife?"

"Stebbs gave me one, yeah."

"Well, get it."

When Eli returned, knife in hand, she motioned to the backpack she'd brought with her. "That's from Stebbs too, he sent you along some vegetables."

"Thank him for me."

"I will."

They regarded each other uneasily over the dead doe's belly. Lynn held out her hand for the knife. "Here, I'll show you."

"Tell me how, let me try."

Lynn shook her head. "Making the first cut is a tricky business. You've got to get through the pelt and the muscle but if you cut down into the intestines you've got a mess on your hands and hell of a smell. Trust me on that. Let me do the first bit, then I'll hand it over."

With a knife in her hand, Lynn relaxed. The methodical work of field dressing restored her spirits, and once she surrendered the knife to Eli the task of instructing him took all her concentration.

His inexpert knife-handling skills would've cost him a finger if she hadn't been there, and the look on his face when she instructed him to reach into the rib cavity and pull out the heart was enough to make her glad she was.

She removed her own gloves. "Here, I'll show you," she said, and stuck half her arm into the warm depths of the deer, emerging with the dripping organ.

"You've got to be kidding me," he said, the color in his cheeks she'd noticed earlier suddenly gone.

"Beats eating grasshoppers," she shot back, and Eli burst out laughing, catching her by surprise and causing an unguarded smile to spread across her own face. "What?"

"Just you, standing there with blood up to your armpit and a heart in your hand, happy as can be." Eli stifled another laugh. "And my mom had a musician all picked out for me."

"Fat lot of good that would do you out here," Lynn said, turning her attention back to the carcass and trying to ignore the pleasant flush that had crept up her cheeks. "Boost me up into the tree and toss me the rope."

The two of them had the deer hung in a few minutes. "It's cold enough now, you can just let it hang for a bit to cure," she said. "One of us will show you how to butcher."

Eli wiped the sweat that had beaded on his brow despite the cold weather. "Thank you," he said, catching her gaze. "For everything."

Lynn kicked snow over the purple mound of organs and grunted. "You're welcome. How about in exchange you tell me about these water maps?"

"Stebbs tell you about that, or Lucy?"

"Both," Lynn said. "But Lucy let it slip first."

Eli sighed and looked up at the carcass. "Neva's got this idea in her head that if she treats her like an adult, Lucy will act like one. But I knew she couldn't keep her mouth shut."

"She needs to learn," Lynn said. "I'm guessing you didn't know she can douse?"

"What's that mean?"

"Witch water," Lynn tried again, but Eli's face remained blank. "She can find water good as any of those satellite things. Better even, since the water she finds is underground."

Eli swallowed once, hard. Lynn was glad to see that city or not, he was smart enough to know what kind of danger that put the little girl in. "It's genetic," Lynn explained. "Someone in your family is able to do it, though Stebbs says it can skip generations. I'm guessing whoever it was never even knew, living in Entargo like you do."

"Did," Eli corrected. "I'll tell you anything you want to know about the water maps, but we're going inside to talk. I can pretend to be tough for two more minutes, but I'm freezing, and I think we've got enough conversation to last the afternoon."

Lynn glanced up at the sun. "I can stay a little," she said hesitantly.

"But I'm not sure how welcome I am inside."

"Neva's not in there," Eli said. "She's out at the grave."

"By herself?"

"I couldn't get her to come away," he said. "Once the snow stopped, she went right to it and started clearing away the drifts. I've been watching the deer upstream, and I knew they came to the same spot every morning, so I needed to be there at the right time. But Neva wouldn't budge, so I had to leave her behind."

"She been there all day?"

"Mostly. I got the deer about right after sunrise, dragged it back here, and went to check on her. I took her something to eat, but she refused to move."

"She dressed well?"

"Well enough," Eli said, and Lynn didn't miss the shiver that went through him. She guessed that Neva was dressed better than Eli, and that he'd given the better coat to her. The idea of being in the small shelter alone with Eli caused a different kind of heat to flush through her. She clamped down on it, the need to know more about the satellites outweighing her nerves.

The little house was warm. She put the pack from Stebbs down next to the stove and stripped off her coat, wet with snow and smeared with deer blood. She hung it over the back of one of the mismatched chairs to dry. "Stebbs got you set up nice," she said as she sat at the little table that was pushed into the corner. She kept her gaze firmly on its top, not allowing her eyes to wander to the loft where Neva and Eli slept together. Not after what Stebbs had told her.

"I got that myself," Eli said as he sat down across from her. "One afternoon when he was over I went out, found it along with the chairs. Of course, every piece came from a different house, so they don't match."

Lynn felt her lips flicker into a smile without meaning to. "You're used to things like matching furniture?"

"Oh, yes, a coordinated dining room," Eli said, fake wistfulness creeping into his tone as he ran his fingers over the tabletop. "I miss it more than tap water."

"Shut it, you do not," Lynn said, a real smile pushing through. "Now tell me about the satellites before I break one of these ugly chairs over your head. Lucy told me you were aiming for my house?"

"Yeah." Eli nodded, all traces of teasing gone from his face. "Bradley said it was big enough for us to survive, not big enough for anyone from the city to bother with."

"Unless the city went south?"

"What's that?"

"Went south," Lynn explained. "It's a country way of saying when something goes bad."

"That was the idea, yeah," Eli agreed. "Basically, the people that my brother and some of the other soldiers hired themselves out to for information had the money to get it, and the foresight to know that the water in the city couldn't last forever. Bradley took their money, then their plan for his own once they knew Neva was pregnant again."

"It'd be a decent plan if you knew the first thing about surviving."

"That was supposed to be on Bradley," Eli said, his eyes not meeting hers anymore. "He knew all kinds of stuff from his training. Berries you could eat, roots even. To eat bugs if you got in a bad enough situation."

Lynn thought of Lucy chasing grasshoppers, her tiny palms smacking against the dry bodies in desperation. "He taught you what he knew then?"

"He tried, back in the city. But I didn't pay as much attention as I should have. He was supposed to be with us, you know? The whole way. I'm good with my hands, but I always learned better actually doing something, so I figured once we were outside I could learn from him as we went a lot easier than trying to remember everything he told me over a table. We couldn't keep anything we wrote down, so I had to memorize it all. I focused on remembering the maps, thought there'd be more time for everything else later. . . ."

His voice trailed off, and Lynn thought about how Eli had watched his brother bleed out in the city while people who were able to help had done nothing. Her own desperation beside Mother's body shot through her memory and she had an unexpected rush of anger at the crowd that had let Eli's brother die in front of them. She cleared her throat.

"In that case, remind me to show you what poison ivy looks like, come spring."

Eli glanced up at her, a teasing smile back on his face. "That's a date."

Lynn's brow furrowed. "It's a season."

"No, I mean . . ." Eli sighed and looked up at the ceiling. "We're going to have to find a shared vocabulary before I can flirt."

"Flirt?"

"Yeah, it's how a boy shows a girl that he likes her. Or vice versa," he said pointedly.

"Sounds like a waste of time," Lynn said carefully, trying to keep the skip in her pulse out of her voice. "Seems like it'd be a lot easier to just say so."

"Easier maybe," Eli said, the smile that came so effortlessly to him spreading again. "But less fun."

"Fun," Lynn grunted.

"Yeah, it's what—"

"I know what fun is," she shot back.

Eli's hands went up in the air. "I'm only teasing."

"Is that part of flirting?"

"A very important part," Eli said with mock seriousness. "Looks like maybe there's a thing or two I can teach you after all."

Lynn rolled her eyes. "Yes, flirting. A necessary part of survival."

"Well, technically—"

"Shut it," Lynn said, and Eli snapped his jaw shut. "Is this what you city kids do all day? Sit around and let each other know how much fun you're having?"

"Sometimes. We go to school, some of us played sports or took music lessons. Read in our spare time. Just normal life, you know?" Eli shook his head. "No, I guess you probably don't know. What I used to do with my day probably seems silly to you."

"No," Lynn said slowly, thinking over every word as she spoke. "It seems like it'd be kind of nice not spending every living minute working against dying."

Eli watched her for a second in the quiet that fell between them. "When we found your place, when I saw you and your mom living there, I didn't even consider taking it from you. I'd lost everything I had. I didn't have the heart to take from someone else."

"Plus I would've sniped your ass."

"That too."

"I guess maybe I'm glad I didn't," Lynn admitted.

"I'll take that as flirting, country girl."

Lynn kicked him under the table before standing. "We're done for today, I need time to get back to the house in the light."

Eli got up quickly. "Could you talk to Neva, before you go?"

Lynn's mouth fell into a flat line that made her resemble Mother. "I'll talk to her, but I can't promise anything."

The little grave was around a bend in the stream, not far from their new house but out of sight because of the meandering path of the water. Lynn could make out the hunched form of Neva, perched on the dead trunk of a tree, keeping her vigil. Lynn purposely stepped on a twig, which snapped under boot like a gunshot. Neva did not move.

"Hey," Lynn called out, suddenly anxious. "You all right?"

There was a small shrug underneath the pile of blankets that Eli had bunched around her, but Neva did not turn her head. Lynn pushed her way through the snow to stand by her side. The ground around the small pile of rocks had been cleared of fresh snow, swept clean of branches and debris.

"That'll be pointless in about two days."

"Then I'll clear it again."

Lynn sighed and sat down uninvited. Neva had changed too, since Lynn had met her, but for the worse. Despite the many layers of blankets and clothing, it was easy to see there was little left of her but bone and skin. A flash of pale showed between her coat cuff and mittens, and Lynn could see that her wrists were tiny, almost as small as Lucy's. Her dark eyes were sunken, the circles underneath them lending to the thought that they might recede entirely into her skull. Even so, she was still alarmingly beautiful.

"So what now? We sit here trying to stop the snow from hitting the ground?"

"You don't have any children, do you?" Neva didn't turn when she spoke to Lynn but kept her eyes riveted on the grave.

"No."

"That man that comes here, the cripple. Is he your family?"

"No, just a friend."

"Do you have any family?"

"No. Mother was killed this past fall." Lynn answered evenly, trusting her voice to stay strong. "She was all I had. I was injured and it was too difficult to put her in the ground by myself. I had to burn her."

Neva was silent for a while, eyes focused on the ground at her feet. "I'm sorry for that," she eventually said. "And I never thanked you for helping bury my son."

Lynn had no response. They stared at the pile of stones together in silence.

"You've still got family left," Lynn ventured. "Your Lucy, she loves you. Eli wants to take care of you."

"My Lucy," Neva repeated, her hollow voice cracking with emotion. "My poor little Lucy. We never should have tried to leave."

"She's all right here. Doing fine, really. She's gaining weight, likes to play in the snow, her feet healed up real nice."

"Her feet?"

"She was a mess when I took . . . when Eli gave her to me to take back to the house for a bit. The shoes she was wearing were way too small."

A bitter smile cracked Neva's dry lips apart. "See? That's what kind of mother I am. My little girl was hobbling around the countryside starving."

"She's all right now, though."

"Because she's with you."

"I do the best I can—but I'm no mother."

Neva didn't answer. Lynn wanted to reach out and shake her, but she was afraid it might cause real damage to the frail body. "She's worried about you."

Neva grimaced. "We're out in the wild and she's the one worried about me. She's all I have left and I am completely incapable of taking care of her out here."

It was Lynn's turn to be silent and stare at the ground.

"She's much better off with you," Neva added.

"A little while longer," Lynn said. "I'll keep her a little while longer, but I want you to try. She's your daughter, not mine."

Lynn got to her feet. "C'mon, that's enough of this. Eli's been making himself crazy thinking about you out here freezing by yourself."

"I'm sure he has. He's always been chivalrous."

"I don't know what that means. Now, am I going to have to move you, or are you going to move yourself?"

For the first time, Neva turned her head and looked at Lynn. "I'll move myself, thank you," she said. Her knees nearly buckled when she stood, but she waved Lynn away and steadied herself. They walked toward the little house together, Lynn pacing herself slowly so that Neva could keep up.

"I know about what those men did to you," Lynn said hesitantly. "It was wrong."

"Yes, it was."

"I brought you something, in case anyone tries that again."

Lynn reached into her coat and brought out a small derringer that she had taken from the gun trunk, which fit neatly into the palm of her hand.

"It's a single shot, but it would do the trick at a short distance. I figured my shotgun would knock you on your ass, and the rifle takes some skill to fire. Even most of the handguns I have got a kick to 'em. But this one will take a man down, if he's close, or at least scare him off."

Neva considered the little pearl-handled gun. "Thank you," she said, reaching for it.

"I'll show you how to fire it."

"Thank you," Neva said again.

"Mother always called that one the whorehouse gun."

"Charming."

Eli shot Lynn a grateful glance as Neva walked past him into their home and shut the door behind her.

"How'd you manage that?"

"I really don't know," Lynn admitted. "I tried to say what I thought was the right things to her, but it just seemed to make her more angry."

Eli laughed a little and shrugged his shoulders. "Yeah, welcome to life with Neva."

"Well, when I finally said something on purpose to make her angry, that's when she did what I wanted her to. So, now you know."

"Guess I'll have to try that." Eli wasn't wearing a coat. His shoulders were hunched reflexively against the chilly breeze, his hands jammed into the pockets of his jeans.

"I better go," Lynn said. "Let you get inside."

"No, really, it's okay," Eli said, although his teeth chattered around the words.

"You have Stebbs' pack? I'm supposed to take it back to him."

"Yeah, sure, hold on." Eli disappeared inside the house. He came back wearing a coat and hat, carrying Stebbs' empty backpack. "I'll walk with you a bit."

"Neva won't care?"

"She doesn't mind being alone. I almost think she prefers it. It's being away from the water that scares her. She's used to having water come out of a faucet."

"Lucy said you have to pay for it?"

"It's expensive, yeah. We are—we *were* well enough off that we could afford the clean water, a nicer apartment building. People who have less money, their water isn't as purified—that means clean."

"Oh, does it?"

"Sorry," Eli said immediately. "I should know by now that you and Stebbs aren't exactly stupid. Any girl who can quote Yeats probably knows what 'purified' means."

They walked without talking a few moments more, while Lynn critically assessed Eli's progress through the bracken. She was torn between wanting to keep him away from the snug sleeping quarters with Neva and wanting to keep herself from being shot in the dark.

"Could you make more of a racket?"

"Sorry," he said again. "I'm just trying to make a path for you."

"I've been walking in the dark a long time, city boy," Lynn said. "You best head back home before full dark. Wouldn't do anybody any good if you get lost out here." She hated the words even as they slipped past her teeth, sending him back to Neva was much harder than she thought it would be.

"Right, okay." Eli blew the air out of his cheeks and turned back the way they'd come. "I'll do my city best to find the only structure out here."

"Good luck with that," she called out after him.

His crashing stopped for a moment, but she couldn't pick out his form in the dying light. "Is that teasing?"

"I thought it was called flirting."

"You're a quick learner."

She could hear the smile on his face even if she couldn't see it.

"Get out of here," she called into the darkness. "Stop encouraging me to yell so much out in the middle of nowhere."

A laugh was the only answer, leaving Lynn to wonder what she'd done that was so funny and reflecting on the fact that he was so noisy she could pick him off at a hundred yards on a moonless night.

She turned toward home and realized that she hadn't missed it. For the first time in her life, she'd been away from the pond and not been rushing to get back. Worries had fallen away while she talked with Eli, and water hadn't filled every waking moment.

And she didn't regret it.

Fourteen

Stebbs was on the roof when she made it back to the house. A pale sliver of moon was rising and she could make out his dark form clambering down the antenna as she emerged from the yard.

"Hey, kiddo," he called to her. "How'd it go?"

"Well enough. Brought your pack back."

"They okay over there?"

"Neva's got problems neither one of us can help her with."

"That's true enough." They walked around the side of the house together. "And Eli? How's he looking?"

"Fine," Lynn said nonchalantly. "He got a deer today."

"Did he? Good boy."

"Why don't you come on in?" Lynn said when she saw that Stebbs was headed toward the field as they approached her door. "No point you walking home cold when you can warm up downstairs before going."

Stebbs rubbed his hands together. "Don't want to put you out."

"Doesn't hurt me for you to soak up some heat."

Their voices dropped as they entered the basement; Lucy lay curled up in her cot near the fire, her small legs making a neat V shape under her blanket. Lynn checked on her, tucking the folds under the small curves of her body. "She go to sleep okay?"

"Not a contrary word. I told her it was bedtime, and to bed she went. That's a good little girl."

"I know it." Lynn opened the door to the stove so they could see each other in the flickering firelight, and set a pot of water to boil. "I'm having some coffee. You might as well have some too."

"I don't know what's caused this sudden rash of kindness, but I'll drink your coffee and thanks."

Lynn fired a harsh look over her shoulder. "I'd kick you if you didn't have two bad feet right now."

"The old Lynn would've kicked me anyway."

"The old Lynn's still in here somewhere, so don't tempt her."

Stebbs laughed and propped his foot up on the edge of Lucy's cot, leaning back to relax. "This isn't a half-bad place you know? Your mom did a fine job getting you two set up."

Lynn sat in the chair opposite Stebbs and began dismantling her rifle. "Long as you're here, I'm going to clean this filthy thing," she said. "I don't feel right having a gun in pieces when someone could come down those stairs any minute."

Stebbs propped his chair back, rested his head against the wall. "Clean away. I'm not going anywhere when there's coffee brewing."

"Neva wouldn't come away from the baby's grave today."

"That right?"

"She said she wasn't capable of caring for Lucy anymore either, and that she's better off with me."

"At the moment, it's true."

"I think she meant forever."

"How'd you feel about that?"

Lynn threaded a wad of cotton through the ramrod before answering. "Not so good, really. I mean, I don't want to give her up just yet. But she's not mine to keep either."

"True."

"I think a girl should be with her mother."

"I do too," Stebbs said. "That particular mother isn't in any shape to care for her daughter as of yet, though."

"I know it," Lynn said, and shoved the ramrod down the barrel. "Is that why you took it on yourself to care for them? 'Cause you don't have family?"

Stebbs blinked at the straightforward question.

"Sorry," Lynn said quickly. "Never mind."

"It's all right. Wasn't expecting it, is all. Where's all this coming from, sudden-like?"

"Neva talking to me about Lucy and her baby that's gone. She asked me if you're my family."

"And you told her?"

"I told her you aren't." Lynn critically inspected the cleanliness of her cotton before continuing. "I don't mind you so much though anymore."

"Thanks for the kind words. You're all right yourself."

Lynn poured them both some coffee and went back to cleaning her rifle without responding. Stebbs warmed his hands around his cup and watched her a few moments. "There's lots of reasons why I help them. Part of it's, yes, 'cause I don't have anybody. But I haven't always done the right thing in my past, and this seems a good a way as any to make up for it."

"Can't imagine you doing something terribly wrong," Lynn said, eyes still on her work.

"There's different ways of doing things wrong, Lynn, and not all of it is choosing to hurt others. Sometimes it's the things you don't do that make you feel the worst."

"All right then, what'd you *not* do that was so awful?"

"How much do you know about your daddy?"

Lynn's hands stopped moving and she glanced up at Stebbs. "Not much. Mother wouldn't really talk about him. All I know is, by the time I got here he'd been gone awhile."

"Does the word *militia* mean anything to you?"

"Are you telling a story or asking me questions?"

Stebbs took a drink of his coffee and settled back in his chair. "If you want to hear it, I'll tell it."

Lynn changed the cotton in her ramrod and kept working on the barrel. "I'm sitting here listening."

"Your daddy was part of the militia. That's not the regular army that the government was in charge of, you understand? There was a chain of command, and weapons, and we would drill much like the proper army, but everything was voluntary, and everyone was local. Sometimes we attracted people who the army wouldn't have for whatever reason. Could be they had asthma or didn't graduate from high school. But sometimes, we'd get the other kind, that the regular army wouldn't take 'cause they couldn't pass the psych exam. Meaning they weren't quite right, up here." Stebbs tapped his temple. "Your daddy, he was part of that last half."

Lynn thought about Mother. Had she wondered how much of Father's instability had rubbed off on her in the end? And how much of his insanity was inside of Lynn, passed on through the blood or Mother's teachings? Lynn thought of the people she'd dropped in the fields, thirsty men and women she'd killed without hesitation.

Was that because of her father's priorities, instilled in her so young? Or was that who she truly was—a smaller, female version of him who took life without regret?

Stebbs was watching her, and she felt her mouth tightening into a thin line under his gaze. "I've known lots of people in my life, Lynn," he said. "There's plenty of good seed sown by the bad."

She cleared her throat, and changed the subject. "You were militia, too?"

Stebbs nodded and moved on. "I was regular army once upon a time, but my convoy got hit by an IED during the Second War for Oil and they sent me home 'cause my hand wouldn't work just right after that." Stebbs held up his left hand, showing Lynn how it wouldn't close properly. "I can't use my index and middle finger for nothing."

"So you became militia?"

"Once you've been in that kind of situation, you don't come back normal. I still wanted that lifestyle, and the militia was the only way to get it."

"That how you met Mother?"

"I'd known your mother before. See, Lynn, even before the Shortage there weren't a lot of people around here. To you, it would seem like a lot, but as far as the rest of the world was concerned we were as rural as it got. Your mom's family, they'd lived here a long time—in this house even—and mine had been around this area for a while too."

"Was she family to you?"

Stebbs looked at her sideways. "You don't know much about her, do you?"

"She didn't talk about herself."

"Well, that's not surprising, considering."

"Considering what?"

"Well, your mom—her family—they did okay. They wasn't rich, but they had enough to get by and then some, which was doing pretty good around here, especially during them times, after the Second War for Oil. Nobody had any money, and there wasn't jobs anywhere either. Our militia started filling out."

"Why's that?"

"Lots of people were unhappy. They was mad at the government about the war, and about the fact that there was no money and no jobs. People always gotta have someone to blame, you see? People without jobs got nothing to do, and they feel like they're not doing anything for their families. Some of them thought the only thing they *could* do was learn how to protect them, keep them safe. Crime was up; everyone was desperate. People started breaking into houses and cars for money, sometimes even just for food.

"Your mom's family though, they didn't have to worry about

money too much, even in the bad times. They was good people, nice enough to give to others, and maybe their good will was part of what kept them safe from the robberies. But Lauren—that's your mom's name, you know—she was always a little skeptical about people, even then, and she came to me to learn about how to use a gun."

"How old was she?"

"Oh, she was a bit older than you. Out of college, and all."

"She was older than I am and didn't know how to shoot a gun?"

"It was a different time, kiddo. Feels like a different place, even." Stebbs took another drink of coffee, looking down into the depths for a moment. "Anyway, she started coming around, careful like, 'cause she knew her family wouldn't care for it if she was hanging out with us roughnecks. That's how she met your daddy.

"He wasn't quite right, like I said. A few of the guys would rather walk through the mud to steer clear of him than pass close by. He was always looking for a fight and knew how to start one even if there was no reason. But he was a charmer too, and better-looking than what the women around here was used to seeing. He got around a bit, I can tell you that."

Lynn blushed at the reference and moved to cleaning the bolt she'd removed from the rifle, keeping her eyes down.

"In any case he and your mom was meant for each other like sparks and gunpowder. She was always treating him like the miscreant he was, something the others lacked the balls to do, and he behaved even worse in front of her just to get her attention. I do think they cared about each other on some level, but neither one would ever admit it to the other. Even once they was together, they tried to act like they weren't, like making that choice was a discredit to them both. And maybe it was.

"Her family, they weren't too fond of her decision either, being as your daddy had a reputation of being cracked in the head. She was still living at home and they did try to stop her from seeing him, but shortly after that her parents—your grandparents—was killed in a car accident. Your aunt had already gotten married and moved out over the way with her husband, so Lauren got the house and it wasn't too long before he was shacking up with her, which didn't go over too well with a lot of people. Your mother was supposed to be a civilized kind, what with her college degree. But your daddy . . . he just wasn't."

"What was wrong with him, specifically?" Lynn asked, now knowing if she wanted the answer.

"Nothing you could put your finger on, exactly. He was the kind of crazy that hid itself well, 'cept in the eyes. That's where you can always see it, if you know how to look."

"What'd he do that was so crazy?"

"Well, now, that's the funny part, really. He'd seen some documentary about how we was running out of freshwater and the government was trying to keep it a secret, so as to avoid a panic.

All over the globe, he said, people was running out of water and the news, they was putting a different spin on it, so we wouldn't know what was going on. All the violence in third-world countries was over water, he said, but they kept telling us stories about tribal wars and religion to keep us distracted, and them poor countries didn't have a way of telling people any different.

"Pretty soon, he claimed, the east would be going down. There was too many people over there and not enough water. Then we'd be next. He said the whole environmental movement had shit-all to do with caring about the planet and everything to do with people giving their money to green programs so that desalinization plants could be built for the rich people to survive the coming shortage. It got so bad with him talking about the freshwater shortage that people started avoiding him out of just plain annoyance along with the fear. Nobody took him serious until the Aswan Dam was blown up."

"Mother told me about that."

"It was a big deal," Stebbs said. "That dam had always been a political problem for Egypt, but the rest of the world was always told it was about power, not water. Well, when the guerrilla group over there took it down, a lot of people over here sat up and took notice. Your daddy finally had an audience.

"He took a group of us up to the lake, Lake Erie, you know?"

Lynn nodded.

"He took us up there to show us this plant that had been built brand-new on the Canadian side to clean up the lake water. We rowed out in a boat, pretending to be fishing, and he pointed out there was armed guards all along that plant's walls, and 'what was a water purification plant doing with a private army holding M16s?' he asked me.

"It was a good enough question, I thought, so once we came home, we started taking him serious. By then he'd knocked your mom up—uh, I mean, Lauren was pregnant with you—and the two of them weren't getting on so well. She needed help at home, but he was all in love with the fact that he had men to lead. He kept saying that the regular army was too busy overseas, and when the time came it was up to militia like us to defend what was ours. Or, in the case of the lake, keep what he felt was Ohio's away from Canada.

"In any case, as it turns out, the crazier he sounded, the closer to the truth he was. One morning, our taps had all been turned off, and we was told if we wanted water we'd have to go into town to buy it. Now, buying water was no new thing—we'd always had to pay for our water, unless you were lucky enough to have a well. But now the water companies was saying they couldn't afford the upkeep of the water lines, and if you wanted it, you'd have to come and get it.

"That's how the Shortage came to be, and it went from there. At first, you had to go into the nearest town with a utility office to get your water. Then pretty soon they said it was too much of a bother to keep those open. So if you wanted your water you had to come to the city to get it, and eventually they just said if you wanted water, you had to live in the city. People started leaving, piling into their cars and going to the city limits to pile on top of each other there. Those of us out here with wells or access to water stayed, and there were bad enough stories coming out of the cities after that to make us glad we did."

"Like what?"

"The cholera, for one," Stebbs said. "Pack all those people together, you're bound to have sicknesses of some kind passing around. They forced a bunch of sick people out of the cities, I heard, but nothing can stop a burn like that once it gets going. Wasn't just the cholera either. Every now and then, people would pass through here that your mother didn't shoot and I'd learn a thing or two. Made it sound like the Black Death had come back again, nearly. But out here, with less people, the illnesses weren't the worst. Out here we mostly just managed to be threats to each other.

"Not long after they drove the sick from the cities, your daddy and I, we had a falling-out. I tried to stop him from taking the men up to the lake to take that water plant by force. He said it'd be a proper war, fought by the militia like the first one in our country was. Enough of the men were on his side that I backed down. He had everybody eating out of his hand by then, and I wasn't half certain that he didn't have it in for me, seeing as he was always looking over his shoulder and wondering who was causing problems in his little kingdom. So I cut my losses, decided to set up on a little piece of land I owned that had a decent vein of water running under it."

"Across the field," Lynn said.

"That's the place."

"You just happened to be able to keep an eye on Mother from there?"

Stebbs shifted uncomfortably in his chair. "Well, here's the part I'm not so proud of, kiddo. Your dad, he said good-bye to your mom, even though her belly was as big as the world with you inside, and he took a bunch of the men up north to the lake, armed to the teeth. Not a one of 'em came back. Not long after I got set up, your mom came walking across that field, gun in one hand, your tiny body in the crook of the other elbow. She said she didn't much see the point in me living in a shack when she had a whole house to offer, and two guns was better than one anyway.

"I could tell she had thought a lot about what she was going to say ahead of time, and made it all come out right so that it sounded like it would be the best thing for both of us, and not like she was asking for my help. I took one look at you, with your eyes so big they filled up most of your face, and your little bare feet so small it looked like they'd fall right through a crack in the ground, and I told her I didn't need no more work than I already had and that responsibility for one was all I had left in me. Your mom, she walked away without asking twice, and I didn't talk to her again until I stuck my foot in a trap."

Stebbs swirled the now-cold coffee in his cup and threw the dregs in the fire, where they sputtered into steam. "I turned my back on her same as her family had done, and the same as your daddy did once there was work involved along with the play. Your mother raised you right, but she raised you hard, and I can't help but think if I'd been around maybe you'd have some softer edges. Maybe you could've actually had a life, and not just *survived* if I'd been here. But here you are, and it seems you don't need any help."

Lynn snapped the stock back onto her rife. "Nope, I don't."

"So that's why I give it elsewhere, I guess. Making amends."

"I remember you being here, after your foot," Lynn said. "I think I might've liked it, if you'd stayed."

"I think I might've liked that too," Stebbs said quietly. "I tried, Lynn. I promise you I tried after I got hurt. I wanted that woman to see sense so bad. . . ." He trailed off, lost in memories made in the very room he was sitting in.

"So why not?" Lynn asked, her voice small. "Why couldn't it happen?"

"She wouldn't have me. It'd taken more out of her than I could've known to ask the first time, and when I shot her down I think it killed everything that was left in her but pride in herself and love for you. She wasn't always a hard woman, you know. It's what she became. You told me once not to speak of her unless you asked—"

"And I'm asking," Lynn said.

"So I guess I'll go ahead and tell you—don't be making the same mistakes she did. Or hell, the ones I did either. Don't be afraid to care for that little one, and don't be too proud to let that boy know what you feel. Otherwise you might end up with neither of 'em."

Lynn propped her rifle in the corner and tossed her own coffee onto the coals. "Seeing how it's pretty late now, you might as well stay here, I guess."

"That's all you got to say after that?"

Lynn gave her rifle a last rubdown with a cloth, hands moving slowly while she thought out her sentence. "I don't know that there's anything to say. I can't change the way Mother raised me."

"I'm not asking you to. I'm asking you to be more than she was. Be strong, and be good. Be loved, and be thankful for it. No regrets."

Lynn sat quietly for a moment, watching the firelight flicker on her oiled rifle barrel.

> "'Yet am I changed; though still enough the same
> In strength to bear what time cannot abate,
> And feed on bitter fruits without accusing Fate.'"

Stebbs watched her carefully. "That's not you talking, I take it?"

"No, that's Byron. Mother always said the winters are long, but poetry anthologies are longer."

Stebbs shot a glance at the bookshelf, where some of the spines were thicker than his hand. "Ain't that the truth. Your mother had something else she said—'It is what it is.'"

A smile spread across Lynn's face at the words, dissipating the sadness. "That's familiar, all right."

"You know well enough what it means, then?"

"Mother always said it when something happened that couldn't be undone, like when I lost that bucket in the pond or broke a canning jar. Means you can't change it."

"Like the past. You can't change the things you've done. It's now and the here on out you've got control of."

Lynn stood up, cracking her back. "All this talking is wearing me out, old man. You gonna stay or not?"

Stebbs got up and stretched as well. "I'll stay, and thank you."

Lynn nodded at him and crawled into bed beside Lucy, curling her body protectively around the little girl. "All right then, good night." She left him to find his way to her cot by the stairs.

She felt tense with an extra body in the room. Stebbs drifted to sleep easily, and she found herself watching him by the waning light of the stove, tracing the fine lines of his face and the spiky grays of his hair, something she would never let him catch her doing while awake. Her affection and gratitude were too subtle and burned away under the harsh light of day. But in the familiar darkness of the basement she let her unspoken feelings pour out of her like water and hoped that somehow the flow would reach him while he slept, and he would know without her having to say. Not long after, the slow, steady breathing of the three filled the basement, in stark contrast to the wild whipping of the wind outside.

Fifteen

Winter came viciously. The snow fell in slanted sheets, sticking to the trees and rocks. Lynn would run outside to deliver more wood down through the basement window into Lucy's expectant little hands and come back inside with a coating of ice on her hair. Weeks passed where they saw no one else, and Lynn would anxiously peer toward the stream to be reassured by the puffs of gray smoke that rose over the trees. Stebbs she could see through her binoculars, when the cold was bearable enough for her to look.

Lynn taught Lucy to play simple card games and they spent many hours making up their own. Lucy demanded a bath, and so Lynn brought in buckets of snow from outside to warm on the stove so that the little girl could have a sponge bath at least. She caved into the temptation herself and even washed her hair, something that Mother had always warned against during the winter, fearing that Lynn would catch cold. But they kept the fire burning brightly and Lucy would hum quietly while putting tiny braids in Lynn's hair and fixing them up with little bows that she'd found among some dolls in the attic.

The little fingers eased through Lynn's hair, coaxing her into a doze that she fought against. Even with the chance of attack at a minimum, she kept her handgun within reach at all times. Lucy hummed a little song while she played with Lynn's long hair.

"Have you ever cut it?"

"Every now and then Mother would, usually just to sprinkle in the yard to scare off the coyotes. Not often."

"I like it long."

"Me too."

Their conversation dwindled off and each fell into their own thoughts as the short daylight hours drifted past outside. Lynn watched Lucy making shadow puppets in the firelight and wondered how Neva was holding up. If not for the little girl, it would've been Lynn's first winter alone, and she wasn't sure how she would have handled it. The long hours of the night could not all be filled with sleep, and the companionship of another was the only thing to alleviate boredom. But Neva had Eli, and Lynn quickly chased the question away of how they might be filling their hours together.

Her heart rejected her mind's attempts to control her emotions, and she tossed without sleep for a long time in the dark. Lucy's rhythmic breathing rose and fell, but the little girl's peace didn't extend across the room. Lynn tossed a few times before slipping her coat on and heading up the steps. At least on the roof she would be forced to be alert, and her mind couldn't wander places she didn't want it going.

The next day dawned cold but clear. For the first time in a while there was a cloudless sky and the sun warmed the air enough for it to be bearable.

"Would you like to go outside?" Lynn asked Lucy.

Lucy bounced off her cot and dressed in layers in a second, eager to be out of the basement. Her thoughts were contagious; they had not been outside long when Lucy shouted up to the roof for Lynn and she saw Eli making his way through the snowdrifts toward them. The snow was sticking, bunching to his clothes in every place that came in contact with a flake, but he kept coming. Lynn climbed down from the roof and walked out with Lucy to greet their visitor.

"Hey, little lady," Eli cried out when Lucy jumped into his arms. "You've gotten big!"

"Lynn says I'm growing," Lucy said proudly. "She's been checking my height on the wall, and I've grown an inch and a half. Do you know what an inch is?"

"I do," Eli said seriously. "That's good work."

"Hey, I want to show you something, c'mon!" Lucy bounded away from them over the drifts toward the corner of the house where she'd begun a collection of bird nests that had been blown from the trees during the fall. Lynn and Eli followed slowly, pushing their way through the heavy snow that went past their knees at times.

"How are you?" Eli asked.

"We're okay, we've got plenty of wood and food stored up. Water too."

"I meant, like, how are you? How's your day?"

Lynn's brow furrowed. "Well enough, I guess. I'm happy that we've got food to eat and wood to burn."

Eli shook his head and smothered a smile. "It's okay that I came, right?"

"Of course it is. You haven't seen Lucy since you handed her off to me, and she's family."

"I came to see you too, you know."

"Well, I'm here," Lynn said, not able to find any other words.

Eli sighed and stopped walking, but Lynn kept struggling through the snow.

"Hey," he called after her.

"What?" Lynn turned and was hit directly in the face by a snowball.

"That's what."

Lynn sputtered as the snow on her face melted and ran in icy rivulets down her neck, finding no words for her surprise.

"Snowball fight! Awesome!!" Lucy came flying at Lynn and knocked her flat on her face in a drift, shaking what was left of her composure completely. She grabbed the little girl by the ankles and pulled her up into the air, tossing her headlong into a drift. Lucy emerged, soaked and laughing, with a freshly rolled snowball in each hand and revenge on her mind.

Lynn ducked the first one, but the second hit her square in the chest. She ignored it and began rolling her own arsenal until Eli knocked her on her side and hijacked her stash, pelting her with her own weapons at close range. She yelped and took out his ankles. Lucy landed on both of them with enough force to knock the breath out of them all. They laid in a breathless heap for a solid minute, soaked and laughing.

"Never thought I'd see one of them in your yard," Stebbs said when he arrived later, motioning toward the snowman standing guard by the wood cord.

Lynn pushed her hair out of her face and shrugged. "Lucy wanted to, and I thought maybe if I put a coat on it, somebody looking might think there was a person standing out there, keeping watch."

"I suppose the carrot sticking out of his face was a tactical decision too?"

"I got a well-stocked root cellar, and that one was not looking great. So don't start thinking I'm as sentimental as you." Lynn delivered a punch to his arm hard enough to penetrate the layers and make Stebbs wince.

"Easy, tiger, don't go beating on the old man."

"The old man needs to hold his tongue."

"He's been without anybody to talk to a long while. I see your pond's found a new use." Stebbs glanced toward the pond where Eli was gliding across the ice on his boots, Lucy perched precariously on his shoulders, hooting like a loon.

"Mother would roll in her grave if I'd been able to dig her one," Lynn said, but there was a smile on her face.

"Nice braids," Stebbs said.

"Shut up."

Their visitors stayed through the evening, and Lynn brought some of the larger wood chunks inside to set upended to use as chairs. The four sat in a comfortable circle near the stove while they ate their supper, topped off with some peaches that Stebbs had brought along mixed with snow.

"It's kinda like ice cream," Lucy said, juice dripping down her chin.

"Kinda," Stebbs answered.

"What's ice cream?" Lynn asked.

"You poor deprived child." Eli shook his head in mock despair, earning a whack on the back of the head from Lynn. She had found herself making excuses to touch him all day. Lucy had coaxed her out on the ice, and even though her balance was good, she'd slipped more than once when Eli was nearby. He always caught her neatly and propped her back on her feet, much to Stebbs' amusement.

"I wish you had your guitar, Uncle Eli," Lucy said, once they finished their peaches. "I'd like to hear a song."

"You know, it's funny, I forgot to grab it when the police kicked down my door and arrested me."

Lucy crawled into Stebbs' lap. "Do you have a guitar down in your secret basement?"

"No, little one, sorry," he answered, smoothing her hair. "Wish I did."

"I think there's one in the attic," Lynn piped up, to everyone's surprise. "Seems like I've seen one up there."

Lucy bounced up and down on Stebbs' lap. "Go check! Go check!"

"I'll come with you." Eli stood with Lynn and followed her up the stairs after grabbing a flashlight. Lynn opened the door into the kitchen.

"I haven't been inside a real house in a while," Eli said, flashing the light off the walls. "Almost feels funny."

"It's weird, sometimes when I think about it," Lynn said. "This is my own house, and I never use it. Mother grew up here, her dad was raised here too, but all I ever see is the basement." She didn't add that having Eli beside her in the upstairs should feel weird too, but it didn't.

"You never come upstairs?"

"Rarely. The bathroom here on the first floor is set up so that we can use it, and Mother stored a lot of stuff in the attic. But mostly no, we stayed in the basement."

"Why's that?"

"Easier to heat in the winter, stays cool in the summer. Only one access door and the windows are too low to the ground to pose much of a threat. Anyone tries to come in those we've got an advantage on them. The windows here on the first floor are a good eight feet long, at least four to a room. Impossible to defend."

They walked through the dining room and into the living room, where Eli looked at the windows in question. "It's such a waste," he said. "I know it's a smart decision, staying downstairs. But this is a beautiful old house; you've got all this space and these high ceilings. In the city, even in the nicer part where we lived, there'd be ten people living in a space this large."

Lynn shuddered at the thought and led him to the curved staircase. "I had a bedroom upstairs for a while. I remember, kinda, what that was like. Attic's here, watch your step."

The door opened onto a narrow staircase that led up into a gabled room. Eli followed Lynn up the stairs, flickering the light in front of her so that she could see. "Look at all this stuff."

The walls were lined with furniture, old bulky antiques that had once filled the downstairs rooms. Steamer trunks were against one wall, tightly rolled area rugs leaned against the other.

"Mother moved most everything up here a long time ago," Lynn said. "She figured anyone foraging for stuff would look in the downstairs windows and think our house had already been emptied of anything useful."

"Who would steal a piano?" Eli asked, striking one lonely key that rang out through the small attic.

"Nobody, probably. But Mother didn't want to take the chance. Everything up here meant something to her, and she didn't want to see it go up in smoke for someone's firewood, or one of her great-grandma's rugs used for a blanket."

"Makes sense, I guess."

"I think maybe she was hoping someday life would be normal again—her kind of normal—and that she'd put everything back the way it was supposed to be. Like sometime in the future, when we wouldn't have to worry about whether or not two people could defend the living room."

"That sounds nice," Eli said sadly, trailing the light over the furniture. "What's in the trunks?"

"Old clothes, mostly." Lynn kneeled down next to one of them.

"This is where I got Lucy's clothes and shoes from. It's my old stuff. Bring the light over here."

Eli followed and Lynn spotted the guitar case, propped behind one of the trunks in between a secretary desk and an old rocking horse. "Knew I'd seen it recently," she said. They made their exit quietly, leaving the relics of a safe past behind them in the dusty darkness.

They'd found the guitar, but the trip had been in vain. Eli strummed the chords, and Lucy made a nasty face. "Ugh. What's wrong with it?"

"Out of tune," Eli said, running his hands along the strings. "I can tu—"

"That's a disappointment, and no mistake," Stebbs said as he rose to his feet. "Can't tell you the last time I heard music. I best get going. I'm sure I've lost the fire, but I can probably stir up some coals yet, if I get back home."

Lucy bounced up when Stebbs did. "Can I come with you? I want to play witch."

"It's all right with me, if it's okay with Lynn."

"You got a gun on you?" Lynn asked.

"Course," said Stebbs.

"It's all right with me then," she said, somewhat reluctantly. "You listen to Stebbs crossing the field, Lucy," she warned as the girl zipped up her thick coat. The child nodded solemnly and took Stebbs' hand.

"You two have a good night," Stebbs tipped Eli a wink as he went up the staircase.

"Slick old guy, isn't he?" Eli said to Lynn when she came back from locking the door behind them.

"What's that?"

Eli ran his fingers over the strings once more, letting their discordant music fill the basement. "I can tune this up in a few minutes, if I want. I'm guessing Stebbs knows that as well as I do, but he slid on out of here and took Lucy with him so we could be alone."

Lynn blushed and blurted out the first thing that came to mind, which wasn't the best choice in the moment. "How is Neva?"

"She's all right, I guess." Eli said, avoiding Lynn's eyes. "It's hard, you know, being stuck in a small space together for a long time. That's part of the reason I came today; I think she needed some time alone. I wanted to see you too though," he added quickly.

"I'm glad you came," Lynn admitted.

"Really? It's not easy to tell with you."

"I am glad."

"Good."

"Lucy seems happy," Eli said.

"She misses her mother. I know it didn't show today, but she was so excited to see you and thrilled to be outside. At night though, she

206

cries after she thinks I'm asleep." She didn't share with Eli how torn she felt, lying in her own bed and listening to the quiet mourning. The basement gave them so little privacy, she wanted to allow Lucy the peace to cry alone. And some nights Lynn's cheeks were wet as well, her own mother near in her mind.

"Will Neva ever be ready to take her back?"

"Do you want her to?"

Lynn leaned back against Lucy's cot and shut her eyes. "No. But she's not mine to keep. I know Neva thinks she's not capable of caring for her."

"It was true at the time she said it," Eli answered. "But she's doing better, physically anyway. All the wildness of this place scares her though. She only leaves the house to visit the baby's grave."

"There's no shame in being scared," Lynn said. "I imagine if I were plunked down in the middle of Entargo I'd probably hide too."

"Our mom thought there was shame in it," Eli said. "Even back in the city, Neva jumped at the smallest things. Mom wanted the best possible wife for Bradley, said he was the kind of person who needed to keep the race going. A girl who cries when there's a mouse in the kitchen didn't exactly fit the ideal Mom had in mind for him."

"What about you? Aren't you the type that's supposed to carry on the race?"

For the first time Eli's smile wasn't a nice one. "Oh, I'm not

Bradley. That's something I've known since I could see. The population schedules are figured according to the male. So a woman could have two kids but each of them would have a different father, one child per male. My dad died before I was born so I don't know what he was like, but he certainly didn't have the place in Mom's heart that Bradley's dad did. If I'd had a child when we were still in the city, it wouldn't have been half the event Bradley's was."

Lynn nodded and looked at Eli in the firelight. She hadn't seen him without layers of clothing since their first meeting by the stream, and he had improved since then. Sinewy muscles lined his arms, the hollows in his cheeks were filled. He caught her looking and she glanced away, clearing her throat.

"But you said your mom had a musician picked out for you?"

"She said my best attribute was my voice, and she found me a nice little pianist."

"I'd say your bow shot is your best attribute," Lynn said.

"That would win me a lot of girls back in the city," Eli said. "They all want a man who can nail a squirrel at fifty yards." They both laughed. "Besides," he went on, "Stebbs says I've got nothing on you."

"True enough," Lynn said, and they laughed again. "I'm better with the rifle though," she added. "I spend so much time prone on the roof peering through that scope my neck's got a permanent crick in it."

"Oh, really?"

"Mmm-hmm." Lynn cracked her neck to illustrate.

"You know, that pianist told me I give pretty good back rubs."

"Oh, did she now?"

"Yup." Eli smiled at her. "Course I imagine you've got more stress than a city musician."

"A bit."

"A fellow can try though, right?"

Lynn eyed him gravely for a moment. "You're not going to try to have sex with me, are you?"

For the briefest moment, Eli was speechless and Lynn felt a flush running up her neck at the thought that she'd said something stupid. The moment was broken when he threw both hands in the air in surrender. "Wouldn't dream of it! Well . . . I might dream—" Lynn tossed her boot at him, cutting him off mid sentence. He swatted it out of the air with ease. "Get over here."

Lynn laughed and scooted over the floor to lean back against his legs. He touched her gently at first, only on the shoulders, and Lynn felt her entire body tense under the contact. He moved slowly but thoroughly, running his thumbs up and down the strong cords of her neck and down to the tops of her shoulder blades. Soon the newness of being touched by him was less alarming and more pleasant, and Lynn sagged against him, allowing all the tension of her life to seep out under his practiced hands.

"Yeah, you're okay at this," she said eventually, breaking the silence.

"Don't be so critical. You're slightly more tense than the pianist."

"Oh, am I?" Lynn asked, but she noticed that Eli had yet to call his old girlfriend by her name. "What was she like?"

"Who?"

"Your girlfriend."

"Oh, well . . ." Eli's hands stopped moving for one second, but he picked the rhythm back up. "She was a nice girl, and we got along fine, but that spark was missing, you know?"

"I don't know. The only people I knew in my life before you guys were Mother and Stebbs."

"There's no real way to explain it," Eli said. "Sometimes you meet a person, and even if you don't know them at all you can't stop thinking about them. And every time you talk to them you get nervous, and when you go home you think about every word you said to each other, replaying it in your mind."

Lynn rested her head against Eli's knee, relishing the feel of his hands against her neck. "I guess I do know," she said.

His hands came to rest on her shoulders. "It wouldn't take all that much for me to tune the guitar, if you want."

"Really?"

"Give me a few minutes," he said, propping her up gently and easing out from behind her shoulders.

She watched his hands moving expertly up and down the strings, as familiar with the instrument as she was with her gun. His head cocked to the side as each note, all new to her ear, was adjusted to his liking. When he was finished, he struck a simple chord, the sound echoing inside the stone walls.

"I feel bad Stebbs is missing it," Eli said. "I know he said it's been a while since he heard music. Not that I don't like having you to myself."

"I've never heard music," Lynn said.

Eli's hand stopped moving over the strings. "Never? Not once?"

She shrugged. "How would I? We had bigger worries."

"No pressure on me then," Eli joked. "It's only the deciding moment on whether or not you reject music for the rest of your life."

"I already like it."

"All you heard was the C chord."

"Then shut up and play something."

Eli tossed a pillow at her but she caught it deftly, the teasing smile on her face dissipating as he began his song, a slow, lilting melody that filled the dark corners of the basement. His voice joined the tune, very different from his speaking voice, lower and throbbing with the depth of the emotions that existed under his jokes. She watched him as he played, studying the small muscles in his arms that jumped as he picked the strings, the slight squinting of his eyes as he concentrated. He came to a slow stop and smiled apologetically.

"That's as far as a I got, back home in Entargo."

"You wrote that?"

"Yup. It's not like holding a deer heart in your hand or anything, but it passes the time."

The sound of spitting ice hitting the window brought them both out of their pleasant reverie. "Shit." Eli stood and tapped at the window, but the freezing glaze on the other side didn't move. "Do you think Stebbs and Lucy made it home in time?"

Lynn rose from the floor and stretched, still lost in the spell of his song. "Definitely, it only takes a few minutes, and he's smart enough to have hurried her along."

"I imagine it'd be pretty unpleasant to be stuck outside."

"If you're looking for an invitation to stay, you don't have to fish for it. I won't send you out in this. Will Neva worry though?"

"Doubt it. She's probably asleep already."

"All right then." Lynn closed the door to the stove, dropping the basement into blackness.

"Damn," Eli said. "I can't see a thing. Is this your plan? For me to break a leg and be your prisoner?"

Lynn found his hand with hers. "Follow me," she said, and led him to Lucy's cot by the fire. "You can sleep here."

"Wait." His hand squeezed hers. "Who said that's the end of the backrub?"

Lynn snorted in the dark. "There's not room for both of us in there."

"We'll make it work." He tugged on her in the dark, and she hesitated. "I don't want anything from you, but I'm not ready to let go yet."

She wordlessly climbed into the cot. Eli slipped his shirt off and slid in beside her, snaking one arm around her rib cage. Lynn had expected to tense up again, with the feeling of his skin so close to hers, the entire length of their bodies. But instead she relaxed and leaned into him.

"You can think of it as heat conservation, if it makes you feel more practical," Eli said in her ear and she giggled. She laid against him for a while in silence, enjoying the thud of his heart against her eardrum, the companionable tangle of their legs. The small differences in their bodies were fascinating to her; the rasping of his stubble against her cheek, the bony outcrops of his knuckles, so much more prominent than her own. She ran her thumbs over them, surprised at how strong his hands had become in the short time since she had met him. Her fingers strayed up his arms to the muscles that had developed there, tracing the lines of his veins.

Long nights spent alone in her bed had not prepared her for the intimacy of lying with him, no matter how comfortable. His hands were doing their own exploring and her breath caught in her throat.

Eli broke the silence. "So . . . I'm not used to asking for permission, but I don't want to get shot either."

"Permission for what?"

"A kiss."

"Oh, sure," Lynn said offhand, surprised that such a small thing had made him uncomfortable. She leaned forward and gave him a quick peck on his cheek; Mother's ultimate show of affection that had followed her down into sleep on rare occasions.

"Uh, that's not quite what I meant," Eli said.

"What then? That's how Mother always kissed me."

"I'm not going to kiss you like your mother. C'mere."

His hand tightened in her hair, and Lynn was surprised when he brought his mouth to hers. Then pleased. He moved against her and she quickly understood that body heat could be made and not just conserved.

He pulled away from her. "Okay, that's enough—or I'm going to have to throw myself into a snowbank."

"Why's that?"

Eli tucked her head under his chin. "I'll explain some other time."

"Fair enough." Lynn settled in against him.

Eli stroked her hair for few minutes more before speaking. "Earlier, when you asked about Neva, I meant to tell you she made something for me to bring Lucy as a present."

"Yeah?" Lynn waited for him to continue, irritated that Neva had come up in conversation yet again.

"She tried to make some kind of doll out of dried grass and sticks, but when I picked it up, it fell apart. Neva went to bed and cried. She said she has nothing to offer her little girl."

"That's ridiculous."

"Maybe, but I kinda know how she feels. I almost didn't come over here today for the same reasons. I didn't . . . I wasn't supposed to be the one in charge when we left the city, you know. Bradley was the strong one, the smart one, the one who knew what to do. We got out here and I could barely keep them alive. I'm learning but I still don't have much to offer, especially to you."

Lynn nestled her head underneath his chin. "You survived. You kept them both alive. You're doing something right."

"And I found you," he added. "That's pretty right, I think."

"I think so too," she said quietly, the sound of his heartbeat loud in her ear.

And they slept.

Lynn woke to the sound of Eli loading wood in the stove, the soft morning light rendering the basement the same gray as his eyes.

"I can do that," she said.

"I know you can," Eli answered, but kept loading it anyway.

She moved to the edge of the bed, where the pillow still smelled like him, and decided to lie there a few more minutes. He'd already dressed in his heavier clothes and was rubbing his hands against the chill of the basement. She burrowed farther under the covers, indulging herself in an unaccustomed lack of responsibility.

"Gets cold down here quick, once the fire goes low," Eli said.

"Yeah, mornings can be chilly. Does your place hold heat okay?"

"I've got no complaints." He shut the door to the stove and Lynn watched him for a moment, glad that she no longer had to hide her interest. He returned her gaze and smiled. "Do you ever wonder what it's like somewhere else?"

"What do you mean?"

"Like somewhere without subzero winters?"

"Mother would talk about going south sometimes," Lynn said. "But I never wanted to."

"Why not?"

"'Cause then we'd be like any other wanderers, carrying the only water you have and hoping you find more before long."

"You'd rather have your pond and tough out the winters?"

"Much rather."

Eli nodded. "When we left the city I was terrified, and we had a destination in mind. I can't imagine walking without a goal."

"How long were you out there, before you found the stream?"

"Weeks. Maybe even a month. I tried to keep track of the days but pretty soon I was measuring time more by how big Nev's belly was getting, not in sunrises."

"See many people out there?"

"Mostly it was just gunshots, some of them aimed at our feet. Although one whizzed right by my ear. No shout, nothing. Just a bullet coming for my head. I didn't even know we were close to somebody's water."

Lynn could see it. Eli slogging through the last of the falling leaves at an incredibly slow pace so that Neva could keep up. Lucy probably trailing behind because of her swollen feet, maybe looking for grasshoppers as she went. And then a gunshot . . . Lynn recoiled as if she'd pulled the trigger herself. "Most people will at least give you a warning shot, like the ones you had—the ones aimed at your feet."

"But not everybody."

"No, not everybody." Lynn got out of bed, put on her warmer clothes, and started a pot of coffee.

"That's tempting," Eli said, watching her. "But I should probably go. Neva will be worried if she wakes up and I'm not back."

"Right," Lynn said, focusing on the pot of water. "Do you ever . . . hold her like that? Like with me last night?"

"No," Eli said immediately. "It's not like that between us. I'm boy enough to know she's beautiful, and man enough to know she'll always be my brother's wife."

Lynn smiled at his honesty. "I had to ask."

Eli opened his mouth to answer her but there was a pounding on the door. Lynn grabbed her handgun and went up the stairs. Seconds later, Lucy came bouncing down. "Hey, Uncle Eli!"

Lynn followed more slowly with Stebbs on her tail. "Hey, Uncle Eli indeed," he said wryly, looking between the two younger people. "Would it be naïve of me to assume that you left late last night and came back early this morning?"

Lynn blushed and began making up the cot, then realized she was bringing attention to the fact that there was only one cot to be made. "Don't start," she said tightly to Stebbs.

"As much as I'd love to spend the morning teasing you, I've got a serious question for you both."

Lynn stopped making the bed. "What is it?"

"How long has it been since either one of you saw smoke to the south?"

"Weeks, easy," Lynn answered quickly, having checked every morning.

Eli glanced at her, thinking. "I don't remember any recently, but to be honest I don't always look."

"I'm with you," Stebbs said to Lynn. "It's been a while, and nothing's surviving without heat in this weather."

"You think they're gone?"

"Gone or dead."

Eli leaned back in his chair. "I feel like shit for saying so, but that's a relief."

"It's a relief, period," Lynn said as she tried to place the unfamiliar feeling of warmth that had spread through her chest at the sight of the people she cared about gathered safely under her roof.

Sixteen

L ynn couldn't remember a winter that had been so content. The plentiful snowfall meant that there was no need to break the ice on the pond to gather water. When they were thirsty, Lynn and Lucy gathered snow in buckets and warmed it on the stove, or ate it in frozen mouthfuls, after pelting each other with it first.

With the threat from the south removed, Lynn joined Lucy on the ground and showed her the different tracks in the snow. Deer and raccoon, the occasional flying leaps of a squirrel that left a sporadic, clumsy trail. The padded track of the coyotes that had been making appearances again. Lucy learned fast and wanted to know more. Lynn taught her how to distinguish the different birdcalls of the hardier birds that stayed for the winter, and how to make a grunt call with her cupped hands to attract bucks.

Lucy was thriving, her thin arms and legs now stocky with muscle from fighting her way through the snowdrifts in search of her next adventure. Lynn followed her, plowing after the little footprints and warning her off the icy pond on the warmer days. They made the occasional trip to Stebbs', though it made Lynn anxious to go. Lucy told her no one wanted a pond that was frozen solid, and they agreed to only be gone a little while. Lynn found her worries melting away once in Stebbs' comforting presence, and they usually stayed long past her time limit.

Eli visited often, making the arduous trek from the stream even on the coldest of days. Lucy would shower him with attention for a while after he showed up, then be distracted by something new, leaving them to talk privately and hold each other's gloved hands. Eli's visits were short by necessity. Neva liked some moments alone, but her fear of the wilderness didn't allow those moments to stretch into hours.

"There's a fine line between enjoying some alone time and just being downright lonely," Eli said as they trailed in Lucy's wake one snowy afternoon.

"Do you think she needs Lucy back?" Lynn asked, even though she wasn't ready to make the offer. "I don't want Neva to hate me, but I want what's best for Lucy."

"Right now—and I hate to say this—being with Neva is not it,"

Eli answered. "She's not entirely stable. She carries that gun that you gave her inside her bra."

"That hardly makes her unstable," Lynn said, letting go of his hand to pat the sidearm she had tucked into her coverall's pocket. "It's common sense."

"Maybe for a girl like you it is, but Neva hadn't even seen a gun until we got here. Now she sleeps with one?"

Lynn shrugged off his concerns, and they walked quietly hand in hand for a while. "Do you think she'd come over here? Maybe she'd leave the stream now that the men from the south are gone."

"It's possible. I can ask."

"Stebbs says there's a warm spell coming. Maybe then?"

"Maybe." Eli squeezed Lynn's hand and stopped her in her tracks. He held her face in his hands for a moment, tucking stray strands of hair back under her cap. "Can we stop talking about Neva for just a minute?"

Lynn agreed with a smile and leaned forward for her kiss.

A small voice taunted them in the distance. "Lynn and Eli sitting in a tree, K-I-S-S-I-N-G."

Eli turned to her, his voice rolling over the snowdrifts. "Do you even know what that spells, brain wave?"

"Uh . . . I think it spells that you're in love."

"Hmm . . ." Eli turned back to Lynn, his hands still on her face. "She might be onto something."

Lucy popped up beside them. "Can I have hot chocolate?"

"Race ya!" Eli challenged Lucy and they started for the house at a dead run that turned into a rolling ball of clothing when Lucy took him out at the knees. Lynn followed more slowly, noting the muted edges of the drifts. The snow was melting, imperceptibly at first, but it was going. Soon the spring would bring warm temperatures, mud everywhere, and a high water mark in the pond due to runoff.

For the moment, life was good.

Though she knew spring was close, the nights were still long and Lynn's dreams were not as pleasant as her days. Sleep came easily but didn't last. After one nightmare, Lynn woke with Mother on her mind. Lucy's even breathing filled the room, and she envied the little girl her deep sleep and innocent dreams. She unwrapped her legs from the sheets, pulled her boots and coat on, and silently slipped up the basement stairs and out the back door.

There was no moon. The utter blackness of the outdoors descended upon her and swallowed all her thoughts, leaving her aware only of her surroundings and what could hide in it. She unshouldered her rifle and sat on the stone step, grateful for the familiar worries of something she could control. Lucy's sleeping form, curled and content, slipped through her mind and she tightened her grip on the rifle, eyes roaming the black expanse of the night.

Her gaze drifted to the south from habit, where a pale glow

made the tree line of Stebbs' woods visible. "What the hell?" Lynn was so taken aback that she spoke aloud, her words trickling away into the night.

She thought for a second that she had worried away the entire night, but the sun wouldn't be rising in the south, and the glow she saw there wasn't the natural pink streaks of the morning. It was a sickly yellow, its pale aura reaching only past the stark black of Stebbs' treetops, and shedding light no farther.

Lynn studied it with a grim face, her mouth tight. She clicked the rifle safety off, all traces of fatigue stolen from her in a breath. This light was unfamiliar and strange.

Which meant it was dangerous.

Stebbs appeared on the horizon a few days later, his limping trail snaking behind him. Lucy had learned quickly how to spot his track, the telltale drag of his injured foot left an easily distinguishable pattern in the snow. For weeks in the dead of winter, he had created crisscross paths, making a game for her to find the right one that ended with him, and a bear hug. She ran toward him the second she spotted him, abandoning Lynn to the task of scraping ice off the doorstep alone.

"Melt giving you much trouble?" Stebbs asked when he made it to the house, Lucy tucked safely in the crook of his arm.

"Not bad. I'm tired of the refreezing in the night, though. Lucy fell walking out the door this morning. I can't have her breaking a leg."

"No, 'cause then someone would have to carry her around everywhere they went," Stebbs said to the little girl, who leaned her head against his shoulder and giggled. "What a chore."

He sat her down and Lucy tugged on his hand. "Come inside and eat with us and see what I made. Lynn's teaching me to knit."

"That a fact?"

"Trying," Lynn said, swatting the little girl's backside as she ran past her down the stairs. "This one's got the patience of a gnat."

"And Eli's teaching me to play guitar," Lucy added.

"Again, trying," Lynn said to Stebbs, as she tossed wood onto the stove and opened a jar of vegetables. Once they were settled and eating, Stebbs brought up his reason for visiting.

"There's another pack of coyotes in the area."

"I know," Lynn said between bites. "We heard them last night." The frantic yelping of the pack had brought Lucy into Lynn's cot, her small body quivering in fear.

Lucy took a bite of her corn and looked from Stebbs to Lynn. "I thought you killed them all," she said.

"Can't get all of 'em, little one. You'd best play closer to the house for a while," Stebbs said. Lucy made a face but Lynn knew she would listen. The wild dogs scared the little city girl in a way that other, less obvious dangers didn't.

"The big one, you know . . ." Stebbs trailed off, watching to see if

Lynn caught his meaning. "He's still out there."

"You see him?"

"No, but I've seen his track."

Lynn didn't want to speak about what had happened to Mother in front of Lucy. "Why don't you run off and see if you can't find that toad in the pantry?"

Lucy's eyes widened. "You think he's still there?"

"I thought I saw him when I went in for the vegetables. Take the flashlight, see if you can catch him."

Lucy jumped at the chance to use the coveted flashlight and disappeared behind the woolen blanket separating the two rooms. Lynn offered what was left on her plate to Stebbs, having lost her appetite. "You think he'd come up to the house again?"

"Not to be crass, but he's found food here before. And Lucy would be an easy kill for a pack like the one I heard the other night."

"I'll keep her close by," Lynn assured him. "I hate keeping her inside though. There's so little daylight as it is and this basement doesn't let much in."

"That's the next bit I wanted to talk to you about," Stebbs said. "The harsh part of winter is over, and Eli is much more capable than he used to be."

"I know it," Lynn said. "And I know what you're driving at. We talked it over the other day, and he thinks maybe Neva will come here to see Lucy. We thought maybe they could readjust to each other kinda, before she moves over there."

"Sounds like a good idea. When?"

"We thought next week maybe, once the weather breaks. You said it would be warmer soon?"

"I'm counting on a total melt, then it'll freeze up again and maybe one or two good snows before winter's done with us."

Lynn ignored the dropping of her heart at the thought of Lucy leaving her. "After the melt then." She glanced toward the blanket dividing the two rooms, where Lucy's voice could be heard calling out for the toad she was looking for. "I saw something to the south, a few nights ago."

"What was that?"

"There was a glow up in the sky. Kinda like the sun was trying to come up in the wrong place."

Stebbs' mouth drew tight and his eyebrows came together. "What color was it?"

"Yellow, I guess. It didn't look right though, like the yellow of a dandelion or anything like that."

"More sickly?"

Lynn nodded slowly. "Yeah . . . that's a good word for it."

"And you saw it when?"

"Just the other night, when there was no moon. Not since then."

"You probably wouldn't, if there was any kind of moon in the sky, it would drown it out."

"Drown out what?"

"The glow of electricity from a small town or even a group of houses. On a black night it wouldn't take much to light up the sky."

Lynn was quiet as Stebbs' words drilled down inside of her to a place that was even darker than that moonless night had been. "They're still alive then? The men from the south?"

Stebbs nodded grimly. "If they've got generators to make electricity, then they've got heat, too. No need for fires."

Lynn closed her eyes against the thought. "Generators, huh? Assholes."

Lynn found herself bestowing small luxuries on Lucy. A new black button nose for Red Dog, the last cup of hot chocolate, a new pair of striped socks that she had knitted for her on the sly. The night before Neva's arrival, Lucy stumbled for Lynn's cot in the dark. Small, cold fingers found her face.

"Can I sleep with you?"

Lynn sighed and pretended to be irritated, but allowed Lucy to climb in beside her. Curled together in the dark, Lynn found the courage to broach the topic she'd been avoiding since Stebbs' visit.

"So tomorrow's going to be a big day," she said.

Lucy's voice, drowsy and content, hummed against her neck. "Wuzzat?"

"Your mother is coming to see you."

"Okay."

"That all you got to say?"

The small shoulders shrugged, and a light snoring soon followed. Lynn wrapped her arms protectively around the small frame. "It'll be all right," she said. "I promise."

Lynn slept in much later than usual, as reluctant to face the day ahead of them as Lucy was. Lucy resisted all attempts to wake her. Lynn had expected resentment, possibly even outright anger toward the mother who had been absent for so long. But the blanket-covered form in the cot was ignoring Lynn completely, presenting her with her back and pretending not to hear when she told her it was time to get up.

"All right, little girl," Lynn said as she pulled on her knitted cap. "I'm going outside. I might hunt a bit but I'll stay within sight of the house. Once you get up keep an eye out for Stebbs. He's coming too, you know."

No reaction.

"And Uncle Eli."

No reaction.

"Fine. But when I come back down here I want you up and out of bed, or I will *get* you up and out of bed, understood?"

The curly blond head on the pillow nodded almost imperceptibly and Lynn stomped up the stairs and out into the late morning air.

Dead grass showed in large patches around the yard, and Lynn had to walk a ways from the house to find a clean patch of white snow to freshen her mouth with.

The sporadic, panicked tracks of a rabbit tore across the yard at one point, nearly obliterated by the blundering leaps of the coyote that had chased it. Lynn was in no hurry to force Lucy out of bed to face Neva, so she took her time tracking the two animals, curious to see if the rabbit had managed to escape. A patch of blood a mile from the house told her it hadn't. Lynn rested under the trees and watched two blue jays bickering. Their harsh voices bounced off the snow, masking the sound of Stebbs' approach.

"Hey there," he said, leaning against the tree with her. "Not used to seeing you out alone."

"Lucy's back at the house." Lynn nodded toward the roof in the distance. "I thought I'd give her some time to . . ."

"Think things over?" Stebbs suggested.

"Yeah, something like that."

"Looks like maybe you're doing the same."

"Maybe." Lynn rubbed the stock of her rifle, but the gun didn't bring the comfort it used to. "Best head back, I suppose."

Stebbs fell into step beside her and they walked in companionable silence until they reached her pond. "Quite the melt," he commented. "Your pond's high. I see you've still got ice on the edges though."

"Can't skate anymore. Lucy'll be disappointed."

"It'll freeze over again, before the winter's over."

Without commenting on it, Lynn noticed that Stebbs was struggling against the snow with his lame leg. She leaned against the house under the cover of a large pine, and he joined her, his breath coming a little faster than usual.

"When you expecting Eli and Neva?"

"Don't know. He said sometime this afternoon, but I slept in quite a bit and then went out tracking for a while. I imagine they'll be along soon enough. I told Lucy I'd be in sight of the house. If she wanted to find us, she could have. I told her Neva was coming last night, and she didn't take it so well."

"It's understandable."

"Yeah well, maybe, but I don't want Neva bent out of shape about it. Or Lucy mad at me, for that matter."

"Want me to go down and try?"

"Better hurry," Lynn said, nodding toward the west, where Eli's and Neva's figures could be made out. Stebbs lumbered to his feet and disappeared inside.

Neva broke into the side yard ahead of Eli, poked a finger into the side of the half-melted snowman by the wood cord and smiled. Eli nodded and said something to her, but it was lost in a cry from the basement.

"Shit! Lynn! Get down here!"

The urgency in Stebbs' voice sent Lynn reeling down the stairs where he was cradling Lucy in his arms, her entire form limp, her closed eyes red-rimmed with fever. "How long has she been like this?" Lynn stared dumbfounded at the unconscious Lucy. "Lynn!"

"I don't . . . I don't know! I thought she was sleeping. I haven't been back down here since I woke up."

Two sets of feet pounded down the stairs, and Eli fell forward into the basement, Neva close behind him. "What? What is it?"

Neva's hands flew to her mouth when she saw Lucy, tears streamed from the corners of her eyes. "Give her to me," she said.

Stebbs handed her over carefully and Neva cradled the light head against her own dark one, rocking her slowly back and forth. "What happened, baby? What's wrong?"

There was no answer.

There was a light touch on Lynn's shoulder. "She's not . . . not gone, is she?"

"No," Stebbs answered Eli. "There's a pulse, but it's light."

"What happened? When did she get sick?"

"I don't know," Lynn said, her voice shaking. "She crawled into bed with me last night and I thought she was fine, but she didn't want to get up. . . . Shit, I'm so sorry, Neva. I didn't know."

Neva waved away the apology. "Get me a cloth," she said as she laid Lucy back on the cot. "We've got to break this fever."

Stebbs looked in amazement at his own hands, still hot to the touch from holding Lucy. "She's burning up."

His words caused a panic in Lynn's mind, dredging up memories of corpses without bullet holes strewn across the fields, bodies that the buzzards wouldn't touch. Cholera burned through people so quickly they died in their tracks, wandering in a haze toward a water source that Mother wouldn't let them near. One man had veered away from the pond and hailed Mother from the yard. Lynn had clutched on to her tightly, fear of the stranger digging her little fingers deep into Mother's tanned skin.

He'd begged for water, pleading that he was not ill like the others and would not contaminate the pond. Mother had refused and sent him off with a warning. Hours later he was back, shit streaking his legs and begging for a bullet instead. This time, Mother had granted his request.

Lynn dug her fingers into Stebbs' coat, her voice a harsh whisper. "It's not the cholera, is it?"

"No, she always does this," Neva said, peeling off a layer of warm sleeping clothes from Lucy. "You can't just get a little fever, can you, baby? You've got to go big." Tears were still sliding down her face, but Neva was moving with purpose. She looked up at her audience. "Move! I need a cold, wet cloth—now. And a thermometer, if you have one."

Neva's conviction broke Lynn's stillness. She shot up the stairs with Eli on her heels. "There's some washcloths in the bathroom," she called over her shoulder. "Use the clean water downstairs in the tank."

"Where are you going?"

"Thermometer," she answered without bothering to explain why she was running up the staircase. Mother had squirreled away all of Lynn's baby clothes, blankets, bottles, and—she hoped—baby thermometer as well. She burst into the attic, throwing open lids to steamer trunks and tossing clothes in the air in a frantic search. The objecting screech of a baby toy told her she'd found the right trunk, and Lynn dug to the bottom, overwhelmed with relief at the sight of the plastic thermometer.

"Please work," she said to it, and the digital screen lit up at her touch.

Her heart was beating so hard, she almost didn't hear the footsteps on the roof. Lynn instinctively dropped down, hand clutched protectively around the thermometer. For a moment there was nothing, only the sound of her own blood pumping through her veins. Then she heard it again.

Someone was on her roof.

Seventeen

She crept down the staircase quietly, dodging the patches of late afternoon light in the living room and slinking into the kitchen. Eli was already downstairs; she could hear his muted voice in conversation with Neva, her tone pitched high with concern. Lynn edged down the steps, handed the thermometer silently to Neva and reached past Eli for her handgun.

"There's someone outside," she whispered to him. He tensed but didn't look away from the cot where Lucy lay, her arm dangling over the side. Neva had to hold her jaw shut to use the thermometer; Lucy was too weak to close her own mouth.

"Where?"

"On the roof, for sure. I'm betting more," Lynn answered quietly, but with her eyes on Stebbs. He noticed and joined their group at the foot of the stairs.

"What?"

"Men on the roof," Eli said, his voice pitched low to not alarm Neva. "What do we do?"

"Not much we can do. They already have higher ground. You run out there firing and they'll pick you off."

"Only if he's a good shot," Lynn countered.

"Assume he is. Put down the gun."

She didn't move. "They're not taking my house."

"I'm guessing they don't want it," Stebbs said evenly. "They didn't meet any resistance coming in. They have the advantage but aren't pressing it."

"So what do they want?" Eli asked.

"We go find out." Stebbs gave Lynn a hard look and peeled her fingers off the gun. "You going to keep your head on straight?"

"Do I have a choice?"

"Don't look like it. You go out first, keep your hands up where they can see them. I'll follow her, and Eli you come last. Be calm, no reason to upset Neva just yet."

Lynn glanced back at the cot before leaving. Water from the cloth on her forehead was streaming down Lucy's face, matching the tears on Neva's. "Hold on, kiddo," she said quietly. "We'll be right back."

She climbed the stairs stiffly, every nerve in her body protesting the absence of her gun. The door creaked open and she walked into the sunlight, both hands open and visible. Three armed men stood in the yard, a woman kneeling in the mud in front of them, a noose around her neck. Lynn walked forward cautiously, highly conscious of the man on the roof and the prickle of hairs on her neck telling her that his crosshairs were focused there.

"Get off my roof," she said.

One of the men spat on the ground and smiled at her, showing off gaps in his teeth. "That the way you greet your neighbors?"

"Neighbors that drag a woman around by her neck, yes."

"Lynn," Stebbs said quietly in warning as he stepped from the doorway. Eli emerged behind him, his hands held up as well. His eyes were on Lynn, a mute entreaty to keep her mouth shut, until he spotted the woman.

"Vera!"

She jerked at the sound of her name, raising her head and allowing Lynn a good look. She didn't need Eli to tell her this was Neva's mother. Her black hair was streaked with gray, the lines in her face were delicate and flattering, a perfect image of what Neva would look like in the future. Except that the light flashing in her eyes was fierce, the determination to live imprinted clearly.

"You got nothing to say to her just yet," Gap Tooth said to Eli. "I'm the one talking right now."

"I got a thing or two to say to that one," a man wearing a blue coat said, nodding at Lynn from his position by Neva's side. "She killed two of my friends."

"I see you brought me more."

"Enough," Stebbs said sharply. "What do you want from us?"

"Don't want nothing with you, old man," Gap Tooth said. "We went to make a trade with your pretty boy there, but he wasn't home. Thought maybe he was making time with the girl, and here we are."

One of the men standing with Vera, who wore a green hat, spoke up. "Where's the little one?"

"She's busy dying," Lynn said coldly.

He looked down at his feet, but not before she caught the flicker of shame in his eyes. "I'm sorry for that."

Vera moaned and her eyes moved to Lynn, a pleading question there that she couldn't answer. Lynn looked away, swallowing hard. "What's your trade?"

"Our business ain't with you," Gap Tooth said.

"You're on my property, and I'm the one asking."

"Goddamn girl, you ain't learned friendly yet, have ya?"

Blue Coat fingered his crotch. "I'll teach her, before we leave."

Eli crossed the distance between them before the men had the chance to cock their guns and delivered a chop to his neck that brought Blue Coat to the ground, gasping. The guns turned on Eli, and he put his hands back in the air. "You came to trade, make a trade. He talks with his dick again, he loses it."

238

Gap Tooth considered his comrade, still fighting for air and curled into the fetal position. He lowered his gun. "We want your fancy girl. Even trade for her momma."

"No," Lynn said without hesitation. "I won't trade a friend for a stranger."

"Ain't your call, girlie."

Eli stood shivering in the chill, his hands still in the air. "She isn't mine to trade. I don't own her."

"I've got food," Stebbs said quickly. "Vegetables, fruit, water. Whatever you need."

"We got water and I ain't hungry, not in that way."

The back door burst open, all guns changed their positions, and Vera yelped at the sight of her daughter. "Her temp is a hundred and four, I need—" Neva jerked to a halt when she saw the men.

"Neva," Eli said carefully, "we need to—"

"Mother!" Neva cried, lurching toward her despite the guns pointed at her. She fell to her knees beside the older woman, tears falling openly. Her fingers wrapped around the noose and began pulling it over Vera's head.

"Hold on there, missy," Blue Coat said, his hand stopping hers. "We ain't done negotiating."

"Negotiating for what?"

"Neva, honey," Vera said calmly. "Listen to me—"

"It's simple, fancy lady," Gap Tooth said. "You come with us,

239

and we leave your mother."

Neva held her mother's bound hands in her own, her face blank as she stared back at him.

Lynn edged toward them, hands still in the air. "Neva, you don't have to—"

Blue Coat swung his gun on her. "Shut it."

"I'll go," Neva said, glancing at Lynn. The rush of energy from Neva that Lucy's sickness spurred had turned into a cold determination, and Lynn barely recognized the eyes staring back at her from the other woman's face.

"Eli, get my coat," Neva said.

"You're not going anywhere," he answered.

"Get her coat or she goes cold," Gap Tooth said.

"Lynn," Neva said, her eyes boring into Lynn's, "take care of my sick baby." Every word punched through the protest Lynn had already formed. Lynn's rage had kept her from seeing what Neva knew too well; Vera was a doctor, and Lucy needed her badly. More than she needed her mother. If the men knew Vera's skill they would never trade her, no matter how badly they wanted Neva.

"Eli," Lynn spoke slowly, disbelieving her own words. "Get Neva's coat."

When he didn't move, Lynn broke Neva's gaze and glanced at him. He searched her face for a moment and Lynn knew he was weighing the fates of Lucy and Neva in the moment before he went to get Neva's coat, head down. Neva bent to take the noose off her mother, but Blue Coat jerked her to the ground and began tying her hands in front of her before she could. Lynn winced, fury at her inability to stop them boiled over.

"You should know that I'll kill you all, and soon," she said.

"Them's big words, little girl, when I'm up here," the man on the roof said.

"My voice carried though, didn't it?"

"Now that looks good on you, Fancy," Blue Coat said to Neva as he tightened the noose around her throat. "Don't go running off on me now." He kicked Vera in the ribs and she fell to her side in the mud. "Been nice knowing you, looking forward to getting to know your daughter just as well."

Vera remained facedown in the mud, refusing to look at him. Neva kept her eyes on the ground, ignoring Eli as he put her coat around her shoulders. The man on the roof clambered down the antenna, keeping his rifle on Stebbs and Lynn as he backed away. The three others followed, Blue Coat dragging Neva to her feet; Green Hat steadied her when she tripped.

"Tell Lucy I love her," Neva said to Lynn as she walked past. Lynn's throat closed up, not allowing her to speak. She only nodded in response, and the figures grew smaller as they moved away, the man from the roof continuing to cover them with his rifle.

"Ma'am, I know it's been a hell of a morning," Stebbs said,

kneeling in the mud next to Vera, "but we've got something to ask of you."

"Lucy's sick," Eli said. "Bad."

Stebbs cut the rope holding Vera's hands together, and she rubbed her wrists. "Where is she?" she asked.

"Downstairs." Stebbs helped her to her feet. "It happened overnight." He explained as they moved into the basement and gathered around Lucy's cot. No one noticed when Lynn quietly picked up her rifle and left.

The four figures were easy to spot from the roof. Gap Tooth led, with Blue Coat dragging Neva behind him, and Green Hat walking beside her. The man from the roof had turned his back on the house, assuming he was clear of her range. He wasn't, but Lynn knew she couldn't make four clean shots before one of them got to Neva to retaliate. All she could do was watch.

Neva stumbled awkwardly over the rough fields, lost her balance, and fell on all fours. Her coat slid off her shoulders as she struggled to her knees. The noose pulled tight, and Blue Coat turned around just in time to see Neva put the derringer to her temple. Lynn saw her body slump sideways before the sound of the gunshot reached her, a flat snap that could have been mistaken for the breaking of a twig.

Blue Coat turned in time for blood to spray his jeans, and he kicked Neva's lifeless body. Wrath rose in Lynn's throat so thickly she nearly choked on it as the other men pulled him off Neva. He turned back to the house, drawing his finger across his throat in an unmistakable gesture. Lynn's finger curled around the trigger, the need to add a dead body next to Neva's so deep that it almost won over her common sense. Mother could have taken them down at that range, but Lynn wasn't confident and a wasted bullet would bring all four of them fanning back around the house, and trouble to Lucy's bedside at a time when every second counted.

But they went south instead of carrying out the threat. Now that Lynn had the high ground and they'd lost the element of surprise, the odds were against them. Green Hat waited until the other men had put some distance between themselves and the body before he knelt down and covered Neva's face with her coat.

Lynn was numb as she fumbled with the door, the image of Neva's lifeless body lying alone in the frozen field stamped on her brain.

"Stebbs," Lynn called down the steps. "I need you out here."

He came to the bottom of the stairs. "What?"

"Up here," she said. He climbed the steps and shut the door behind him when he saw the look on her face.

"Neva's dead."

"How?"

"Did for herself, with the derringer I gave her. Not long after they walked off. They left her out in the field."

Stebbs sat down on the stone steps, resting his head in his hands.

"What do we do?" Lynn asked.

"We'll have to go get her, but right now we've got worse problems."

"How bad is Lucy?"

"I don't know much about sickness, but by the look on her grandma's face, I'd say it's bad."

Lynn sat beside him, ignoring the freezing water that soaked through her jeans. "What do we do?"

Stebbs put his arm around her, and she leaned into him. "Kiddo, you and me don't do so well in situations we can't control. There's nothing you could've done for Neva, and we can't help Lucy now. It's not up to us."

She rested her head on his shoulder, tears of futility pricking at her eyes. "Don't think I care for that."

The door burst open behind them, and Vera ripped past, Lucy's shaking, naked body clutched in her arms.

"Jesus, woman!" Stebbs yelled.

"She's seizing!" Vera screamed, and disappeared over the bank of the pond. They ran after her, Eli on their heels, and crested the bank to see Vera plunge the white form into the icy blackness of the pond.

Lucy's eyes snapped open and she screamed, scratching frantically at the strong arms holding her body under the water. Lynn grabbed Vera and yanked her backward, but her strength was outmatched by the older woman's determination. She landed on her back, the wind knocked out of her.

"Get off me!" Vera yelled. "We break the fever or she dies."

Lucy kicked weakly, her efforts sending ripples through the water that broke against the ice still covering the depths. Vera pulled her out, and her limbs fell limply to the side, spraying Lynn's face with freezing droplets.

"Take her," Vera handed her off to Eli, who raced back inside.

Vera slumped next to Lynn on the bank, clutching her wet arms to her sides. "It was the only thing I could think of," she said. "Once the fever gets past a hundred and five there can be serious brain damage. I had to cool her, fast."

"Did it work?" Stebbs asked.

"She stopped seizing, but it will spike again."

"What's wrong with her?" Lynn asked.

"I'm guessing it's a bacterial infection, though it could be viral. Her medical history makes me think the former; she's always been susceptible to the bacterial kind."

"Neva said Lucy's fevers always went real high," Stebbs said.

"Some people's bodies burn higher than others." Vera rose to her feet, looking at the ice crystals re-forming where she'd broken through with Lucy's frail body. "It'll spike again, and I'll have to dunk her."

"I have some medicine," Lynn said. "It's mostly expired, but there is some aspirin. That can bring down a fever, can't it?"

245

"It can, but if it's old it can't do much against what she's facing. It's probably too much to hope that you have some antibiotics?"

Lynn shook her head and followed Vera as she started back to the house and her patient, wet arms clutched against the rising wind. The older woman kicked in anger at a frozen clod of dirt. "I smuggled some medicine out of the city when I went, but I hid my pack when I ran into those men on the road."

"Is it far?"

"Too far on foot to do Lucy much good. They picked me up in their truck and we drove awhile before we got to their camp."

"How long?"

Vera gave a shudder that had nothing to do with the temperature. "Long time."

"Did you have a general sense of direction? Could you find it again?"

Lynn opened the door for Vera and they descended into the basement together. Eli had wrapped Lucy in the extra blankets and had her lying in the cot near the fire. Vera put her hand on her forehead, frowning. "I had a compass on me, and a map. They took them both. I know we traveled east to get here, and I could recognize the area again. By the time we found the meds and came back though, it would be too late."

"I have a truck," Lynn said. "I'll drive you."

Vera tucked the blankets tightly around her granddaughter, her decision made the second she put her hand against Lucy's burning flesh. "We leave now. Eli—stay close to Lucy. If she seizes again, you'll have to dunk her. I know it's ugly, but it's the only way to keep her temp down. Let me see those aspirin."

Lynn handed the coveted bottle over to Vera, ashamed at the rattling of so few pills inside.

"These are years past effectiveness," Vera said critically. "Usually I'd say the drug is broken down past any use, but we don't have a lot of options." She handed the bottle to Eli. "Crush up two of these and mix it with some water, try to get Lucy to drink it. You—" She pointed to Stebbs. "Strip the other cot and start some water boiling so there will be clean bedding ready. And keep the water boiling to sterilize the dirty. If this fever breaks, she'll be covered in sweat, and vomiting will probably follow. That's the best-case scenario."

"What's the worst case?" Stebbs asked.

"It doesn't break."

The truck started without a problem, and Lynn let out a sigh of relief.

"You were worried?" Vera asked.

"Don't drive much, except for emergencies," she answered. "Truck doesn't always want to start up, and that's the kind of day it's been."

"Right."

Lynn headed straight west, her hands drumming against the

wheel in an effort to channel her energy. Words bubbled up from her chest, looking for an outlet. "We're lucky they didn't come until after the melt. Even in this truck we couldn't have managed the roads in all that snow." The idea that something as simple as a snowmelt could dictate whether Lucy lived or died left her feeling shaky and unanchored.

"They talked about coming sooner," Vera said calmly. "But Roger—the one who did all the talking—"

"Gap Tooth?" Vera gave her a blank look. "The one missing teeth?"

"Yes—that's Roger. He said they should wait. They wanted Neva, but they knew they would have to take you by surprise. If they used the trucks, you'd hear the engine and be on the roof in a second, and they couldn't make the walk until the snow melted a little. Roger said from what they knew of you they had no guarantee you wouldn't shoot us all, including me."

"A couple of months ago, I might've," Lynn admitted.

"How did Lucy end up with you?"

Lynn was quiet for a moment, weighing her words. Vera still didn't know Neva was dead, and it would fall to her to tell her.

"They couldn't care for her," she said slowly. "Surviving out here is hard, and they weren't ready for the weather. They thought they'd have shelter sooner."

"Why didn't they? It seems like there's plenty of abandoned houses around."

"Their original plan was to stay in my house, near a source of water. When they saw I was there, they knew they couldn't take it. They were worn down and weak. Neva didn't want to leave the stream, so they stayed there."

"Living where?"

"Eli did a decent job of building them a little shelter. Stebbs—that's the man back at my house—he talked me into coming over and visiting them. Eli and Neva decided that Lucy would be better off with me."

"They should have never tried it," Vera said, placing her hand against the passenger window and splaying her fingers. "I could've aborted her pregnancy and they would've stayed in the city."

"Why didn't you?"

"Neva wouldn't do it. She said she'd rather have her baby out here than stay in the city and give it up."

"She lost it," Lynn said. "It was a boy."

"Carried to term?"

"Uh . . ."

"Was she really big when she had the baby? Was the baby fully formed?"

Lynn remembered the fading warmth in the little bundle that

Stebbs had handed her, and Eli unwrapping it to see whether he'd had a niece or a nephew.

"I think it was, yeah."

Lynn thought about Neva's hunched form at the tiny grave, faithfully visiting every day no matter how cold it was. The same determination had been in her face as she traded her life for her daughter's, and Lynn felt her gut twist at the thought that Neva had known what she was about to do even as she walked away.

They drove through a crossroads, Lynn blithely ignoring the stop sign at the corner. "There's a town up here, to the south, but it's abandoned. Was there anything like that where you were?" She didn't know if prompting Vera would help or hurt, but blind driving would get them nowhere. Lucy's chances dipped with the sun and every turn of the tires.

"I don't remember any towns. I was in the bed of the truck most of the time, and on my back, but I had a little peripheral vision and I wasn't looking anywhere else."

Lynn's stomach rolled at the implications. "If you didn't see much, it probably was west. There's not a lot in this direction."

They drove awhile in silence. Lynn's hands were tight on the steering wheel, her knuckles white. "Any of this looking familiar? Are we too far out?"

Vera stared out her window, shaking her head. "Nothing looks right, but I think we were farther out than this. I do remember seeing a church spire, and thinking it was odd to see a church that big out here in the middle of nowhere."

"Was it white?"

"Yes, but the bell had fallen out and crashed down the front of the tower."

Hope blossomed in her chest like a crocus pushing through the winter's ice, and Lynn swung to the right. "I know that place, it's the old Methodist church. When I was really little, Mother used to take me hunting with her, 'cause she was afraid I'd wander outside alone if she left me behind. She'd hunt there for wild turkeys. The bell was still hanging then."

"Your mother?"

"Gone now," Lynn answered. "This past fall."

"I'm sorry."

Lynn drove fast in the fading light, scanning the horizon for the spire of the church. She hadn't been this far from home since Mother had brought her out as a child, and though her sense of direction was keen, she didn't trust her distant memories in the dark.

"I need to tell you something," Lynn said. "About Neva."

"I can't think about her right now," Vera said. "I can't stop what they're doing to her. It's best to focus on Lucy and something I can help."

"She's dead."

"What?" For the first time, Vera looked away from the window, her strong composure breaking with the single syllable.

"She shot herself in the field, not long after they took her."

Vera closed her eyes and rested her head against the cold glass. "Neva, my poor girl. I'm so sorry, baby."

Tears pricked at Lynn's eyes and she stared ahead, uncomfortable in the small truck cab with Vera's mourning. The church spire stood black against the setting sun, the red rays of evening pouring through the hole that the falling bell had torn.

"Here's the church," she said, driving past slowly. "Do you know where you are now?"

Vera opened her eyes and wiped away a few stray tears. She cleared her throat. "I wasn't far from here, there was a little cemetery around the corner. I had just passed it when I heard their truck coming. I was smart enough to hide my pack behind a tombstone, but stupid enough to not hide myself. I was hoping I'd be able to get a ride."

"It's not like the city out here," Lynn said. "You're better off to distrust everyone at first and make them earn it."

"Then it's exactly like the city."

Lynn drove to the little cemetery silently, parking so that the headlights cut across the graves, giving the stones long, black shadows.

"You remember which one?"

"I've got a general idea," Vera said as she opened her door. "Everything was in my backpack and I ditched the whole thing."

"They didn't think it was odd you were traveling empty-handed?"

"They weren't thinking with their brains once they caught me."

Vera and Lynn fanned out through the center section of the graveyard in the long evening shadows. Lynn's feet sank into the soft ground as she walked. The backpack was hunched sadly against the back of a leaning tombstone, the underside dark with moisture. "Got it," she called out, hefting the backpack up with one hand.

"Careful," Vera called out. "There are syringes in there. If they break, it's pointless."

Lynn handed the pack over to Vera and watched as she checked the contents. "They're injectable liquids, we'll have to hope they haven't frozen since I left this behind."

"Will they still work?"

Vera shrugged. "Only thing we can do is inject her and wait."

They headed south, Lynn's foot heavy on the pedal now that they weren't looking for landmarks anymore. Full dark fell, and she noticed that Vera tensed every time they flew through a crossroads.

"Sorry," she said when she noticed Lynn looking at her. "It's an old habit. When I see a stop sign, I still think 'stop.'"

"Mother used to stop at every one," Lynn said, smiling. "She said running them felt wrong."

"It's a different world now," Neva said. "I am sorry about your mother."

"I'm sorry about your daughter."

"Right now, I'll concentrate on saving Lucy, and mourn later."

Lynn sped up.

Eighteen

The needle sank into Lucy's fevered skin, leaving a pucker behind. "She's dehydrated," Vera said. "Did she keep anything down?"

Eli shook his head. "I crushed up a few of those aspirin and put them in some water, but she lost it pretty fast."

"Keep putting fluids in her. Her temp is dropping but it will spike again, even if the antibiotics are working. It takes a steady stream of medicine in her system to start fighting the infection. I can inject her with what I have maybe twice more, but that won't kill the bacteria on its own. They'll multiply and we'll be back in the same situation in a week or two."

"So we need more antibiotics," Stebbs said.

Vera nodded and pushed a curl of Lucy's hair behind her ear.

"I've heard horror stories of people dying out here from the simplest things; I didn't want to escape the city only to be killed by a scrape I overlooked one day too many. My own lab had the injectables, so it was easy enough to take some and adjust the inventory. But trying to take more or to take pills from someone else's lab would've been suicide."

A heavy silence filled the air at Vera's last word, and she put her hand to her mouth as if to force it back in.

Stebbs cleared his throat and shared a glance with Lynn. "You'll have to search some houses for the pills she needs."

Lynn began lacing her boots back up even though she'd just sat down. "I'll go now."

"I'm coming with you," Eli said, dragging his own boots out from under Lucy's cot.

"You do this sort of thing often?" Vera asked, her composure regained.

"Sometimes," Lynn said as she shrugged her coat back on. "If we need something we don't have handy. I haven't been out scavenging in a long time though, no idea what the nearby houses look like these days."

"Those men who took me . . . that's what they were doing—scavenging. They'd go house to house and clear out anything that seemed useful—medicine, blankets, and tools. They had it all stockpiled back at their camp."

"Why'd they need all that stuff?" Lynn asked blankly.

"They don't. They're taking it so that others that *do* need it have to come to them for it."

"To trade," Stebbs finished for her. "Sons of bitches."

Lynn remembered the traveler on the road, the stranger whose boots had been taken off his feet in order to be stockpiled somewhere. "I won't trade with them, even for medicine."

"Doesn't matter," Vera said. "You don't have anything they want. They're on the stream. It's flowing well right now from all this melt so they don't need water. But you're going to have to drive a long time before you get to a house they haven't cleaned out."

Lynn tucked her handgun in her waistband, slung her rifle over her shoulder. "We'll drive then," she said. "Surely there's somewhere they haven't been."

The evening was cold and she leaned into Eli as they walked out to the truck. "Did Stebbs tell you?" Lynn asked quietly.

"About Neva? Yeah."

Lynn rested her head against the steering wheel before starting the engine. "I can't believe she did that. Eli, I swear I never thought she'd use it for that."

He touched her cheek. "I know you didn't. It's all right."

"You don't blame me?"

"No. If that was her decision, she would've found a way eventually."

Lynn squeezed his hand, then started the truck, a weight sliding from her shoulders with the idea that Neva's face wasn't among those she should feel guilty for. "I don't know how far to go. Vera seemed to think those men cleared out a lot of the houses around here. They picked her up to the west, and their camp is somewhere to the south. We'll go east for about half an hour and start checking houses."

Eli watched as the fields and woods flashed by. "You're not going to do anything stupid, are you?"

"Not while I'm driving."

"You know what I mean. I was standing there when you threatened them."

"I will kill them, Eli. Now's not the time, but I will do it."

"It won't bring Neva back."

"I'm not trying to bring her back. They walked into my place and took something from me, and I let them. They'll do it again and again, for as long as I have something they want. Leaving them alone guarantees my own destruction."

"Vera said you don't have anything they want."

"Today they wanted Neva. Now she's gone. They could come back for me or decide they want Vera back. And if they knew Stebbs and Lucy could witch—"

"But they don't."

"They've tried to take the house before, when Mother was still alive. They want it; they just wanted Neva more. The stream won't flow well forever, and if their whole purpose is to gather things other people need, they'll come for my pond eventually."

"So what are you going to do against a camp full of men? You don't even know how many there are or where they're at."

"Vera will know."

Eli was quiet for a while as he stared outside at the darkness. "Stebbs won't like it."

"Stebbs doesn't run me. Sounds like you're the one who doesn't like it."

"Damn it, Lynn what do you want me to say? Yes, please attack a bunch of angry men who outnumber you and won't kill you fast?"

"You say what you like," Lynn said. "I'm trying this one." She braked and pulled into a driveway on the left, even though they hadn't been moving for thirty minutes. She didn't want to fight with Eli, but she wasn't caving either.

Lynn hailed the house before walking in. "I don't want to be shot for a burglar after living this long," she told Eli. There was no answer and they went through the front door. It was obvious the second that they walked in the men had beat them there. The sofa cushions were tossed on the floor; the stuffed furniture had been slashed.

"Why'd they do that?"

"Looking for valuables people would've hidden, I guess," Eli said.

"Anything truly valuable is in the kitchen."

"Well, it's empty," Eli's voice echoed off the walls in the next room. Lynn followed him to see cupboard doors hanging open. The drawers had been pulled out and dumped onto the floor. The utensils were gone. A few plastic straws rolled on the floor in the wake of her steps.

"Bathroom," Lynn said, but it was equally bare, except for a toothbrush in the sink whose bristles were splayed and permanently hardened.

"Shit," Eli said, looking into a cupboard by the shower. "They took everything. There's not even a washcloth in here."

The next house was the same, and the one after that. Lynn's resolve hardened and their conversation stopped entirely as the night wore on. They were nearly two hours from her house when they found a modest Cape Cod tucked behind a copse of trees that had not been rifled.

"Well," Eli said when they walked into an immaculate living room. "It makes me feel bad to say this about someone who kept such a clean house, but I hope they had an infectious disease and a well-stocked medicine cabinet."

They skipped the kitchen and went straight to the bathroom.

"Jackpot," Eli said when he opened a drawer under the sink. Lynn bent down to see rows of orange prescription bottles lined up carefully, with days of the week marked on the white lids.

"Any antibiotics?"

"I only know the names of a few," he said, holding a handful of bottles in the beam of Lynn's flashlight. "Here's one at least—amoxicillin. The others I can only guess at."

Lynn dumped her empty backpack at his feet. "We'll take them all, Vera will know what's what." They stripped the drawer bare, and checked the rest of the bathroom. They found Band-Aids, gauze, bandages, plus a first-aid kit with sample packages of painkillers inside.

The kitchen yielded plenty of canned food, and Lynn took a new pot, a skillet, two plates, and some utensils as well. "Usually I wouldn't take so much," she said, somewhat sheepishly. "But I could use a new pan and I keep expecting Lucy to break one of my plates."

"Better you than them," Eli said, and helped her carry their stash out to the truck.

"What do you think?" Lynn put the last bag in the bed of the truck. "Should we try another or head for home?"

"Home," Eli said.

Lynn nodded in agreement and reached for the driver's side door. Eli stopped her. "Let me drive, you're beat."

She didn't argue, and her head slipped to the side as they drove south, the heater lulling her into a much-deserved rest. When the truck came to a stop she jerked awake, disoriented by the strip of sun rising. Eli turned off the engine and rested his forehead against the steering wheel. "You awake?" His voice reverberated off the dashboard.

"Yeah."

"Good. I dropped the medicine off at your place. Right now I need your help."

"Help?"

Eli nodded and got out of the truck, motioning for her to follow. Neva lay on the ground, the derringer frozen in her palm. Even though Green Hat had done his best to cover her, a hard frost had fallen in the night, closing the wound in her temple and freezing her unseeing eyes open. Eli wordlessly scooped the lifeless body from the ground.

They laid her in the back of the truck gently. Lynn pried the gun loose from her fingers and put it in her own pocket, tucking Neva's hand under the coat. She rode in the back with Neva as close to the stream as the truck could go, and then took turns with Eli dragging the stiff body back to the grove of ashes. They hacked away at the ground through the morning hours, placing Neva next to her nameless little boy.

"Seems like we spend a lot of time digging graves together," Eli said, wiping the cold sweat from his brow.

"I don't think I can do another."

"She'll make it." Eli gathered the exhausted Lynn in his arms. "She's a strong kid."

They left the graves, walking hand in hand past the log where Neva had refused to leave her baby, now the sole sentry keeping watch over them both.

Lucy's fever broke in the river of sweat and vomit that Vera had promised. Stebbs was kept busy running stinking bedclothes out to the cast-iron pot suspended over the fire. Lynn held Lucy in her arms in between bed changes, cradling the blond head in the crook of her elbow and rocking her gently back and forth. As the sun went down, fatigue caught up with her, and Lynn collapsed onto her own cot.

She woke in the dead of night to feel little fingers combing through her hair. "Lynn?" The parched little voice was barely a whisper.

"Hey, little one, what are you doing up? You should be in bed."

"Thirsty."

"Okay. You lie down." Lynn pulled Lucy into her own cot and got to her feet. Eli and Stebbs were slumped together against the stone wall, their heads leaning against each other. Vera was on the floor at the foot of Lucy's cot, her head resting on the frame. Lynn tiptoed past everyone for Lucy's cup. She knew she should wake the others and share the relief of Lucy's recovery, but she wanted the small miracle to herself. Lynn filled the cup with clean water from the pantry, then propped Lucy's head in her hands while she sipped at it.

"Done," she said, and fell weakly back onto the pillow. "Can I sleep here with you?"

"Sure." Lynn slid into bed, and Lucy cuddled against her, the warmth that radiated from her small body no longer carrying the taint of fever.

"You said my mommy was coming. Where is she?"

Lynn rubbed Lucy's back quietly for a moment. "How much do you remember?"

"Just that you said Mommy was coming, and then I didn't feel so good. I thought I saw Mommy, but then when I woke up just now I saw Grandma is here sleeping, so I think maybe I was just confused."

"No baby, your mommy was here to see you."

"Is she gone now?"

"Yeah, sweetheart, she's gone." Lynn kept rubbing Lucy's back in concentric circles, trying to lull her back into sleep.

"So Grandma found us?"

"She did and she saved you from your fever. You're sick, little girl. You're going to have to take some medicine."

Lucy stuck out her tongue.

"Eli and I had to drive a long way to get the medicine, so it's important, all right? I want you to take it and no argument."

"'Kay," came the halfhearted reply, followed by a light snoring moments later. Lynn wrapped her long arms around her, muscles tightening in a futile attempt to shield the girl from all dangers.

"I'm going to make sure nothing can hurt you ever again."

Nineteen

"It's insane," Eli protested the next morning as Stebbs eyed them both over coffee. "I can't believe you'd even consider letting her go."

"I'm not in charge of her," Stebbs said. "If Lynn wants to go, she'll go, and neither of us can stop her."

"You could at least tell her you disagree."

Stebbs took a long drink before answering. "I'm not so sure I do."

"Thanks," Lynn said.

"You're kidding," Eli said in disbelief.

"Quiet," Vera chided them from Lucy's bedside, where the exhausted patient slept restlessly. "She's out of the woods but can still see the trees. Would you go outside?"

"Sorry, ma'am," Stebbs said, rising to his feet.

"Stop calling me that, mister," Vera said, and tossed a dirty pillowcase in his direction. "Feel free to wash that when you're done with your coffee. And once she's asleep, your pants are coming off."

Eli and Lynn both froze in mid stride, looking at each other in shock.

"I think she means to look at my leg," Stebbs explained, and winked at them.

"I might be able to rebreak the original injury and set it correctly," Vera said in an attempt to cover the blush that crept across her cheeks.

"Well, that'd be good," Lynn said lamely, and hurried up the stairs, Eli close behind.

Stebbs ignored their teasing glances when he followed them outside. "Look, Eli, I know you don't like the idea of Lynn going over there to check out their camp, but she's right. Their strength will grow. If we're going to do something about it, we need to do it now."

"And what will we do?"

"I can't say for sure until I go and look," Lynn answered. "Could be they're so strong we can't do anything. Except leave."

Hope sprang into Eli's gray eyes. "You'd do that?"

"Worst-case scenario—maybe."

"Listen, both of you," Eli said, glancing between them as he spoke. "In Entargo, there was always this rumor that California was still . . . normal. That they had so many desalinization plants by the sea that they were self-sufficient, had excess even. If that's true, we should go."

"Rumor?" Stebbs asked, hitting hard on the word. "Where'd you hear this?"

"It was something that would get repeated a lot, you know? Bradley had heard it through military sources, but he said mostly it was kept quiet so that people wouldn't leave, to keep them paying for water."

"Or it's a mercy to keep fools from wandering out west in search of something doesn't exist," Stebbs said. "You'd take Lynn and Lucy thousands of miles on foot without water, exposing them to God knows what on the road?"

"It's an *idea*," Eli said defensively.

"Sorry, Eli," Lynn said. "I'd rather shoot people in Ohio than walk to California."

Eli snorted and looked at the ground.

"Look," Stebbs said, trying to ease the tension between them. "I know you're not used to the way we live out here. You've learned a lot, but the next lesson is a bitch. We've got to defend what's ours, or we die. Lynn's always known that, she's lived that way to an extreme that I never went to, but there's some sense in it. I was too comfortable, too content to see the danger those men posed. Once the smoke stopped to the south, I didn't think about it anymore."

"And I wasn't smart enough to know that what I saw in the sky was the glow from electricity," Lynn said bitterly.

"You can't beat yourself up about that, kiddo. Vera said they're running generators. They've got heat going in the houses, on top of electricity. We assumed they died; really they traded up. You had no way of knowing what you were looking at, having never seen a working lightbulb in your life."

"Where are they getting the gasoline for generators?" Eli asked.

"Trade," Stebbs said. "They've got a few women over there. Vera said a gallon of gas gets you half an hour. They're set up in South Bloomfield," Stebbs said. "Lynn, you familiar with that place?"

Lynn nodded. South Bloomfield was a small village by the stream to the south. It was nothing more than a bridge, a cluster of houses and a township hall at the crossroads. She'd raided the houses years ago in search of a pair of scissors.

"I'm going," she said stubbornly. "Soon as possible."

"At least let me come with you," Eli said. "I don't like the idea of you going alone."

"Sorry, Eli, but I might as well drive right through town honking the horn as take you with me. You're as delicate as an elephant in the woods. And Stebbs would slow me down, no offense."

"I'm getting my leg rebroke. You'll eat those words one day, missy."

"'Til then I can still outrun you," she said, ignoring the dark looks Eli gave her. "I'm going to check on Lucy."

Vera was sorting through the prescriptions they had found when Lynn got downstairs. "How'd we do?"

"Pretty good, actually," Vera said, holding out a bottle for Lynn to see. "This one is Augmentin. Normally I'd say it's a little too strong for someone Lucy's size, but it's expired so some of the potency is lost. I'll start her on it and see where it gets us."

She handed her another bottle, with only a few small pills inside. "That one is amoxicillin, it's an all-purpose antibiotic that I'd prefer to give her, but it lacks the punch of the Augmentin and there isn't enough to keep a stable amount in her bloodstream long enough to kill off all the bacteria. You keep it, and if you ever get a cut that looks bad, take the pills until they're gone."

Lynn looked at Lucy, peacefully curled into a ball under her clean blanket, a freshly boiled Red Dog tucked under her chin. "This bacterial infection . . . how did she get it? Was it in the water? Something I gave her to eat?"

"I can't say for sure how she got it, Lynn. But I can tell you that if you hadn't been feeding her these past few months, she'd be dead for sure."

"Right."

"It's not your fault. It's just something that happened."

"It is what it is—that's what Mother would always say."

"She sounds like a smart woman." Vera smiled at Lynn and touched her shoulder. "I don't want to upset you, but I'm going to

269

move Lucy over to the stream house. The damp air down here could lay the groundwork for an opportunistic infection."

"You could move her upstairs," Lynn offered. "Plenty dry there."

"Maybe, but the nights still get cold and judging by the ductwork I see here in your basement, there aren't working fireplaces up there, right?"

"No," Lynn admitted. "There's not."

"Eli said that little shed that he and Stebbs built is tight as a drum, holds the heat and has no drafts. I'm sorry, but in Lucy's condition it's the better bet over an old farmhouse."

"It's all right," Lynn said. "I want her healthy. I'll be fine. When are you leaving?"

"I'd like to take the meds back to the stream today, and get a proper bed set up for her there. If we could all be safely tucked in by nightfall I'd be pleased."

"Take the cot she's been using."

"You're sure?"

"No need for it here," Lynn said. "It'll just be me."

She made it a point to be up on the roof when they left. Vera sloshed through the muddy yard, a sleeping Lucy slumped over her shoulder. Eli followed with the cot and Vera's backpack. Stebbs walked beside him, weighed down with medicine, extra blankets, and Mother's rifle, with instructions to leave it with Eli at the stream house. Lynn knew he would've refused it if she'd tried to give it herself, and was relying on Stebbs' prolific common sense to overrule Eli's objections.

Eli made it as far as the wood cord before he put down the cot and turned back. Lynn sighed and put her eye back to the scope for a distraction. Vera and Stebbs had stopped to wait for him, and she saw Vera leaning close to Stebbs while he spoke to her. Closer than necessary. Lynn bit her lip to keep the smile from spreading. "Wily asshole," she said under her breath.

"Hey now," Eli's voice came from behind her. "I know you're not happy with me, but I don't think I quite deserve that."

"Not directed at you," Lynn said, nodding toward the older couple standing in the distance. "Don't make them wait too long. Lucy needs to get indoors."

Eli sat beside her on the shingles, ignoring the fact that her attention was focused on the rifle and not him. "I don't want to go."

She made sure she had control over her voice before she turned to him. "Vera and Lucy need you."

"And you don't."

The words came out clipped and bitter as the air they landed in, dropping between the two of them like icicles. Lynn dropped her head back to the scope, close enough that her eyelashes brushed the cold metal.

"I didn't mean it like that."

"It's true though." Eli looked to the south. "I'm worried about what you'll do once we leave."

"What's that mean?"

"Just promise me you won't do anything stupid."

"Done."

Eli sighed and put a hand on her shoulder. She hesitated a moment, then gripped him back. "Come back," she said, her shaky voice betraying her. "When you can. When they're safe."

"Soon as possible," he said, his voice husky. Then he was gone. He emerged in the yard, shoulders hunched against the cold, head down against the wind. Lynn covered them with the rifle, not allowing tears to blur her vision until they were out of sight.

When darkness fell, she put on hunting camo, strapped her rifle across her back, and filled a canteen. "It's not stupid, Eli," she said as she closed the door and headed south across the field.

South Bloomfield had once been a nice place to live, according to Mother. From her perch in the tree on the ridge, Lynn saw in the rays of the rising sun that most of the homes were brick two-stories with ancient, sagging porches. A few had swimming pools that now stood empty, except for the carcasses of the animals with the bad luck to fall into them. The town was upstream from Eli and Lucy, at a point where the water widened. The bridge spanning it had been rebuilt just before the Shortage, reinforced with steel guardrails that still held a reflective sheen. A relic of the past loomed over the village—a cell phone tower where Lynn had spotted a sentry once the sun rose.

She envied the tower sentry his position. From his height, the only thing preventing him from seeing forever was the curve of the earth. The bare branches didn't offer much cover. Lynn knew that once spotted she'd be dead, so she was stuck in the tree until dark fell again. The sentry had been exempted from the daily work in town, which meant he was an excellent shot. Lynn marked him as her first target.

The first activity in town came mid morning. The man she thought of as Blue Coat led three women out of a yellow house near the center of town. He was armed. They were barely clothed. They shivered in the chilly air but didn't try to cover themselves. The men passing by hardly glanced at them; they'd already seen everything on display.

As much as she wanted to kill him, Blue Coat wasn't her highest priority. He seemed to be in charge of the women and though he was armed, she doubted his capabilities under fire. He'd run his mouth too much when they'd come for Neva, and Lynn had noticed how his eyes were always squirreling away from hers, bouncing off everything in sight. Blue Coat didn't have the cold stare of someone who could shoot well, or the sense to keep his mouth shut to cover up his nerves. He deserved a bullet, but she'd have to give him his after those more capable.

Blue Coat marched the women to the stream, and they disappeared down the near bank. Lynn watched through her binoculars as they emerged minutes later, dripping wet and clutching themselves to conserve heat. Green Hat walked alongside the youngest girl, and Lynn saw him slip something into her hand before she disappeared into the house again. As tightly as the girl clutched the gift, Lynn guessed it was food.

Lynn kept the binoculars on Green Hat and the line of women filing back into the yellow house. His actions caused a ripple of doubt on the placid surface of her cold rage. He had said he was sorry for Lucy's illness when they came to take Neva, and Lynn could tell by his eyes that they weren't empty words. The child's illness had bothered him, and he had helped Neva up from the frozen ground as she'd stumbled toward her death.

In the past, it had been easy to know who her enemies were—anyone not Mother. But even though he was clearly a part of the group of men, Lynn couldn't bring herself to watch him through the rifle scope with her finger curled on the trigger. Slipping extra food to the starving, nearly naked young girl wasn't an action she could account for in someone she needed to kill, and so she marked Green

Hat as a question mark. She'd kill him or not, depending on how he reacted once the lead was flying.

The man who had been on her roof watched everything from his position in front of the town hall, the only building under guard. He sat in a lawn chair in the parking lot with a rifle across his knees. Green Hat wandered away from the yellow house and made conversation with him for a few minutes but didn't succeed in fully gaining his attention. The guard was constantly watching the movement in the streets, the other men, and the people who had come to trade. Green Hat couldn't distract him, and he changed his position when men not a part of their group came into the village so that he could cover them with his gun. Lynn marked him as her second target.

Traders were filing into town as noon approached, the sun glinting off the melting snow and giving Lynn a headache. People filtered in and out, more than she would have guessed existed in their small corner of the world. She couldn't see well enough to know what everyone had brought to trade, but red gasoline containers were easy to spot, as were the round portable propane tanks.

A man and woman appeared on the road, walking hesitantly toward town. She held a bundle protectively against her chest. Lynn squinted into the binoculars and could see a tiny fist jutting from the top of the blanket, entangled in her hair. As they approached the center of town, a man emerged from the largest house and hailed them from the porch. Lynn switched to her rifle.

He was unknown to her. Tall and broad through the shoulders, with red hair and a confidence about him that immediately said he was in charge. He greeted the couple with familiarity. Lynn could see by the wary look on the woman's face that she knew enough about him to be frightened. The husband gestured toward the baby in his wife's arms. The redhead nodded and smiled as if he understood but shrugged off their questions, pointing to the church next to the town hall.

The woman disentangled the baby's fist from her hair and handed the bundle to her husband. She walked to the church with her head down. Lynn could hear the high-pitched wailing of the baby from her position in the trees, even as the father rocked it in his arms. The woman knocked on the door of the church, and Gap Tooth—Roger, Vera said his name was—opened it.

She caught a flash of black and white behind him, and Lynn nearly rolled out of the tree in surprise. There was a cow in the church, a dairy cow. There was a pail swinging from the father's elbow as he walked the baby up and down the porch of the brick house. The mother disappeared inside the church with Roger. Lynn hoped the doors were thick enough to stop the cries of her child while she did what she had to do to feed it.

Other traders came. Tall Red stayed on his porch, where a line began to form. He sat at a table with a pencil and paper, figured out what the traders wanted, what they'd brought to trade for it, and whether it was acceptable. One man brought a five-gallon jug of gasoline to the table and walked away with an entire deer carcass over his shoulder.

Those less lucky traded their own bodies or the bodies of their women. Tall Red never took them into the house himself, but Blue Coat, Roger, and a man with a black beard each took payment at different times during the day. One woman came begging for water, empty buckets in her hands and children clinging to her legs. Green Hat played with the children to distract them while Black Beard took the woman down to the stream far longer than necessary to gather water.

Lynn decided not to shoot Green Hat.

Tall Red dickered extensively with a man who had driven a truck loaded down with blankets, pallets of canned vegetables, and a mattress. Tall Red kept shaking his head, and the man walked back to his truck, emerging with a pack of cigarettes, which turned the tide. Tall Red scribbled on a piece of paper and handed it to him, directing the man toward the town hall. The guard there looked at the paper, spat, and stuck it in his back pocket. Roger and Black Beard emptied the truck while the man followed the guard out of town toward the east. They appeared minutes later dragging a wood splitter behind them.

The sound of an engine caused Lynn to jolt. A huge truck with no muffler roared into town, the bed so loaded with goods that it rested on the back axles. Two men jumped down from the bed and began unloading the truck, carting their loot into the town hall where the guard kept a tally. Two more men emerged from the cab. Lynn began counting on her fingers. The presence of the looters swung the odds in their favor. A long way in their favor.

The sun was beginning to swing back toward the horizon when one man took a bundle of food to the cell tower, where the sentry lowered down a bucket for his lunch, taking a leisurely piss off the side afterward. Roger led the cow from the church to an overgrown yard and tied it to a post to graze. The looting party gathered on the porch with Tall Red, their feet propped on the railings, heads lolled back in idle conversation. The stream of visitors slowed, then stopped entirely as the long shadows drew dark marks in the old snow.

The sentry came down from the tower after dusk, his skills rendered useless. The guard at the town hall switched out with a less vigilant looter, and the unfamiliar glow of electricity came from inside the houses. The cow lowed to be let back inside and Roger returned it to the church. The slight breeze that had been blowing died down enough that Lynn could hear the squeaking of bedsprings and the whir of generators, while Tall Red remained on the covered porch, keeping watch over all.

There were lights still on in some houses when Lynn tumbled out of her tree, legs numb with disuse. She flexed her neck and arms, keeping her eyes on the town below her. There was still a guard in front of the town hall; with her naked eyes, she could make out his dim, dark shape beneath the electric light that shone over the parking lot. The houses at the west and east ends of town each had a guard on the porch. Beyond the arc of the warm glow of electricity, Lynn could see nothing. There could be guards in the dark; there could be no one.

Lynn crept east through the woods. The man who traded for the wood splitter came prepared with a truckload of goods in exchange. If the men were willing to part with one they probably had more, and a guard to watch over them as well. She'd counted eleven men in all, and didn't need the surprise of a twelfth if she and Stebbs chose to attack.

She crossed the road to the east and fought her way through brush to the stream. The moon came out, illuminating in stark brilliance that there was no choice.

She burst through Stebbs' door without knocking, causing him to whirl on her with a frying pan raised above his head.

"Christ child, Lynn! What are you doing?"

"They're building a dam."

Twenty

"Shit," Stebbs said when they crested the ridge. "You weren't kiddin'."

"Nope."

Machinery littered the meadow on the far bank of the stream, skeletal and pale in the moonlight. A dark scar marred the earth around the stream where they'd widened a reservoir area, a massive pile of stone stood nearby, menacingly solid. Stebbs took Lynn's binoculars and squinted into them.

"Shit," he said again. "They've got a decent-size reservoir dug already, and plenty of stone to stop the river anytime they want. They probably couldn't work in this mud, so they're waiting either for a freeze or the ground to dry out."

"Either way, they'd have Eli and Lucy out of water in a week," Lynn said.

"Them and anyone else downstream who counts on it for water." Stebbs handed the binoculars back to Lynn, and surveyed the dam area. "Shit."

"When Lucy was sick, you said you and me aren't the kind of people who don't like situations we can't control. You said we need to be able to do something."

"I remember."

"I think it's time we did something."

"I know it. But what?"

She regarded him critically for a moment, biting her lip. "How've you been feeling?"

Stebbs shifted his weight awkwardly on his bad foot. "I've been better, mostly back before I was cripple."

"Can you lay still for a while?"

"Laying still is something I'm good for."

"You eat anything lately?"

Stebbs forehead creased in confusion. "I ate well enough tonight. Why?"

"C'mere. I want to introduce you to a tree friend of mine."

Stebbs was true to his word, making less rustling than Lynn, and even managing to fall asleep on his perch in the tree. Lynn had given him the long, wide limb she'd used earlier to stretch out on. She was nestled comfortably against the trunk where the limbs made a V, hugging her knees against her chest. She rested her head against her canteen, allowing the gentle swaying of the branches to lull her into a decent rest, if not sleep. The taut muscles in her back and legs screamed for a break, and she took turns flexing them as the gray light of dawn appeared on the horizon. She hissed at Stebbs to wake him, and they watched as the sentry climbed the cell tower.

"He come out at dawn yesterday too?"

"Earlier."

Stebbs made a noise in his throat and borrowed her binoculars again. "Keep them," she said. "I've seen."

Through her rifle scope she watched the men go about the same duties as they had the day before. The guard who had been on her roof reclaimed his position in front of the town hall, and Roger brought the cow out of the church to graze.

"Milk," Stebbs muttered to himself. "Almost forgot such a thing existed. Looks like they're keeping their stockpile in the town hall, since it's the only place that's guarded. The cow and the women being the exception. You got to realize that we start shooting, some of those girls could get hurt."

"I'm willing to take the risk. Bet they are too."

Stebbs shifted on the limb, moving his gaze to the group of men headed toward the truck. The same four looters started it up and headed out of the village with an empty bed. "Those the scavengers?"

"Yup. I imagine we hit while they're gone?"

"I would. They leave about the same time yesterday?"

"I didn't see them go. They might even spend the night outside the village, the farther they've got to travel to forage."

"We'll want to hit on an off day, once they're gone and not expected back."

Lynn followed the truck through her scope, ignoring the urge to pull the trigger. "That was my thinking."

Stebbs watched the village in silence for an hour, finally handing the binoculars back to Lynn and propping himself on one elbow. "Well, I'd say so far you're right on. Take out the tower sentry first, then the guard at the hall. After that, the guy with the beard and then the one in the blue coat. The guy in the green hat we wait and see."

"What about the big guy? The one in charge?"

"Didn't see him."

Lynn handed the binoculars back to him, gesturing toward the town. "Across from the church, there's a big brick house, with a porch. He was out there yesterday, doing his dealings with the people."

She raised her rifle back to her eye again but found the porch empty. Movement in one of the windows caught her eye. "Heads up," she said. "He's coming."

One of the women from the yellow house opened the front door, clutching a blanket around her thin shoulders. She crossed the road limping, even though she'd been uninjured the day before. Tall Red walked onto the porch holding a cup of coffee and leaned against one of the pillars.

"That's him," Lynn said, but there was no response. "What do you think? Should we pick him off before the guard at the hall?"

Silence.

"Stebbs? What's the call?"

He pulled the binoculars away from his eyes slowly, handing them back to Lynn. "That's got to be your decision."

"Why?"

"'Cause that's your daddy."

"You're sure?" Lynn asked as they slipped back to her house in the dark on stiff legs.

"There's no mistaking him. This change anything? He's the only blood you've got left in the world, you know."

"He's my blood, true. But I've been thinking lately that maybe he's part of what makes up the bad bits, the things I've done that never bothered me until you said they should."

Stebbs thought about it as he trudged along beside her. "I knew your father, Lynn, and I know you. What you did, you thought you had to. Wasn't no part of you enjoyed it, or liked hurting for the fun of it. If there's some of him in you, it's been for the good—the will to survive and the brains to figure out how. There ain't ever been one person who was all good or bad, not me or you, not your mom or your daddy either. So I say again that it's up to you—does this change anything?"

"Good blood or bad, he's a stranger to me and a threat to my friends," Lynn said. "We take him out."

Their shoes crunched through the evening dew that had frozen the scanty patches of snow still left on the ground. "There'll be a hard freeze in a few days," Stebbs said. "That truck with the scavengers went out this morning. If you're right about them spending the night outside of the village, we'll need to do this right quick. I say we talk to Eli now. We can be in place by morning."

"He doesn't want any part. You and I can handle it."

"Maybe. Maybe not. Two snipers are only good to have if they're reinforcing someone on the ground. There's no guarantee we'll make every shot, and after that first one, they'll scatter. We'll be hard pressed to nail three right off, and then we're in for a long wait while they're undercover. We'll be sitting in trees with only what we've got on our backs, and a truck with four more men in it coming back anytime. And that's the best-case scenario, assuming neither one of us gets shot. One of us goes down, the other is dead."

"I don't like it. I know you've been working with him, but Eli's not good with a gun."

"No, but it's his water we're fighting for. Don't you think he'd want the chance to defend it himself?"

Lynn thought of their exchange on the roof, the bitter tang of uselessness that had threaded Eli's words. "We'll put it to him, see what he says."

"Where you go, he'll go," Stebbs said.

"I know it."

"Tough caring about people, isn't it?"

Lynn considered the long, cold winter that had passed happily, with Lucy sharing her basement and a stolen night with Eli sharing her cot. Without them, she would've been alone for the dark hours, staring into the blackness fighting off grief and madness. "Wouldn't trade it," she said.

"You're sure this is necessary?" Eli asked, dissecting the crudely penciled map that Stebbs had drawn.

"They'll only grow stronger. The scavengers will keep looting the countryside until there's nothing left for anyone in the area. We'll all be begging them for something sooner or later," Stebbs answered, bouncing a grinning Lucy in his lap. Not even the seriousness of the adults could cut through her happiness at avoiding bedtime.

Vera stood at the stove, boiling stream water for Lucy, with a concerned frown. The stove heated the little stream house so well that Lynn felt a trickle of sweat running down her chest.

"I know you don't like it," she said to Eli. "But you need to know

I wouldn't do this if we didn't need to."

"You sure about that?"

"I'm not killing people for spite. This is about living."

Eli weighed her words, his gray eyes searching hers for answers. "What do you want me to do?"

"The important thing is going to be distracting the ones on the ground. Once the tower sentry is out, they'll be blind," Stebbs said. "The man guarding the hall is capable, so he goes next. But that still leaves us with five men that can find cover and wait us out."

"Four, if we assume Green Hat is a decent fellow," Lynn added.

"Assume he's not," Stebbs said. "If he is, all the better."

"So I create a distraction?" Eli asked. "Something to draw everyone out?"

"Exactly," Stebbs nodded, pointing to the map. "I'm sending you out to set a fire at the hall. The stockpile is there. They need it to retain a position of power."

"Wait," Lynn interrupted. "A fire? It'll take a while to get one started. How's Eli safe while he's trying to set it? And how does he get past the guard?"

"Your momma ever teach you anything about Molotov cocktails?"

"Uh, no."

"Easy enough—gasoline in a glass bottle, stoppered with a rag that Eli lights. He tosses a few of those onto the roof and those shingles will go up in a flash."

Eli nodded in slow agreement. "Sounds good, but that still leaves the guard."

"It's all in the timing. You hear that first shot take out the sentry and you're running toward the hall. The men will be trying to figure out where that shot came from. The guard at the hall will leave his post to see if it's the tower sentry doing the shooting. That's your window to get in there and toss the fire."

"What's his window to get out?" Lynn asked.

"You and I and our rifles," Stebbs answered as Vera pulled Lucy from his lap. She gave Stebbs a dark look that he either missed or ignored.

Lynn shook her head. "I don't like it."

"I'm the best option," Eli said. "I'm quicker than you, and you're a far better shot. With you and Stebbs in the trees, I'm probably safer there than I am sitting here talking."

Lynn looked down at her hands and didn't answer. Stebbs continued. "The two important shots are the sentry and the hall guard. Once Eli sets the fire, they've got a choice; let their easy life go up in flames or risk our bullets. They'll risk it, but her daddy's a smart bastard. He'll know what we're up to and send people to find us while the others fight the fire.

"Lynn, you take three good shots and then I want you to move to a new position. Best case, he only sends one man up after you and you can pick him off as he comes, then concentrate on the town."

"What about you?" Vera asked, her worried eyes searching his face. "How many shots will you take before you move?"

"Sweetheart, I'm too old and twisted to be moving. Once I'm set up, I'm there for the duration. Hell or high water."

"Probably be hell," Eli said. "We haven't seen a lot of rain lately."

Lynn found his hand under the table. Her gratefulness for his humor couldn't be expressed in words.

"When do we go?" Eli asked.

Stebbs and Lynn exchanged glances, the lightness of the moment vanished. "Before the sun comes up," he said. "Eat well, rest, clean your guns."

Lynn squeezed Eli's hand; she wouldn't let go of him until she had to.

They left the stream house together, not making excuses for their departure. They walked silently hand in hand toward her home. Lucy had been sleeping as they finalized their plans, and Lynn had settled for placing her hand on the little forehead in farewell. Her skin was soft and cool to the touch. Lynn didn't think she'd ever be able to touch the little girl again without fear of feeling fever burning underneath her skin.

"What did Vera tell her, about Neva?"

"The truth, to a point. She told her that her mother made a sacrifice in order to save her, because she valued Lucy's life over her own."

"That is the truth," Lynn said, thinking of the last lingering glance Neva had given her, along with instructions to tell Lucy she loved her. "How is Lucy doing with it?"

"As well as can be expected. She asks questions that are hard to answer, and she's quiet for long periods."

Lynn snorted. "I'll believe that when I see it."

They went downstairs together. "I want to give you a handgun," she said. "I've got a few. I won't have you on the ground unarmed."

"Stebbs has been letting me borrow his rifle to shoot, but I've never even touched a handgun, country girl."

"We'll practice now."

He took her hand, guiding her over to the cot. "There's better ways to spend our time. I'm not standing out in the cold and the dark shooting a gun when I could be warm in here with you."

"You'll regret it."

He pulled her down next to him and she rested her head against his shoulder. "I'll regret it more if these are our last hours and we spend it with a gun instead of each other."

Lynn leaned into him. "Don't talk like that."

"Besides, Stebbs told us to rest."

"Yeah," she teased. *"Rest."*

"I don't want anything more than to hold you, Lynn."

His arms encircled her and she felt the calm that always came with him welling up from a place she'd thought only Mother could touch.

She turned her face into his chest so that he couldn't see her tears as she cried quietly, knowing that Mother would have never risked her own skin for the sake of others. In a few hours, Lynn would climb a tree miles from her own pond to fire bullets she couldn't spare so that Eli, Lucy, and countless strangers downstream could have a drop to drink. She inhaled Eli's smell, buried her face deeper into his chest, holding on to him until the world would make her let go.

Twenty-one

It was bitterly cold when they emerged in the dead of night to meet Stebbs. They huddled together for warmth, not even bothering to tease the older man when he came from the direction of the stream, rather than his own house. When he handed a backpack to Eli, the fumes of gasoline rolled off him in waves.

"Careful with that, that's the last of the gasoline I had stored up in my basement," Stebbs warned as Eli shouldered it. "Here's a lighter. Didn't want to take the chance of a breeze with matches."

"How long've you had a lighter?" Lynn asked.

He shrugged. "Since forever."

"Asshole."

They headed south and walked in silence, except for the clinking of the bottles in Eli's backpack. When they reached the ridge, Stebbs gave her a foot up into her tree and Lynn settled onto a thick bough. They moved off toward the east, where Stebbs had found a suitable place to take his own shots, nearer town. Eli would wait with him. Eli's good-bye was quick and silent, the flash of a white hand through the darkness as he waved. Lynn unstrapped her rifle and tucked her handgun into the back of her waistband. A light snow began to fall as she waited for the sun to rise.

When it did, it came fast, the gray predawn haze burning off quickly as the sun peeked over the horizon. Lynn could see men moving inside the houses, their dark forms anonymous behind the curtains. The sentry had not come out yet. She shifted position and dried her palms on her jeans. The hall guard emerged, pissed in his yard, and made his way to his post. Roger led the cow out to pasture. Her father appeared on his porch, coffee in hand. Her gaze skittered off him, nervously.

They had agreed that though he was the leader, it was important to take the sentry and hall guard out first. Her father had won third place in that lottery. Lynn's first shot was for the sentry, Stebbs' the hall guard. After that they would fire at will, each picking their own target. Lynn had not argued, though she hoped it would be her bullet that downed her father.

She watched him through her scope, wondering what Mother would feel to know that the smoke from the south was caused by a fire from her past. Father was a conversation that never happened, a ghost that had never lived. Lynn had always believed he was dead, and perhaps Mother had as well. But he was alive and had never come for them. He'd abandoned them, and the only thing she'd ever give him would be delivered through the talents Mother had wanted her to master. There was comfort for her in the idea that the shot she'd fired too late for the coyote might be redeemed yet. His face in the crosshairs made her finger curl around the trigger, anxious for the only comfort Mother could offer from the grave.

Father spat out his first mouthful of coffee and crossed the road to where the hall guard sat, rifle across his knees. They exchanged words. Her father shook his head and walked over to the yellow house where the women were kept and pounded on the door until Blue Coat answered. He went inside, and the tower sentry emerged moments later, shrugging his coat over his shoulders.

Lynn tracked him to the tower, waiting for him to settle onto his perch before clicking the safety off her gun. She could only assume that Stebbs was watching as well, that Eli was prepared for her shot. She flattened her torso and inhaled, holding the breath.

She fired. From that distance the features of the sentry's face were unclear, but the bullet's exit was easy to see. A spray of blood rained down from the tower, followed quickly by his rifle, then his corpse. They reacted to the shot before his body hit the ground. Men erupted from the houses like bees from a disturbed hive; pale faces pressed against the windows in the upper floor of the yellow house.

Lynn spotted Eli speeding up the near bank of the stream as the hall guard rose from his chair, head cocked in a question. The guard shouldered his rifle, shouting at the other men as he crossed the parking lot for a good look at the tower. Her father ran toward the men, shouting directions. Lynn drew a bead on him just as Eli came into their view, the lit Molotov dangling from his hand. He threw it in a graceful arc, all eyes trailing it as it exploded in a river of fire onto the shingles.

Her father's reaction was immediate. He yelled at the hall guard, who spun on his heel. Stebbs and Lynn fired at the same time, her crosshairs trained on Father. He fell, clutching a shattered shoulder. His hand dangled lifeless from the dead arm, his gun useless on the ground. The hall guard dropped to his knees and fired at Eli before Stebbs' bullet could reach him. The guard's brain exploded through the back of his head, but not before his bullet hit Eli's backpack.

Eli became a living ball of fire.

Lynn screamed from her perch, watching helplessly as the arms that had held her only hours ago pinwheeled in agony. Drops of liquid fire flew from his fingertips and sputtered out on the road. She knew exactly how many bullets she had and could afford to waste none. One shot could deliver him from his own gasoline-soaked skin.

The bullet seemed to fly slowly, protracting every second of his torment. Lynn kept her eye to the scope, unable to look away from the path of the only bullet she had ever fired with love in her heart.

Lynn dropped to the ground and rushed downhill toward town. The smell of smoke was strong in the air. Black plumes rose above the hall roof. Stebbs was firing, but she had no view and didn't know if his shots were finding their targets. She flew downhill, arms spread wide to keep her balance as she ran.

Roger was running uphill to meet her, rage contorting his face. She ran directly at him, her own fury disregarding the gun he held as she launched herself directly at him. Their bodies collided, and the stale reek of male sweat folded over her as they rolled downhill together, hands grabbing for purchase on each other's bodies. She gained her feet first, but he took her knees out from behind with his rifle stock. Lynn landed on her belly, the breath knocked out of her. He straddled her back and her lungs flattened farther as he pulled her head back by her hair.

"What'cha think you're doing, girl? Playing war games?"

He drove her face downward into the ground and she struggled against him. She tried to breathe, but inhaled only dirt. He pulled her face back up, taunting her.

"Men got two guns, you know. One for now," he tapped the barrel of his gun against her nose. "And one for later." When his free hand went to his zipper, she twisted underneath him, bringing her knee into his groin and pulling her knife from her boot.

"Mother taught me to carry a knife for always."

She left him holding his intestines in disbelief as she disappeared down the hill, his gun tucked securely in her waistband.

She slid to a stop in a clearing and dropped onto her belly to scan the village. Blue Coat disappeared inside the yellow house, emerging at a downstairs window with his rifle. He was pulled down in a flurry of white hands and kitchen knives. Green Hat was the only man attempting to stop the fire, but he was armed with a single bucket and losing the fight. Black Beard was running to the east, whether to escape or find Stebbs she didn't know. One bullet dropped him; her second shot finished the job. Her father had staggered into a blue house in the middle of town. Lynn saw a bloody hand draw curtains on the first floor, but it was the only flicker of movement. Green Hat had given up, his bucket sat at his feet while he watched the hall go up in flames.

Lynn scanned the trees, spotted Stebbs awkwardly making his way down from his post to the east. She fired a warning shot at Green Hat's bucket, sending it ten feet in the air. He backed away, his hands up. Lynn emerged from the brush at the foot of the hill, her rifle trained on him.

"I got no issue with you," he said, voice shaking. "Though I know you got reason to have one with me."

Lynn wandered onto the road, uneasily scanning the houses on either side of her. She spat some dirt from her mouth, ignoring the trickle of blood running down her neck from a gash that Roger had given her as they fell. Green Hat eyed her uneasily, raised hands shaking.

"You armed?" Lynn asked.

"No." He spread his jacket to show her. "Never much liked the feel of a gun."

She relaxed her grip on the rifle as Stebbs came into town from behind the church, his own gun trained on Green Hat. "He all right?"

"Don't think he'll be a problem," she answered, and Stebbs lowered his gun.

"Jasper's in the little house there," Green Hat said, gesturing toward the blue house Father had gone into. "You winged him good, but he was moving okay last I saw. He lost his gun when you shot him, but that don't mean he's not dangerous as hell. There's still a truck out, too," he went on. "Four men, though I doubt they're the type to come back if there's trouble."

"We know," Lynn said stiffly, handing her rifle to Stebbs. "There's a man up the ridge that might call a bullet a favor."

Stebbs glanced at her bloody face. "I s'pose I don't feel much like granting favors today."

Lynn nodded and backed away from him, forcing herself not to look at the smoldering black heap that had been Eli. The door of the yellow house opened and the youngest girl stepped out, the edges of a blanket clutched in her bloody hands.

"Emma!" Green Hat yelled, Stebbs and Lynn having vanished from his mind as he ran toward her. "Are you hurt?"

She shook her head and leaned against him. The other two women appeared in the doorway, glancing warily at Stebbs and Lynn.

"What are you going to do?" Stebbs asked Lynn.

She checked her handgun before answering, handing Stebbs the extra she had taken from Roger. "I'm going to go have a talk with my father."

"Careful."

"I will be."

"I'm sorry as hell about Eli," Stebbs said, not meeting her eyes. "I got that shot off as soon as I could."

"It is what it is. I got other worries right now," she said as she walked away from him, her hammering heart screaming at the lie in her words.

"Careful there, lady," one of the women yelled at her. "He's a mean bastard, that one is. And tricksy." She touched a darkening bruise on her face as she spoke.

Lynn tightened her grip on the gun as she opened the front door.

Bloody footprints led her to the kitchen where her father sat at the table, slumped and pale. His right hand cupped the remains of his left shoulder; bone fragments jutted out between his fingers. He summoned the energy to look up at her as she walked in, but his head dropped back to his chest immediately. A slow smile spread across his face.

"The boys told me you was a pretty girl," he said with his eyes closed.

She approached the table cautiously, her finger curled around the trigger and ready to fire. "You know who I am?"

His eyes cracked open and he gave her a long, assessing stare before they closed again. "Have to be blind not to. You look just like her. Don't think there's a bit of me in you."

Even bleeding and maimed, he was an imposing man. The bulk of his body spoke of capability, the shine of his eyes held unvented malice. "There may be a bit yet," Lynn said as she circled around behind him, checking for weapons.

"I don't have a gun," he said. "Funny thing about your shoulder exploding, it makes you drop whatever you're holding. You ever been shot?"

"Not yet."

"You may as well have a seat and relax," he said calmly, closing his eyes again. "Not like I'm gonna harm my own flesh and blood."

"'Cause you can't or 'cause you wouldn't?" Lynn asked, lowering herself into the seat opposite him, her gun still trained on his chest.

"It really matter? Either way, you can rest a spell."

"If that's your answer, I believe I'll stay out of your reach for now and keep my gun out, if it's all the same to you."

One of his eyes opened to a slit and he regarded her warily for a moment. His answer came in a shrug from his uninjured shoulder. "You do as you please, girl." He licked his lips, and she saw the sheen of blood coating his tongue.

"My bullet still in you?"

"Went down through a lung, I'd say. Maybe little Emma over the street could patch it up, if you're inclined to let her."

Lynn didn't answer. He cleared his throat. "S'pose you're wondering why I left?"

"What I'm curious about is why you came back."

"Don't it make sense for a father to return to his only child?"

Lynn's mouth twitched, she flexed her finger on the trigger. "Maybe. But you didn't."

"I'm here, ain't I?"

"I think you came back to where there's water. Somewhere you could control the flow and knew the country."

A small smile pulled at the corners of his mouth. "It is a good place, isn't it?"

"It's our place."

"Who's that? You and your mother? What all she tell you about me?"

"Nothing too nice."

He grunted and spat a wad of blood-tinged phlegm on the floor.

"She tell you I bought you that puppy, when you was still in her belly, so's the two of you would have some protection? She tell you that? Full-blooded German shepherd he was, woulda been brown with black ears. I trained him up to keep you safe, gave him to your momma before I left."

"Yeah." Lynn shifted her gun with his movements, her sweaty palm sliding along the stock of gun. "We had to put him down, 'cause of the rabies. Living thing goes mean like that, nothing for it but a bullet."

Both his eyes opened and he watched her carefully before speaking again, gaze trained on her unwavering gun.

"I came myself, you should know, once or twice. The boys thought your momma was gone, but I wasn't so sure. I didn't want to wander too close and find myself in her crosshairs, with no love for me in her heart. Couple nights I stood out by the pond, wondering whether you were inside, hurting or grieving, whether you'd take any comfort from my hand if I came to you."

"That it?" Lynn asked, her eyes cool behind the barrel. "That's what you were thinking out there by my pond? Or were you waiting to smell me rotting before you came any closer?"

He ignored her question. "I kept the boys from you too. Roger woulda liked to done more than fire a warning shot at you over that downed tree."

"Roger's got bigger worries now."

"You kill him?"

"Partway."

His eyes slid shut again, and he stifled a laugh that brought a froth of blood to his lips. "Damn, you're a cold bitch. Nothin' but contempt for your own flesh and blood, but you'll overnight a cripple and snot-nosed kid in the house I made safe for you."

"It's mine. Make no mistake."

"Nothing's nobody's out here, little girl. Those that can, take. And there ain't no justice or higher power to appeal to."

"'Til now," she said softly.

His eyes opened, what blood there was left in his body burning in their heat. His lips twisted when he spoke next, the words slurred with angry memories. "And your momma, she set up a lemonade stand after I left, huh? That what she did? Offer comfort and a drink to every poor soul that wandered your way?"

"No, but we never did any taking either, or hurting for the fun of it."

One eyebrow twitched in response, but he had nothing to say to that. He rested his eyes for a moment. Fresh blood seeped out between his fingers, dripping from his elbow to the floor, where a small pool had begun to form between his feet.

"You've done some low deeds, Father."

"All's fair in love and war, my girl. What I had with your mother amounted to about the same thing. Guess it's down to you and me now, so which is it gonna be?"

"You hoarded water when people were dying of thirst, stole things you didn't need when you were surrounded by want."

A slow laugh rumbled through his chest and he opened his eyes to stare her down across the table. "I don't know that your momma would approve of your soft ways."

"Maybe not," Lynn admitted, "but she'd like this next part just fine."

She shot him neatly in the forehead, leaving behind a black hole that was still smoking when she shut the door behind her.

The frozen ground at the little cemetery beside the stream was stubborn, but Lynn had adrenaline on her side as she hacked out a grave beside Neva's. She worked relentlessly, ignoring the steady climb and descent of the sun, focused only on the task at hand. Blisters formed and burst on her hands, pus, followed by blood, flowed down her fingers. She ignored the pain, intent on her digging.

Stebbs had wrapped Eli in a blanket while she was inside with her father, sparing her the sight of his cracked, blackened skin. She lifted the body from the bed of the truck, disgusted by how light it was. She laid him tenderly into the hole in the ground and returned to work, throwing shovelfuls of frozen dirt on top of him, though she could not get the charred smell out of her nostrils long after he was covered. She toppled the stones she'd stolen from the dam site out of the truck and rolled them over the grave, resting her hand lightly on the last one.

"I'm sorry to be doing this one alone," she said. "I'm sorry it's yours."

Lynn collapsed onto Neva's log, staring at the little cemetery while the billowing smoke rose to the south, the ashes of material things and men mixing with a light powdering of snow that dusted her shoulders as she wept.

Epilogue

Lynn climbed the antenna to the roof and stepped over Lucy's long legs to stand beside her as she surveyed the horizon to the east. "What do you see?"

"Not much going on tonight," Lucy answered. "Looks like Brad's cow got out again."

"Emma'll give him hell."

"And he'll love it," Lucy added, smiling. She set the binoculars beside her on the shingles. "The new family that came in over to the south—what's their name?"

"Robinson."

"Yeah. The Robinsons got a fire going, so the chimney must not've been blocked in that old house she picked."

Lynn picked up the binoculars and looked at the thin column of smoke. "They're burning dry wood at least. Didn't figure him for an idiot, being's as he kept them alive wandering in the winter."

Lucy shivered against the chill that permeated the air, even though crocuses had begun blooming on the west bank of the stream, over her mother's grave. "Not sure how he managed, with three children and all."

"From what we're hearing, things are bad in the city," Lynn answered, her mouth tightening. "Man takes it on himself to wander into the wilderness with his family, tells me it's true."

"Cholera?"

"Your grandma says it seems so, by the sounds of it. That girl Audra that wandered in last fall? She had stories to tell Vera that made her hair curl."

"Her hair's already curly."

Lynn glanced sideways at the younger girl. "Aren't you the smart one this evening?"

Lucy picked up her rifle and glanced down the sight, smothering the little smile that played over her lips. "Stebbs said the Robinson house had a good vein of water running under it too."

"That's good, he can drop a line soon as true spring comes."

Lucy's mouth twitched as she peered into the scope of her rifle. "Bet I could find a better vein."

"I bet you could keep your mouth shut about that," Lynn said. "Anything else?"

"Grandma said there's a new man over at Stebbs' old place, across the field."

"I saw him."

"Did you now?"

Lynn ignored Lucy's raised eyebrow. "I imagine we'll walk over there and introduce ourselves soon enough."

"Sure could use a hand getting that piano out of the attic," Lucy continued. "That's the last thing to come down. The Bennet lady said she'd teach me, if I wanted to learn."

"That's a fine idea, but I'm not going to go inviting a strange man into the house for the sake of hearing you bang on a piano night and day."

Lucy pulled herself into a sitting position, resting the rifle across her lap. They'd begun living in the upper floors of the house years ago, but Lynn only allowed Stebbs and Vera inside.

"I s'pose we could get it down ourselves," Lucy conceded. "If we're careful."

"And I suppose I could let the Bennet woman come on over, if we can get it down without smashing it to pieces," Lynn said, eyes still on the horizon. "It would be nice to hear music again."

Lucy nodded but didn't speak. The newfound safety of community had left Lynn with something she'd never known before: spare time. A few years earlier, Lucy had followed the ghostly notes of misplayed music up to the attic and found Lynn in front of the piano, awkwardly picking out a song that Mother had attempted to teach her on a rainy afternoon in the distant past.

The next tune Lynn had tried had brought tears to Lucy's eyes as she recognized a song from her childhood, sung by her uncle in the dying firelight of the camp as he tried to distract Lucy and Neva from the hunger pains in their bellies. Lynn's fingers hesitated across the keys, and the notes had come out haltingly, played from a memory punctuated by more gunshots than melody.

Lucy cleared her throat. "I'm on watch for the first time tonight. East side."

"Stebbs didn't post you alone, surely? Isn't Maddy or one of the other Johnson girls going to be there with you?"

"I imagine Carter will join me after a bit."

"I imagine he will," Lynn said. "You mind yourself."

Lucy let go of the rifle long enough to cross her heart and wink. "Promise."

There was movement in the yard, and Lynn squinted into the dying sun. Lucy peered through her scope. A massive coyote, old and frail, picked his way down the bank to the pond, placing his mud-caked paws carefully with every step.

Lucy aimed the rifle. "What's the call?"

Lynn watched as he reached the pond, his long tongue hungrily lapping at the life-giving water. "Leave him be," she said. "He's just trying to survive. Same as us all."

Acknowledgments

This book is my debut baby and it took a village to raise it.

I used to roll my eyes when writers thanked their editor for helping make the book stronger. I thought they were probably still boiling inside about the comma on page 246 they were told to delete. Now I get it. A huge thanks to Sarah Shumway for making *Not a Drop to Drink* a better book. I'm over the comma.

And of course who doesn't thank their agent? If I hugged people, I'd hug Adriann Ranta of Wolf Literary. Thanks for taking a chance on me!

I had two crit partners who were with me on this one for the long haul, RC Lewis and Caroline Poissoniez. The former helped comb out the comma splices and the latter told me I'd better give Lynn a little more emotional accessibility before the bullets flew. I also need to point out that it's a lovely thing to discover that you get along with your online friend in real life as well. RC Lewis's couch is comfy, and we even like the same food. She was willing to fetch and re-fetch me from the airport . . . good thing I have a keeper.

No author is an island, except in their heads. I couldn't have found the shore without the support of debut author groups like Book Pregnant, the Lucky 13s, the Class of 2k13, and most especially Friday the Thirteeners. Members of online groups know that sometimes your inbox can get clogged, but I read every email in every thread from that last group of ladies. When you're dealing with the Thirteeners, you don't want to miss a word.

I must acknowledge the entire community of writers at Agent-Query Connect. There could not be a more positive learning environment for writers, and I credit it with my success. I especially need to thank my fellow moderators there, who donate time out of every day to help others and support one another. Specifically, huge MG & YA love to moderators RC Lewis, MarcyKate Connolly, and Cat Woods. I have friends in real life, too. Amanda, Mel, Erin, Debbie, and your respective men—I miss college and I want it back.

Lastly, I kind of lied two paragraphs above. Authors really can be little islands occasionally. Thanks to my family for understanding that sometimes they have to get in the rowboat to come get me if they need me. Patience is a virtue. I'm glad you have it, but it's not genetic.